The roar of gunfire brought them both to high alert. Cotton tossed Jack a rifle, pulled a shotgun from the rack, and they both started for the door. Cotton stopped before stepping outside.

"That could be some of Cruz's men. I'd say there are two of 'em. They may be trying to draw us out the front door so they can gun us down. We'll go around back and down behind the livery," Cotton said, grabbing Jack by the arm.

Cotton opened the back door slowly. He was in no hurry to present a target to someone who might have guessed he'd come out the back and be ready for him. Seeing no one, they eased into the shadows behind the jail and moved quickly down the alley toward the livery. The way was clear and they sprinted for the safety of the next building. That's when bullets rang out, tearing chunks of pine from the livery's walls . . .

". . . *Cotton's War* is an old-fashioned, barn-burning, gutwrenching Western story that moves at a gallop over dangerous territory. Phil Dunlap's sharp prose packs the punch of a Winchester rifle."

—Johnny D. Boggs, four-time Spur Award–winning author of *Northfield* and *Hard Winter*

"Phil Dunlap's latest novel, *Cotton's War*, is a rip-roaring yarn that realizes the best traditions of the Western genre: strong, well-defined characters, the color of the West vivid and perfectly researched, and the writing entertaining and quick as a bronc set free to run wild. A surefire read for Western fiction fans."

—Larry D. Sweazy, Spur Award–winning author of *The Badger's Revenge*

"This is a well-crafted story with a good, clear writing style. It hits a good pace and keeps it up."

—John D. Nesbitt, Spur Award–winning author of *Stranger in Thunder Basin*

COTTON'S WAR

Phil Dunlap

BERKLEY BOOKS, NEW YORK

THE BERKLEY PUBLISHING GROUP
Published by the Penguin Group
Penguin Group (USA) Inc.
375 Hudson Street, New York, New York 10014, USA

Penguin Group (Canada), 90 Eglinton Avenue East, Suite 700, Toronto, Ontario M4P 2Y3, Canada
(a division of Pearson Penguin Canada Inc.)
Penguin Books Ltd., 80 Strand, London WC2R 0RL, England
Penguin Group Ireland, 25 St. Stephen's Green, Dublin 2, Ireland (a division of Penguin Books Ltd.)
Penguin Group (Australia), 250 Camberwell Road, Camberwell, Victoria 3124, Australia
(a division of Pearson Australia Group Pty. Ltd.)
Penguin Books India Pvt. Ltd., 11 Community Centre, Panchsheel Park, New Delhi—110 017, India
Penguin Group (NZ), 67 Apollo Drive, Rosedale, North Shore 0632, New Zealand
(a division of Pearson New Zealand Ltd.)
Penguin Books (South Africa) (Pty.) Ltd., 24 Sturdee Avenue, Rosebank, Johannesburg 2196,
South Africa

Penguin Books Ltd., Registered Offices: 80 Strand, London WC2R 0RL, England

COTTON'S WAR

A Berkley Book / published by arrangement with the author

PRINTING HISTORY
Berkley edition / June 2011

ISBN: 978-0-425-24177-6

BERKLEY®
Berkley Books are published by The Berkley Publishing Group,
a division of Penguin Group (USA) Inc.,
375 Hudson Street, New York, New York 10014.
BERKLEY® is a registered trademark of Penguin Group (USA) Inc.
The "B" design is a trademark of Penguin Group (USA) Inc.

PRINTED IN THE UNITED STATES OF AMERICA

10 9 8 7 6 5 4 3 2 1

Chapter 1

————◆————

Emily Wagner stepped onto the porch when she heard riders approaching in the distance. As she squinted into the waning sun to find a reason for their arrival, something about them didn't seem right. A sense of impending danger arose in her, and an unexpected chill skittered up her spine.

As the riders got closer, she could make them out as complete strangers, scruffy and dirty. The one riding at the head of the bunch looked vaguely familiar. Feeling inexplicable alarm at their advance and rough appearance, Emily hurried inside the ranch house to locate her late husband's double-barreled scattergun just in case these visitors *did* prove to be less than friendly.

She had to use a stepstool to reach the shotgun that hung above the fireplace. When she freed it from the pegs where it rested, she snapped open the breech to make sure it was loaded. It wasn't.

Now, where did Otis keep those shells?

As her eyes scanned the room, she remembered him saying something about a box in the desk drawer. She rushed across the room and tugged at the stubborn drawer pulls. There, in a wooden box, she found a handful of double-aught buckshot shells. With shaking hands, she gathered up two, then, with the shotgun breech still open, she fumbled with the shells, trying to insert them. She dropped one. It clattered to the floor and rolled under the table, out of reach. *Get hold of yourself, Emily.* She cursed under her breath before taking a second to gather her wits and calm her nerves. She wrestled with the box to extract another shell. She nervously took one out and slipped it into the breech. Snapping the barrel closed, she hurried out onto the porch.

She was shocked to see the four tough-looking cowboys sitting quietly astride their horses less than ten feet from the railing. The one who had been at the head of the small column tipped his hat and gave her an insincere smile, revealing a gold tooth, one of the few teeth he had left.

"Why, howdy do, Miz Wagner. Lovely weather we're havin', ain't it?" he said.

"Fair to middlin'. What is it you've come about?" Emily said, holding the Greener tightly as she cocked both barrels. "And how do you know my name? I sure as shootin' don't know yours."

"Why, we was acquaintances of your dearly departed husband, ma'am. Sorry to hear of his misfortune. Just stoppin' by to pay our respects."

"I don't reckon that's necessary. So, why don't you boys just keep on riding? Go on about your business."

Emily raised the barrel of the Greener toward the leader, moving it as if it were a cattle prod. Just then, from behind, a strong arm reached around her and yanked the shotgun from her grip. One barrel discharged into the porch overhang as her fingers were yanked off the trigger. The pellets blew a hole clear through the shake shingles. Startled, she tried to back away but was quickly surrounded by the strong arms of someone twice her size who emitted the distinct odor of skunk.

"What the . . . ? You let go of me this very instant or

I'll scream my head off. My boys will come pouring out of that bunkhouse any second now. You scoundrels will wish you'd never come by this ranch." She started to scream but was struck on the head with such force her knees buckled and bright colors danced briefly before her searching eyes. Her world faded to black as she crumpled to the floor.

A stabbing pain in the back of her head was the first thing Emily felt as she awoke. Still groggy, she tried to sit up but found that her hands had been bound behind her. Her ankles, too, were securely bound, and her shoes had been removed. She was lying on a bed, facedown on blankets that smelled musty and thick with dust. *These aren't my blankets and this sure isn't my bed.* Panic began to overcome her as she struggled to raise her throbbing head to get her bearings. But the room was pitch-black. She cried out.

"Where am I? Is anybody there?"

At her cry, a creaky door opened, and a shaft of sunlight shot into the room. It took a moment for her eyes to adjust to the brightness. She could make out that the room was sparse, with only a table and a couple of chairs near a cast iron stove. A few sticks of firewood sat nearby, and a coffeepot, a couple of tin plates, and an empty whiskey bottle sat on the table. In the doorway stood the man with the gold tooth, silhouetted by the waning sun behind him.

"Welcome to *my* hacienda, Miz Wagner."

"What am I doin' here? Why have you kidnapped me?" she screamed.

"Ah, the little lady has so many questions for which I have no answers, at the present, anyway."

"Who the devil are you? I've never done you any harm, although the sheriff will when he gets here."

"We'll worry about him when the time comes, lady, not that it's likely. In fact, unless you settle down and be a proper guest, I might get mad enough to kill you instead of keeping you safe and sound until our mission is finished. Oh, and since you asked, my name is Virgil Cruz. I think you may have heard of my brother, Vanzano Cruz, eh?"

Emily's blood ran cold at the name. Vanzano Cruz was the polecat who had gunned down her husband, Otis Wagner, on the streets of Apache Springs less than a year back. Otis had just left the barbershop next door when the robbers came busting out of the National Bank's front door. One man came face-to-face with Otis and shot him in the chest for no reason other than he was there, standing between the gunman and his horse. Otis died on the spot. Emily had seen it all from the window of the dry goods store.

"What do you want with me?" she said through gritted teeth.

"Well, I'll tell you this, Miz Wagner, you are gonna help me get rich and get even with the man who shot my brother down like a dog," Cruz said.

"I wouldn't help you climb out of a pit of vipers."

"Oh, you *will* help. I promise you that."

"As soon as Sheriff Cotton Burke finds out what you've done, he'll be at your doorstep. Then you'll wish you were someplace else."

"Don't be countin' on Cotton Burke for help. No, ma'am. We got that angle covered. He'll not be ridin' to your rescue, leastways not until after the sixteenth, not if he cares a whit for your safety," said Cruz.

Emily puzzled over what Cruz meant. Had something happened to the sheriff? A look of deep concern fell across her face.

"Well, for sure my men will be out scouring the hills looking for me. They'll come, sure as shootin'," Emily said.

"Them men of yours could scour the hills for a month and never think to look here. A posse of marshals with hound dogs couldn't track us to this spot."

Emily struggled to hide her alarm at her situation. *I must put on a brave face.*

"You don't know my men. One of them is an Indian,

pure Mescalero Apache. He'll be lookin' for certain. And he *will* find you."

"Gotta track me down first, and that ain't gonna happen. So you might as well make it easy on yourself, settle back and enjoy your visit with us. It'll all be over before you know it." Cruz turned and went back outside, leaving the door ajar. Emily could hear him talking to one of his men.

"You keep a keen eye on her. I don't want anything to happen to her before the sixteenth. If she gets away, I swear I'll gun you down myself. If there's any questions, get 'em out now, Scat," said Cruz.

"No questions, Boss," said the other man. "She ain't goin' nowhere."

"See that she don't. I'm on my way to deliver our *invitation* to the sheriff," Cruz said.

Emily could make out the squeak of leather as Cruz mounted up. Horse's hooves striking a rocky trail echoed off nearby walls. *Sounds like we might be in a canyon*, she thought.

A chill ran through Emily at the possibility of remaining captive to this band of scum until the sixteenth—a date nearly two weeks away. *Where are you, Cotton? I need you.*

Tears dampened the filthy blanket as desperation overcame her.

Chapter 2

———⟫•⟪———

Henry Coyote stormed into the sheriff's office with fire in his eyes. The door slammed against the wall, rattling the window, then stayed open. The sheriff looked up only with his eyes at the Indian's abrupt entry. The short, wiry frame and stark black hair hanging to his shoulders beneath a red headband could make any person unaccustomed to coming face-to-face with an Apache very nervous. But Cotton had known Henry for some time and felt no threat from his fierce demeanor. Though it was looking like this time could be different.

Henry was a full-blooded Mescalero with walnut skin, a deeply lined face, and a Bowie knife slipped through a woven belt. He was a man of few words and not a man to trifle with. It was clear to Cotton, however, that someone had done just that.

"You're here about Emily." As Cotton Burke looked into those dark eyes, he saw more than just anger. A time for calm and reason needed to be arrived at, if the expression on Henry's face was any indication. Now, if he could only get Henry to come to the same conclusion.

"How you know?" Henry's eyes echoed the question.

"I'm the sheriff. I get paid to know things."

"I, too, know things."

"Tell me."

"I no see Miss Emily since sunup. When I go look for her, she nowhere to be found. House door open and shotgun on floor by door. I feel bad thing happen. What we do?"

A grim expression clouded the sheriff's face, as he scooted back in his chair and motioned for Henry to sit across from him. "Henry, we have a serious problem. I do know about Emily. Sit. We'll talk."

"No time talk. Must find Miss Emily. You come, or I go alone."

"At the moment, neither one of those choices is goin' to work," Cotton said.

Henry shook his head, obviously rejecting the sheriff's vague words. He shuffled his feet and clenched his fists. He showed no intention of wasting more time jawing. Cotton knew if Henry thought something bad had happened to Emily Wagner, he'd waste no time doing something about it. Cotton watched the Indian grip the hilt of his Bowie knife and set his jaw. His dark eyes narrowed at the words he was hearing.

"Not good enough," he said and turned to leave.

"Hold on, Henry! You *must* hear me out. This piece of paper has to do with Miss Emily. And, for now, we must both make very careful moves, so as to keep her from harm."

"What words say?"

"It says that she has been kidnapped by dangerous men. It warns against retaliation, or she will be killed. If we do as they say, they insist she will remain safe."

"What demands?"

"The paper says that she will not be harmed and will be

released after the sixteenth of this month. It says I am not to look for her or send anybody to look for her."

"Who send paper?"

"I'm not certain, but I'd bet it came from Virgil Cruz."

"He very bad man. Work for Brennan outfit."

"That's right. Now, I need your help to keep her safe. We must be careful not to push these men too far, or I am certain she will be harmed. They are a vicious bunch. I can't let anything happen to Emily. You know how fond of her I am."

"I know she feel same. But how I not try save her?"

"First of all, I have no idea where she is being held. If I start digging around, scouring the county for the hiding place, I would surely be spotted. It's likely you would be, too. Cruz has men all over. If that happens, Emily will be killed."

Henry looked at his feet for a moment, then back at the sheriff. "I go alone. No one see me. I bring Miss Emily home safe."

"I need you to hold off for now, pardner. I *do* have a plan, but it will take a few days to put in place. You'll have to trust me and be ready when the time is right. It could mean Emily's life," said the sheriff.

"I do anything for Miss Emily."

"Here's what I want you to do. First, ride out of town and go straight back to the ranch. Don't let on to any of the other hands what I've told you. We have no idea who all might be involved in this. If you don't hear from me within six days, you are free to scout out where she might be held. You must do this on your own. You must be very secretive about it, probably only going out at night. But you can't do anything until I have the rest of the plan in place. This involves more than Emily, it could mean the lives of others, too. Do I have your word you'll do as I ask?"

Henry appeared reluctant to commit to the sheriff's request. His eyes clearly harbored many more questions than had thus far been answered. He shifted his gaze from Cotton to the floor. Finally, he nodded in agreement.

"Good," said the sheriff.

"All men from ranch gone," said Henry.

"Gone?" Cotton was startled by this news. "Where?"

"When I no see others, I come here."

"That's not good news. Either they were in cahoots with whoever grabbed Emily, or—"

"They in danger."

"Could be. Keep an eye out for anything that might suggest an ambush or a shooting. In fact, you must be on the lookout for *any* signs of trouble. If something has happened to the other hands, you may be the next target."

Henry grunted as he stood to leave. The sheriff stopped him.

"Go out the back way. The fewer people who know we've talked, the better."

Henry shut the rear door quietly behind him. He slipped away without being seen.

Cotton knew full well why Henry Coyote had such a deep desire to see that Emily Wagner was returned safely. Three years back, Otis Wagner had discovered the Indian lying in a gulley, sprawled facedown in the dirt, shot and bleeding. In a couple more hours, Henry would have been dead. Otis and Emily took him to the ranch, cared for him, and nursed him back to health. In Henry's mind, he owed his life to this woman and her deceased husband. He would be determined to do everything in his power to make her safety his priority.

I only hope he'll give me the time I asked for before he goes off on his own.

When Henry got back to the Wagner ranch, he began looking around for any signs of horses other than those of the regular ranch hands. Near the porch, mixed in with hoofprints of many others, he found the distinctive pattern of a horse with a broken shoe. *I not forget this print*, he thought, *and will kill the man whose horse made it.*

He'd promised the sheriff not to act impulsively, but

Henry Coyote found himself already struggling to keep
that promise. There were no words, no promises that could
allow him to leave Emily's life in the hands of scoundrels
one minute longer than necessary. He began his search for
the missing ranch hands.

Chapter 3

———>•«———

Cotton Burke stared at the Colt .45 in his hand. He loved the feel of the smooth walnut grip and the perfect balance. It was the only tool he'd ever been really good at using. He wondered if that was a skill to be proud of. Killing wasn't something he'd set out to do, but some men seemed bent on behavior that made it inevitable. The day he shot and killed Vanzano Cruz was a case in point.

He turned the revolver around and half-cocked it. He snapped open the loading gate and slowly rolled the cylinder to make certain it was fully loaded. Five bullets, with the hammer on the empty chamber to prevent an accidental discharge. He slipped the Colt back into his holster as he stood. Near the door lay his saddlebags, an extra box of cartridges, and a couple of blankets rolled and tied with leather thongs. A Winchester rifle leaned against the wall. He pulled out the note he'd found nailed to the door of his office and read it once more.

Looks like I'm destined to kill me another Cruz. His

mouth contorted with loathing for the man. He refolded the paper and slipped it into his pocket.

Before gathering up his things, he tore an old wanted dodger in half, turned it over to the blank side, touched the point of a stubby pencil to his tongue, and began scribbling a note for his deputy, who was out of town collecting taxes from some of the ranches to the south. Deputy Keeno Belcher would be back the next day, but Cotton wasn't going to wait around to talk to him in person. He placed the note in the center of his desk where it was certain to be found. He mulled his words over one more time.

> *Keeno,*
>
> *Something's come up. I'll be back in a couple days. Don't say nothing to nobody about me being gone. If you do, you'll be back cleaning out stalls at the livery stable. Anybody asks, you say I'm conferring with the mayor, or getting up a petition, something of the sort.*
>
> *And keep that Remington in its holster. The last time I was gone, I come back to find you'd darned near shot your foot off. Try talking them drunks into coming to jail peaceable like.*
>
> *Cotton*

I hate threatening that fool deputy, but I can't risk him stumbling onto what's happening.

Cotton walked to the livery to get his horse saddled. As he approached, the stable owner came out with a pitchfork in one hand and a bucket in the other. The man was muttering to himself. He didn't see the sheriff coming toward him. He looked up abruptly, startled at the shadow that had fallen across his path.

"What the . . . Oh, it's you, Sheriff. Didn't see you."

"I could tell your mind was elsewhere, Dooley. What's got you so deep in thought?"

"This here is a bucket of grain from one of the bags I

bought two days ago from the feed store. It's so full of them blasted mealy bugs, it ain't fit to give any animal a fellow'd expect to make it home on. Make 'em sick, it would. I swear I don't know what's gotten into ol' Delbert. He's actin' like his loyal customers don't mean a hill of beans no more."

Cotton peered into the bucket and, sure enough, crawling all over the grain were the pesky bugs that drove ranchers crazy when they got into their feed, usually when it had gotten wet and started to rot. But it wasn't the bugs that had the sheriff worried, it was the pitchfork Dooley was wielding like a spear.

"What do you intend to do with that frog-sticker, Dooley?"

"What? Oh, this here pointy thing. Uh, I figure it'll give him the incentive to fork over the money I gave him and come down and haul off that pile of rotten grain he foisted off on me."

"Maybe I ought to saunter on down there with you. Just to make sure nothin' happens to make you sorry you didn't think this through real good."

"Aww, that ain't necessary. Here, you take the pitchfork with you. You can lean it against the first stall if you're goin' thataway. Say, you leavin' town or somethin'?"

"I have to ride over to the Brennan place. I hear he thinks his cattle have been disappearin' a few head at a time. Says his men have been tryin' to catch the rustlers in the act, but so far they've had no luck. I'll be back later."

Dooley gave the sheriff a backhanded wave and continued his march to the feed store.

Scat Crenshaw squatted on the porch of the tiny, remote cabin. His mind was going a mile a minute. There were three things that Scat seemed to have little control over: his temper, his impulsive use of a gun, and his infatuation with the ladies. He didn't have anything to lose his temper over at the moment, and since he was stranded out in the wilderness alone, he had no one to get angry at and shoot. The only thing left to divert his mind was that good-looking lady lying inside, all strung up and helpless.

And Emily Wagner certainly *was* occupying his thoughts.

Scat Crenshaw had joined Cruz and his band after being sent a wire to come down to Apache Springs from Colorado to help with what Cruz referred to as "a killing." Of course, the gunslinger wasn't certain how many Cruz meant to kill, or who they were, but since dodgers with Scat's face on them hung on walls and posts all over Colorado, it didn't really make any difference that Cruz was vague about whatever the job was. And since he'd ridden all the way down to Apache Springs on the word of a man with a reputation even worse than his own, he aimed to get his fair share of whatever crooked deal Cruz had in mind. If he hadn't already been solidly on board, Emily Wagner was shaping up to be quite an added bonus.

In fact, the only thing that stuck in his craw was Virgil's talking down to him, like a father to an errant child. *He don't know me well enough to go makin' threats, no sir. The time'll come when I'll make him eat them words.*

Scat began making plans to have Emily *and* his share of whatever loot might be coming his way. And whoever this Cotton fellow was that Emily mentioned, well, he better watch out because Scat Crenshaw was nobody's fool. And he could hold his own against any law dog from here to the Mississippi. He'd shot enough of them to know.

Chapter 4

The tall, rail-thin man wearing a long, black duster reined in his horse out front of the dry goods store in Gonzales, New Mexico Territory. He sat for a moment before dismounting, searching about with narrowed eyes, taking inventory of every face that might seem unduly interested in his arrival. Satisfied he hadn't been followed, he dismounted, drew his carbine from its scabbard, draped a pair of saddlebags over his shoulder, and strode toward the hotel, directly across the street.

In front of double pine doors painted dark green, with brass doorknobs and frosted glass window lights, he smiled at how improved the facade was since he'd last been there. Before entering, he slapped at his coat to shed some of the dust that had accumulated over the past seven hours, then took off his black, floppy-brimmed hat, and brushed at it a couple of times before settling it back on his head.

He entered to find a wide lobby with two circular, padded seats in the middle. A large planter with fanlike palms filled a corner, and several velvet-covered armchairs sat around. *That fancy oriental rug gives this place more opulence than this dusty New Mexico town deserves*, he thought.

The check-in desk to his left was attended by an attractive, blue-eyed woman with too much makeup and long blond hair piled on top of her head, held by two silver combs. Several strands dangled loosely to her shoulder. She looked up from studying the register, and seeing him, she broke into an effusive smile and rushed around the counter to hug him.

"Oh, my lord, is it really you? Can it really be?" she stuttered. "You *are* a sight."

"Yep, it's me, Melody."

She stepped back, holding him at arm's length, and shook her head and clucked her tongue.

"Cotton Burke, alive and kickin'. We heard you were dead, that you got shot up in Texas. It's good to see a soul can't always believe what she hears."

"Uh-huh. Good to see you, too, Melody. Looks like the, uh, *hotel* business has been good."

"My girls are stayin' busy."

"Yeah, I saw a couple of them out front. Is Jack around?"

She stopped smiling. Her face suddenly grew hard, revealing a life her smile had masked.

"Now, Cotton, you ain't still sore at him for something he didn't do, are you?"

"Is he here?"

"Cotton, it wasn't him, it was me. He didn't steal me away from you. I-I just couldn't take it no more, you bein' away all the time, never knowin' whether you'd been shot down in some filthy cow town street. I went to him because I was lonely. Women get that way, you know. Please, Cotton, don't . . ."

"It's got nothin' to do with you. Now, I asked if he is here. Can I get an answer or am I goin' to have to kick in every door in the place?"

Melody stepped back, her forehead lined with worry, the years since he'd last seen her suddenly added physically to his memory of her. She turned away from him with tears in her eyes.

"Second floor, number three."

"Obliged," he said as he headed straight for the stairway.

"Go ahead, Cotton, kill him. Kill him for nothin'. You're good at that, aren't you, you gunslingin' polecat," she shouted after him.

Cotton ignored her pleadings. He didn't even look back as he took the steps two at a time. When he reached number three, he turned the knob. It wasn't locked. He shoved it hard. The door slammed against the wall as he stepped inside with his rifle at the ready. He found Memphis Jack Stump lying on a brass bed, naked to the waist, sound asleep. At least he was until Cotton Burke nearly busted the door off its hinges. Stump awoke with a start, reflexively reaching for a Remington .44 on the table beside the bed.

"That'd be a big mistake, Jack," said Cotton, cocking the Winchester before the still groggy man could get the Remington under control and bring it to bear.

"Cotton! What the devil are you doin' here? I-I heard you got yourself blown to pieces over in Texas," said Jack.

"Somebody lied to you, Jack. Someone else just said you can't believe everything you hear. Even you should know that by now."

Jack dropped the Remington on the sheets and sat up. He rubbed at his eyes and reached for a bottle of whiskey that was also on the small, round table where his gun had been. He pulled the cork, took a long swig, and then thrust it toward Cotton.

"Drink?"

"Too early."

"Suit yourself. So, Cotton, what brings you back to Gonzales? You ain't still sore at me for takin' up with Melody, are you? Shucks, you was gone so long, how was I to know you was still alive. A man has to have female company, pardner, or he shrivels up and goes crazy. Besides, wasn't that her job, lookin' out for us poor lost souls?"

"Like I told her, and of course she didn't listen, it's got nothin' to do with that business."

Cotton leaned the Winchester against the wall and pulled up a chair. He pulled back his long coat to reveal a Colt .45 in a cross-draw holster. He wore a brocaded vest over a black cotton shirt. On the vest pocket, a silver badge was pinned.

"W-whoa. What's that danglin' from your vest? Y-you ain't sold out to the law again, have you? Tell me it ain't so," said Jack.

"Catron County sheriff. And I got a problem, Jack."

"Catron County is up north, ain't it? What brings you down here? Why, I ain't never even been up that way."

"That's what I'm countin' on, Jack. Nobody up there knowin' your ugly face."

"What are you talkin' about?"

"My problem."

"What problem?"

"The one you're goin' to help me with. That problem, Jack."

Jack blinked, took another swig of whiskey, corked the bottle, then lay back down and rolled over onto his side, facing away from Cotton.

"Be sure to let me know how it all comes out, ol' friend. Right now, I've got to get some sleep before the poker tables open this evenin'."

Cotton stood up, took one step toward the bed where Jack had just settled his head back on the pillow, and reached out, grabbing a handful of long hair. Jack was yanked off the bed with a yelp as he crashed to the floor. Cotton picked up his rifle and pointed it at Jack's head. Jack lifted himself up on one arm, rubbed his shoulder where he'd fallen on it, and gave Cotton a scowl.

"Now, what'd you have to go and do a thing like that for, Cotton? Damn, my poker arm'll be sore for days, and I'm no good at dealin' when I got a sore arm. Probably can't draw worth a hoot, either. Could get myself outdrawn by some drunk on a losin' streak."

"Get up, Jack. Get some clothes on and let's get goin'. Oh, and you better stuff a couple of clean shirts in your saddlebags. You'll be gone for a spell."

Chapter 5

———◦•◦———

Virgil Cruz and four others reined in in front of the ranch house at the Double-B ranch. They dismounted as ranch owner Hank Brennan stepped out through the heavy oak door and onto the wide, stone porch. A yapping fox terrier shot past him into the yard.

"Where you boys been? I thought you were checking on the cattle in Saucer Valley."

"We, uh, was just headed out that way when we came across some tracks that looked to be leading to where we lost them forty head last month. Thought we'd track 'em, see where they led us," said Cruz.

The little dog began nipping at the horses' heels. Cruz's roan began crow hopping, dancing sideways to escape the noisy nuisance.

"And, what'd you find?" said Brennan, giving the dog the side of his boot. The dog yipped and retreated to the porch, where he continued his vocal disagreement at sharing his yard with smelly horses.

"Nothin'. They sorta faded into the rocks where all that

slick-rock and shale has fallen into the pass at boundary marker seven."

"You think the rustlers came that way?" said Brennan.

"It's likely."

"What do you Tulip boys think? Cruz got it right? You two are the only real trackers I got around here."

The Tulip brothers looked at each other for a second before one of them spoke. "We weren't with them during their trackin'. We was down by the creek movin' that bunch of steers to the pens. But I reckon if Virgil said it was so, it likely was."

"That's right. The Tulips joined up as we was ridin' in," said Cruz. He shot a scowl at the twin brothers that he hoped Brennan wouldn't see.

"Well, get yourselves a bite to eat, then head out to where I sent you in the first place. You got that, Cruz?"

"Why yessir, *Mister* Brennan."

The five of them walked their horses to the pens behind the bunkhouse. Brennan watched them for a moment before going back inside. Hank's eighteen-year-old son, Cappy, sat at a table, reading a book.

"You hear all that, Cappy?"

"Uh-huh. You think they're lyin', Pa?"

"Can't say for certain, but I'm goin' over and cut them Tulip brothers out of the herd. I'll get to the bottom of it."

"Want me to tag along?"

"No. You stay here. I don't want them figurin' out you're keepin' an eye on Cruz and his bunch of cutthroats."

"Whatever you say, Pa."

Hank caught up to the only hands he truly trusted, the Tulip brothers, as they were coming out of the cook shack. Cruz was nowhere in sight.

"Hold up, boys. I want a word. Was that the truth when you said you weren't with Cruz and his boys and don't know what they were doin'?"

"Yeah. We was doin' like we said. Now, Cruz, uh, well–" stammered one of them.

Hank shook his head and walked away. "Never mind. I

figure I oughta knowed better than to expect the truth from that bunch. Never shoulda hired that no-account Cruz."

Cruz came out of the cook shack in time to see Hank walking away from the Tulips. He was picking his teeth with a toothpick and glaring at the two brothers.

"What'd the old man want, boys?" Cruz said.

"Nothin', Virgil. Just passin the time of day, that's all."

Virgil squinted at them both, then said, "You two are a-lyin'. I can see it in your eyes. And I don't hold with no liars. Now, get mounted 'cause we're headin' up to Saucer Valley like old man Brennan told us to. We'll put on a good show for him."

The Tulip brothers went for their horses as Ben Patch approached Cruz.

"How long we gonna have to put up with that old fool's orders, Virgil?" said Ben.

"Till the sixteenth. That's all. Then we'll be rich beyond belief." He looked over at the Tulip brothers with a sneer.

The Tulip brothers always did as they were told. This time, though, they were nervous and hesitant, both knowing they would be without jobs if they didn't follow the foreman's orders, and while they weren't certain what Cruz was up to, they were certain that it likely wasn't legal. But jobs were too scarce to take a chance of getting kicked off the ranch. All five of the men whipped their mounts to a trot. They noticed that Hank Brennan had pulled aside the heavy drapes on the front window and was watching them leave.

Hank and Cappy stared after the departing riders for several minutes before Hank allowed his feelings to spill out.

"I've never had a good feelin' about that bunch, Cappy. I surely haven't."

"Why don't you just run 'em off? We can get a new crew together in no time. Why there's men in town who'd give their right arm to get on with the Double-B," said Cappy. "I've been asked lots of times if we got any need for wranglers."

Hank turned away with a sigh, failing to answer his son.

* * *

After they arrived at the ridge that overlooked Saucer Valley, Cruz reined in and swung his horse around to face the Tulip brothers. He had been silent for the whole time since they had left the ranch house. Now, after letting his anger build to a fury, he was ready to say his piece.

"You two dumb sons of bitches. Why didn't you back me when I was tellin' Brennan where we were?"

"I don't understand," said one of the brothers. "Why would we say we was with you when we wasn't? We was doin' what we said. Fact is, you shoulda been with *us*, but you took off and hightailed it to who knows where, leavin' us to shoulder all the work. We ain't takin' the blame for you fellas messin' in business you shouldn't ought to. You was comin' back from the direction of Saucer Valley, and that's the truth of it."

Cruz got off his horse and led the roan over to a tree where he tied off the reins. The others followed suit. The Tulip brothers sauntered over to the edge of the overlook.

"It don't look to me like there are two hundred head down there. Where do you suppose the others could have got to?" said one of the brothers. "Do you know anything about this, Cruz?"

"Well now, it ain't nothin' you two need to worry yourselves about. You got other worries right now," snarled Cruz. The Tulips turned to see Cruz pointing his six-shooter at them.

"Wh-what the hell! You–" was all that one of them was able to spit out before Cruz emptied all six shots into the brothers. They were dead before their dusty slide to the bottom of the hill ended in a tangle of brush and prickly pear cactus.

"Damn!" said Ben, his eyes wide in surprise. "I sure didn't see that coming."

"Neither did they," said Cruz, with a snicker.

Chapter 6

———⟫◆⟪———

"Where are you taking him?" Melody grabbed at Cotton. "You got no right to haul Jack outta here. He ain't done nothin' to you. I'm the one you want. Beat me, slap me around, shoot me if it'll make you feel better. But don't take it out on Jack, please. I love him," she screamed, and took a wild swing at his chest.

Cotton grabbed her hand, pulled her close, and looked her right in the eye.

"Stay out of this, Melody. It's got nothin' to do with you." He released his grip and pushed her back onto one of the overstuffed chairs in the lobby. She jumped up angrily and stomped her foot.

Cotton turned to Jack and gave a jerk of his head to say it was time to leave. But Melody rushed around the counter and grabbed a .41-caliber Colt derringer from an open drawer. She pulled back the hammer with both thumbs, leaned her elbows on the sign-in book, and took shaky aim at Cotton.

"If you don't let go of Jack, I swear I'll blow a hole through your gizzard. So help me, I will."

Seeing that the situation was escalating and that someone could get killed, even from a stray shot, Memphis Jack held up his hands.

"Now, hold on, Melody. He ain't worth gettin' you strung up for a killin'. If he says it ain't got nothin' to do with you, then I gotta believe him until I find out different. I reckon I do owe him for keepin' me from a prison cell. That don't mean I like him, just that I trust him to keep his word. Now put that thing away and come kiss me good-bye. Cotton says I'm goin' on a little trip to help him out, although he ain't said how I'm supposed to do that."

Melody eased the hammer back and placed the pistol on the counter. She had tears in her eyes as she spoke.

"Cotton, you got to promise me nothin' will happen to Jack. Please, Cotton."

Cotton pushed Jack toward the door and then turned to Melody.

"Ain't no guarantees in this old world, darlin'. You of all people ought to know that." He shoved Jack ahead of him out onto the boardwalk. The blast from the little single-shot derringer shattered the glass in the door frame and lodged in a porch post not two feet from Cotton's head.

As he hurried Jack toward the stable, Cotton said, "Good thing she never really learned to shoot." He smiled as he remembered the day several years back when he had tried to give her shooting lessons. *She never could hit the broad side of a barn, but the way she looked and the things she could do, who cared?*

As they reached the other side of the street, Cotton untied his horse's reins and led him to the livery. Jack stopped just inside the door and turned to Cotton.

"I want to know where we're goin', and I want to know now, before I take another step."

"You'll know when I'm good and ready to tell you, Jack. Now, move it."

Jack's eyes narrowed, and if he'd had a handful of six-shooter, he would probably have taken that opportunity to plug his old friend Cotton. But Cotton was no stranger to

Jack's mercurial changes in mood or attitude and was prepared for whatever might come.

Jack's swing at Cotton came with the suddenness of an aroused rattler. Cotton merely dodged the roundhouse punch and jammed the Winchester in Jack's ribs.

"Oww! Damn, Cotton, you don't have to get rough. I'm comin' along, ain't I?" Jack doubled over in pain.

"I suppose that fist was just your way of sayin' thanks for the invite."

Jack hung his head for a minute. "Naww. maybe I was just thinkin' about havin' to leave sweet Melody all alone. Nobody knows better'n you what happens when she ain't got a man around for a couple of weeks. She goes on the scout for a replacement, that's what."

"Yeah, I reckon I do know how Melody is. But you'll get over her. I did. Now, let's get a move on."

"When do you intend on tellin' me what I'm gettin' myself into? Or are you scared I'll light out on you after findin' out?"

"Jack, you won't light out, because if you try it, I'll blow you to kingdom come without another thought. You were right back there, you *do* owe me a favor and a whole lot more. So get that gelding saddled and be quick about it. The devil's a-waitin' and I don't want him to have to twiddle his fingers."

Jack swallowed hard and threw the saddle on his horse. He tied his bedroll on the cantle along with the saddlebags and then climbed aboard.

"Okay, Cotton, I'm ready to ride. But you better make it worth my while, because I'm an unforgiving sort."

"It ain't like you're in that corral all by yourself, pardner. Now, let's move out."

They rode for several hours, heading north through scrubby desert land that no farmer could ever make pay. What few cattle they spotted were spread so far trying to find a patch of edible grass, a man could ride for days just rounding up a handful of them.

"Can't see what would bring anyone out here in the first place, unless they got a hellish hankerin' to dig up what's beneath the ground," said Jack, turning in his saddle to give his sore back a rest. "'Cause there sure as shootin' ain't a thing above ground a soul could yearn for."

"There's lots of things a man with a twisted sense of what he wants can dream up."

"We goin' after someone like that, Cotton? I'm itchin' to know what I'm headed into."

"You'll know in due time, Jack."

"Cotton, for old time's sake, you know I never did hold with walkin' into a bad situation blind. At least give me a hint at what's goin' on."

"You want a hint? Okay, Jack, I'll give you a hint. You remember back about eleven years ago, when you and me found ourselves smack dab in the middle of a cattle war? The outcome wasn't all that certain."

"Uh, yeah. You sayin' we're walkin' into another one?"

"No."

"Then what?"

"Not a cattle war. But it likely won't feel much different," said Cotton.

Jack looked away as he muttered something foul under his breath.

Chapter 7

———◆◆◆———

Virgil Cruz and his thugs dug two graves in the rocky soil. The dead bodies of the Tulip brothers lay several feet away, awaiting burial at the bottom of the ravine where they fell, the stench of death already beginning to encircle them.

"This hole's ready. How're you coming over there?"

"About finished. Not quite deep enough, but I can't stand the stink any longer. This one musta relieved hisself just as he died. Let's get the bodies underground and be done with it, Virgil," said Ben Patch.

Virgil spat a stream of tobacco juice into the hole and nodded. He'd had all he could stand of digging holes, anyway. He climbed out of the trench and motioned for the other two to drag one of the bodies to the edge of the fresh grave. He wiped his sweat-drenched brow on a filthy shirtsleeve.

"You two get a hold on his feet and toss him in," he said.

They grumbled at the sight, bloody and beat-up as if the dead brothers had been dragged through a field of cactus.

But they bent down, grabbed each of the corpses by its near worn-out boots, and did as they were told. All three began shoveling dirt into the holes as fast as they could. When they were finished, Virgil smoothed over the dirt so it wouldn't attract any special attention.

"Help me gather up some brush and a few rocks to scatter on top, so no one will figure these for fresh graves and get curious enough to do some diggin'. Hell will freeze over before anyone finds the Tulip brothers, poor dumb souls that they was," said Virgil.

"You sure are right about that, Virgil. Reckon they shouldn't oughta suggested you weren't on the up-and-up. They surely was a couple of fools," said Ben.

"Yeah. And you can see what it got them. Let's mount up and go into town for a couple beers before heading back to the ranch," said Virgil. "Bring their horses."

The three of them barely glanced back at the freshly made graves of two men who only hours before had been a couple of hardworking cowboys. They'd never been considered members of Virgil Cruz's very small circle of friends. But then, that circle always did seem to have a way of shrinking, often suddenly.

Cruz and his men rode into the dirty little town of Apache Springs, Catron County, New Mexico Territory, as if nothing had happened, as if their fellow cowboys had merely ridden off into the desert and never come back. Virgil Cruz led the others into the saloon and up to the bar. Bartender One-Eyed Billy Black took note of their presence and wiped the bar top in front of them.

"What'll it be, gents?" said Billy.

"Beers."

Billy drew three beers from a barrel on the end of the bar, blew the foam off the tops, and sat them in front of his customers. The sound of three coins hitting the wood completed the transaction. Billy stood for a moment, then sauntered back down toward the end to reenter the conversation he had been engaged in when Virgil and his two cohorts had come in. An old man leaned over to Billy and whispered something, masking his mouth so as not to be overheard.

"Ain't that ugly one Virgil Cruz?" he mumbled.

"That's him," said Billy. "But I wouldn't let him know you're asking about him, 'cause he's meaner than a rabid coyote. I saw him gun a man down just for lookin' at him wrong."

"What is it that makes a man that mean?"

"With some men, it usually results from life dealing them a lousy hand. With Cruz, it just come natural."

The other man laughed and slapped the bar top.

Virgil got an itch. It was one of those feelings like a bug crawling on his skin that he couldn't actually see. He just knew it was there. "Drink up and let's get out of here. I feel like we're becomin' the talk of the town," he said.

The others did as he said and they all three started toward the door. Suddenly, Virgil stopped, dropped his hand to his Colt, drew, cocked, and fired in the blink of an eye, shattering the glass that sat between Billy and the other man.

"Next one will split your skull, old man. Don't you ever talk about me when I'm within earshot. You understand? Never!"

The old man just nodded rapidly, shaking like an aspen in a gale. Billy didn't move, didn't even look up. He'd seen Virgil's antics before, and nothing surprised him. In fact his only having one eye had a lot to do with Cruz. It was something he knew better than to talk about when Cruz was around.

Virgil and his crew of misfits sauntered down the boardwalk, crowding other pedestrians out into the street to avoid being shoved aside. Women, of course, were different. If Virgil and his men came upon a woman leaving the dress shop or mercantile, they politely stepped aside and tipped

their hats, being certain the lady heard whatever crude re-
mark they made about her as she passed. Women usually
checked the walkway before venturing out, to avoid any
such contact with bullies if possible. Even the town's soiled
doves kept their distance so as to not attract the kind of
trouble these three were known to dish out.

"Blade, I think it's time to turn a profit on some of
them beeves we got hid out in the hills. Our funds are getting low, and the sixteenth is still a ways off," said Virgil.
"We're goin' to have to move a few of Brennan's cattle for
a quick sale."

"I ain't sure we can rustle much more from these hicks.
Folks are pickin' up and leavin' left and right. Pretty soon,
there won't be any brands left to work," said Blade Coffman, a long-faced, hollow-cheeked gunman who walked
with a limp from a piece of lead that was lodged in his
thigh. He'd been shot during a bank robbery attempt in
Arizona that almost took his leg off. He'd found he was no
match for a sheriff with a Winchester. He was left alive, but
gimpy. After spending a year in prison, he was pardoned
when a man came forward to give testimony that Coffman
had simply been an innocent bystander in the bank that
afternoon and had been shot by mistake.

Coffman was so grateful to the man for getting him out
of prison, he joined up with him as soon as he was set free.
He never asked why it had taken him a whole year to come
forward. The man who had sprung him was Virgil Cruz,
one of the bank robbers who hadn't been caught.

Chapter 8

"Blade, as soon as we get back to the ranch, you and Ben go on up to the line shack and look in on things. Make sure Scat ain't been messin' around with that gal. The only way this is goin' to work is if it goes according to my plan and she stays unharmed until we're through. After that, well, it's a different story. You understand me?"

"Virgil, you cut me deeply. Why, even my sainted mother knows there weren't nobody ever born that's better at followin' orders than me." Blade's mouth twisted into a brown picket fence of a grin, with several pickets missing.

Virgil had handpicked Blade Coffman and Ben Patch because they were two of the meanest gunmen west of Amarillo. Between them, they accounted for eleven dead men, not including an estimated dozen more that didn't count in their minds because they were Indians, blacks, or Mexicans. One of the six deaths attributed to Blade was a soiled dove in Fort Worth. Blade wasn't picky about who became one of his victims. And he never showed remorse.

"Where'll you be when we get back, Virgil?"

"Not that it's any of your business, Ben, but I'm goin' to tell old man Brennan how the Tulip brothers got themselves shot up defendin' the herd from rustlers. That and how we saved the day by ridin' in just in the nick of time to save all but a few head of his prize cattle."

"Say, that's a good story, Virgil. Think he'll buy it?"

"He'll swallow whatever I tell him, boys, ain't you figured that out yet? Now, get along with you." Virgil swung his horse around and headed for the Double-B ranch.

When Virgil and his two hard cases had first blown into Apache Springs, Hank Brennan's spread looked like the perfect place from which to launch their nefarious acts. Brennan gave in and hired them on because times were tough and finding desirable hands was all but impossible. New Mexico Territory was rife with vagrants and scum. And Virgil Cruz was the worst of the lot.

As Virgil rode through the front gate, Hank Brennan stepped out of the bunkhouse followed by two of the other ranch hands. Hank stopped, cupped his hand over his eyes to see who was riding in so late, and then turned to the two cowboys at his side.

"Here comes Virgil. I need to talk to him. You two go on down to the creek and gather up them calves and bring 'em in for the night."

Both cowboys nodded and mounted up. They were well on their way when Virgil rode up leading the Tulip brothers' horses.

"Took you long enough to have a look at the western range. You take a little side trip into town? And where are the Tulips? And why do you have their horses?"

Virgil dismounted and wrapped the reins of all three horses around a hitching rail. He hiked up his holster and walked up to Brennan. He took off his hat and wiped perspiration from his brow with his shirtsleeve.

"Mr. B, I got back as soon as I could. We run into a little trouble when we caught up with the herd. There were some rustlers havin' at them cattle, and we just naturally needed to stop 'em."

"Well, come on inside and tell me about it." Brennan led the way into the large whitewashed frame ranch house he'd built himself ten years ago. Two stories tall, with a curved stairway and an oak railing he'd had sent all the way from Chicago, a carved oak mantel for the fireplace, and an oak front door with etched glass, the ranch house was an imposing structure. It was, in fact, the envy of ranchers for miles around. He motioned Virgil to the drawing room and a high-backed, overstuffed chair, and shooed the terrier off the couch. The dog growled lowly at Virgil, then hopped off the sofa and scurried beneath it.

Virgil settled into a chair, looking grim at what he was about to tell his employer but with confidence in his ability to continue blowing smoke in Brennan's face without fear of discovery. Virgil was well known for his silver tongue, and while he was pretty puffed up at his ability to pull off one successful scam after another, his boss wasn't always the easy mark Virgil assumed. Hank Brennan had proven adept at seeing through other men's bluffs on more than one occasion.

"Well, Mr. Brennan, here's the way it happened. We rode down into Saucer Valley where them cows was being ranged, when we noticed a spindle of smoke just kinda climbin' up through the still air like a rope a-twistin' around on its way to the heavens. Then we saw some hombres with runnin' irons plannin' to make changes to your brand. So we rode like the wind down into that valley, firin' and yellin', so's they'd know what they was up against and run for their lives."

"That what they did?"

"Well, yes and no. They had already cut a few head out and had driven them off to who knows where, but them that was left was stopped in their tracks when we got there. Only thing was, there was more'n we figured on and those poor Tulip brothers were cut down right before our eyes. And them in their prime, and all." Virgil faked at wiping a tear from his eye.

"You say the Tulips was killed? Both of 'em?"

"That they was. That was before we scattered them sidewinders to the four winds. Shot a couple of 'em up real bad, too. But they got clean away while we was gatherin' up what was left of the herd."

"What did you do with the boys?"

"Buried the poor unfortunate souls right at the bottom of the hill where they was shot to pieces, so their spirits could gaze out on this fair land for the rest of eternity. That's what we did. I jes' knowed you'd approve."

Brennan said nothing as he stared Virgil down, trying to figure out just how much of his story could be believed. He slumped in his chair, with a suspicious frown wrinkling his forehead, his jaw tightening as he chewed his lower lip. He waved Virgil on out of the room as he sat in morose silence.

I never should have hired that lyin' rattlesnake. Now I'm stuck with him and his murderin' ways. But I can't keep puttin' up with it. I have to do something to correct my error.

Chapter 9

The two men rode in silence. Cotton wasn't eager to tell Jack about the trouble he was about to be dragged into. He would have to soon but, for the moment at least, his thoughts were all about Emily. From the first, he'd been smitten with her. Even before Vanzano Cruz, Virgil's brother, had killed her husband Otis. And now Cotton felt there was yet a score to be settled. At least as long as there was a Cruz still alive.

It had broken Cotton's heart to see the sadness on Emily's face and the flood of tears that had stained her cheeks when her husband died, all of which served to make him hope some woman would care that deeply for him one day. But he'd been careful never to appear interested in being more than acquaintances after her husband's death; that is, until she stopped by his office one day with a very unusual request.

"Good morning, Sheriff Burke," she said, gliding into the room like a breath of fresh air.

Cotton busted his kneecap on the edge of the desk in his

awkward attempt to be a gentleman and stand in the presence of a lady. He stumbled forward in pain, while at the same time removing his hat. She smiled behind a delicate, gloved hand at his attempt at being mannerly.

"M-Miss Emily, I'm delighted to see you. Uh, won't you have a seat? Would you like some coffee?" His words were like a teenager's first encounter with the prettiest girl in town. To add to his misery, he suddenly remembered how most people referred to his coffee.

"No, thank you, Sheriff. I'll just sit a minute to cool off from the terrible heat. I'm afraid coffee would add to the distress. I *would* trouble you for a cup of water, though."

Thankful she'd turned down his coffee, he fumbled through his desk for something resembling a clean tin cup. Later, with her sipping the cool water, and both of them seated so as not to have any more mishaps, he was eager to hear whatever business had brought her to his office.

"Now, Miss Emily, what can I do for you?"

"Well, as you know, several ranchers have been trying to persuade me to return to St. Louis, a place more suited to a lady, they say. I suspect it is a desire to get their hands on my land. However, I was fully aware of the possible dangers to be found in a hostile land when I agreed to come in the first place, and I came willingly. The fact that my Otis fell victim to a brutal act has in no way deterred me from fulfilling his dream of building a ranch here. I venture to say it has hardened me to the task."

"I'm delighted that you've decided to stay, but I reckon I have to agree with the others; it's a tough life for most men, let alone a woman," he said, with some hesitation that his words could bring with them an unintended meaning.

"There's no use in trying to talk me out of my decision. I am staying, and that's that."

"H-how can I be of assistance, then, ma'am?"

"My husband had complete confidence in you as a man of strong character. It is for that reason that I would like for you to look over the men I have working for me and tell me which ones might chafe at taking orders from a woman, and which would be reliable, hardworking gentlemen."

"You want me to tell you which wranglers to keep?"

"And help me hire any new ones that are necessary."

Cotton had swallowed hard at the prospect of acting as an employment agent, but since it would allow him to get to know Emily Wagner better, he'd acceded to her wishes, spending about three days culling her hands to a very reasonable seven men in whom she could have confidence.

From that day forward, friendship had slowly grown into something more than just a passing interest on both their parts.

Cotton and Memphis Jack rode into Silver City just before nightfall. They stopped in front of the Cloverleaf Hotel and dismounted, dropping their reins loosely over the hitching rail.

"I'll get us a room. You go in and order us some grub," said Cotton.

"I'll be over in that saloon across the street. Come get me when you've got a room. My hand's itchin' for some action, and I feel lucky."

"We'll eat first, then you can go lose your money."

Jack gave Cotton a cold look. "Look, Cotton, you ain't my keeper. I'm along as a favor, although I can't figure out for the life of me what favor I owe you. So, if I was you, I'd scrape up every bit of good will I could to keep me taggin' along on whatever scheme you got in mind for us, and it better be profitable, too." Jack turned and headed straight for the saloon. He stopped after he heard the distinctive sound of a Colt .45 being cocked.

"Food first, Jack, or you'll be eatin' dirt. You ain't slippin' out on me."

Jack threw up his hands as he stared down the barrel of Cotton's revolver.

"Okay. Okay. Make it a steak, and I'm yours."

Cotton holstered his Colt and Jack followed him into the

hotel. Cotton went to the counter, turned the register book around, picked up the pen, dipped it into the inkwell, and started to write their names.

A man came through a curtained doorway. "Excuse me, sir, but we are full up for tonight. I'm real sorry."

Cotton looked at an empty register, frowned, then looked the man straight in the eye.

"I don't see any other rooms taken." Cotton pulled back his coat to reveal the sheriff's badge. "Where are all these folks that are supposed to be booked for the night?"

The man began to fidget nervously. "Uh, well, they aren't actually here right now, but Mr. McMasters reserved the whole hotel."

"McMasters? Who the devil is he?"

"Why, everyone in these parts knows Mr. McMasters. He ramrods the biggest mine around, ten miles east. He has several fellows that work for him, and they're all real handy with a six-shooter. He's expected anytime now, and if he found out I'd rented out one of his rooms, why, I'd be a dead man. Please, sir, Miss Betty runs a boardinghouse a block down. I'll bet she has a room available." He mopped at his sweaty brow and the top of his balding head with a large white handkerchief, looking like he was about to jump out of his skin.

Cotton thought about what the man had said, then shrugged, tossed the pen down on the counter, where it made an inky splatter, and turned on his heels and stormed out. He could hear a relieved sigh all the way out into the street.

"That badge of yours sure did turn that feller to your way of thinking, Cotton. He was mighty impressed."

"Oh, shut up, Jack, and move it on down to that boardinghouse."

"Uh-huh. And how about that steak? You're the one said you was hungry, and now you got me to thinkin' about wettin' my whistle *and* fillin' my belly. There's a restaurant right over there, next to the livery. What say we stop there first?"

"If it'll make you quit your whinin', we'll do it. You surely do talk a bunch. Is that what attracted Melody to you?"

It was apparent by the look on Jack's face he didn't like that last crack, but he let it drop. His eyes gave him away, though. He wasn't about to forget it. There'd be a day of reckoning, of that there could be no doubt.

When they reached the restaurant, Cotton went to a table in the corner, away from the other customers seated closer to the front window.

"How come you want to sit all the way back here? You afraid somebody from your shady past will come through them doors and decide to kick your backside?" said Jack.

"No, I'm afraid someone will want to kick yours and spoil my dinner."

"Uh-huh."

Cotton leaned over and talked just above a whisper.

"I need to tell you what you're up against before we get to Apache Springs, and I don't want the whole world knowin' about it. *That's* why we're sittin' in the back, you ornery cuss."

"I mighta figured it would be something so despicable, you'd have to keep it secret till I was hip deep in it. Well, spill it. I'm hungry, but I'm all ears."

A man with a badly stained apron came over to their table. His sleepy eyes suggested he was eager for the day to end. His unenthusiastic recitation of the menu items probably accounted for the few diners at a time when the place should have been full.

"Gents. I got a couple of steaks with your names on 'em, and some black-eyed gravy, and I can heat up some beans, too, if you've a mind. What'll it be?"

"Steak and beans for me," said Jack, "and you can skip that gravy. Coffee, too, if it ain't too much trouble."

"The same for me," said Cotton, waving the man off.

"Okay, get to it, Cotton. Give me the bad news so's I can get on with bein' even more angry at you than I already am."

"Better limber up that gun hand of yours, because you're about to fall in with the grimiest, smelliest, ugliest bunch of owlhoots you ever laid eyes on. They'll slit your throat for snorin', and gun you down for your boots. And they got a powerful hate on for me. Before it's all over, you can figure on getting real cozy with that bunch."

Jack sat there with a withered look on his face.

"What did I ever do to you to deserve such a rotten, lowdown friend?" he mumbled.

"What *haven't* you done?"

Chapter 10

———◆◆◆———

Scat Crenshaw was wanted in three states. He had slipped into New Mexico Territory to join Virgil Cruz and his men for what Cruz had said would be "well worth your time." And time was about all Scat had. He had been holed up in a cabin in Wyoming for nearly three months, trying to stay clear of a posse that had sworn to string him up quickly when they caught up with him. There were posses scouring the countryside for him and his brother, Dogman, for a string of stage robberies that had netted nothing but pocket change but left a number of dead bodies across Idaho, Montana, and Wyoming. When Scat got word that Virgil Cruz had work for him, he and Dogman slipped across the border into Colorado.

Now, as part of that work, Scat had been left in charge of Emily Wagner. He had a weakness for pretty women, and she fit the bill perfectly. Cruz's admonition not to lay a hand on her didn't scare Scat one bit. After Cruz rode off, Scat had a grin on his face that could mean only one thing: Emily was going to have to learn to enjoy his company or stay tied up for what could amount to many days. He snick-ered to himself at that thought.

He lit the wick of the kerosene lantern, grinning as the light revealed the woman's face. Emily was staring at him with a mixture of defiance and fear. He sat on a flimsy chair he'd pulled over beside the cot she was lying on, still bound tightly.

"Well, missy, I'd like to introduce myself. They call me Scat, and I'm going to be the only thing between your safety and comfort and a whole lot of trouble, if you catch my drift." The flickering lantern picked out a thin, pockmarked face with lines so deep they could have been planted with corn. "So, I hope you'll be rememberin' that when I ask kindly for a little favor now and then."

"If you lay a hand on me, Cotton Burke will flay you like a venison steak, you filthy pig," Emily snarled at him.

"Hmmm, you're a feisty little thing, ain't you? Well, we'll see how things go when you start to get hungry, real hungry." Scat got up with a chuckle and went outside to sit on the porch and smoke while he figured out just how to handle the pretty lady with an attitude more like a cata-mount than a member of a ladies' choir. That was when he saw two riders coming up the trail.

Virgil left Brennan's house reassured that he had success-fully just blown smoke in the old man's face once again. *I could get that old fool to use his last dollar to buy stock in an iron pyrite mine*, he thought. *Maybe I'll just up and try to locate one to sell him one of these days.* That brought out a laugh as he stomped toward the bunkhouse, leading his horse to the corral and raising a cloud of dust as he kicked clods of dirt out of his way.

After leaving his still-saddled roan tied to the cor-ral fence, he went inside to find three cowhands playing cards.

"Hey, Virgil, sit down and haul out some of that bundle of yours. We're a little short after last night's trip to town.

We could use some of your money," said Cappy Brennan, Hank's son.

Cappy was an amiable sort, easygoing and slow to anger. But everyone knew he wasn't an experienced manipulator of the pasteboards. Virgil often tried to push the young man to his limit, but he'd thus far failed to sucker the boy into betting more than common sense would dictate.

"Cappy, I swear, you're dumber'n an east Texas sodbuster if you think you can take a red cent from me."

"Well, sit down and let me give 'er a try. I *may* be smarter than you think."

As Virgil pondered whether it would be a good idea to try cleaning out the boss's son, he heard riders approaching the bunkhouse. He went to the single window and looked out to see Ben Patch and Blade Coffman riding up. They dismounted and started for the door. Virgil got to the door first and went outside, shutting the door behind him so that those inside wouldn't hear what was being said.

"Everything all right up there at the line shack, Ben?"

"Uh, well, I ain't just certain that our guest is any too happy bein' tied up and all," said Ben. "But I think we put the fear of God in Scat if'n he was to touch the lady."

"He's gettin' a little itchy, you know, waitin' on the action. I ain't sure we can keep him away from Miz Wagner," said Patch.

"Maybe I'll try to enlist a couple more men, help keep an eye on things."

"Ain't more just gonna cut down on our share of the money, Virgil?" said Ben.

"What did I ever do to get burdened with a couple of dirt-dumb saddle bums like you two?" Virgil shook his head as he kicked at a clump of dirt, exploding it across the ground. "Sometimes I swear I gotta spell everything out to you two."

"Well, don't it?"

"How many times do I gotta tell you, the only way it works is if the sheriff stays out of it. And the Wagner woman, and her safety, is our insurance."

"Uh-huh. We understand."

"Leave your horses saddled; we're goin' into Apache Springs."

As the three of them mounted up and started to ride off, Hank Brennan stepped out onto his wide porch. He was smoking a stogie and had his revolver strapped on.

"Virgil, where are you and the boys goin'?"

"Why, uh, Mr. B, we were just about to go back out to check on the herd, make sure they ain't been visited by them rustlers again."

"Hold up while I saddle my horse. I think I'll ride along with you." He stepped off the porch and headed for the corral. "You can show me where you buried the Tulip boys."

Virgil chewed on his lower lip as he thought about old man Brennan riding along with them and what he'd do if he found out that Virgil had been lying to him about rustlers running off with almost a quarter of his herd down in the valley. Ben and Blade looked to Virgil for guidance. All that showed them was a slowly building panic welling up in their leader, which didn't do much toward calming their own fears.

"That's a real rough ride up there. You sure you're up to it, considerin' your lumbago an' all?" Cruz asked as Hank rode up to them.

"Don't you worry none about my health, Virgil. I was pushin' beeves and bustin' broncs while you were still crawlin' in the dirt. Let's get goin'."

As the four rode, little was said between them. Ben and Blade exchanged questioning glances. Hank Brennan didn't abide deceit and was not a man unfamiliar with firearms. Ben grew more and more unsettled, squirming in his saddle like he had fleas. They all knew if old man Brennan caught on to what they'd been doing for several months, there'd be a hanging for sure, especially if he figured out they'd dry-gulched the Tulip brothers, twins that Brennan had hired on when they were but a couple of scraggly, bow-legged teenage orphans. Sweat streamed down Ben's face as he looked to Blade for some comfort. He saw nothing. It was clear from the expression on Virgil's face that he, too, had misgivings as to what they were riding into. They continued to follow the narrow trail through the jagged rocks and steep drop-offs. The trail came perilously close to the edge in several places. Virgil rode beside Hank.

Just as Ben was certain they were all dead men, Virgil yanked his horse to the right. Hank's horse shied, losing its footing in the rocky shale. The old man was thrown from his saddle. Both horse and rider tumbled over the edge and down the side of the sheer cliff. Hank slammed to a stop against a cluster of boulders that jutted out from the cliff twenty feet from the top. Brennan groaned at the impact, then he lay still, unconscious.

Virgil dismounted and peered cautiously over the side, shaking his head, though he was unable to see Hank's body. Brennan's horse had plummeted all the way to the bottom of the canyon, nearly a hundred feet, and lay dead from the impact. Virgil grinned at the sight of the broken animal.

"I told you this was dangerous country, Mr. B. An old man like you should have stayed at the ranch, where it's safer."

Chapter 11

———➤◆◄———

Cotton crawled out of bed at dawn and pulled on his pants. Stifling a yawn, he pounded on the wall that separated his room from Jack's.

"Rise and shine, Jack. We've got to get movin'. There's a long ride ahead of us."

He heard no sound coming from the other side of the wall. With a grunt of anger, he pulled on his boots and stepped into the hallway. He turned the doorknob to Jack's room and pushed. The room was empty, and the bed hadn't been slept in.

Cotton mumbled as he gritted his teeth. He struggled into his shirt, grabbed his rifle, gun belt, and hat, and hurried downstairs toward the sound of voices and the smell of cooking.

The dining room was at the rear of the house, and he could hear several men in conversation. As he stepped inside, he saw four men laughing as they ate. They were gathered around the table, stabbing potatoes from a bowl in the center, slicing chunks of fried pork, or spooning out a slab

of butter for their bread. One man was laughing and slosh-
ing coffee around so vigorously, some of it splashed onto
the table. This seemed to increase their raucous laughter,
and in the center of the hilarity, sitting with his back to the
door, was Memphis Jack Stump.

Cotton was relieved that he wouldn't have to go chasing after Jack; but that didn't calm his annoyance with the
man. He moved to the other side of the table and pulled
out a chair.

"Well, here he is right now, good ol' Cotton Burke,
the best damned sheriff in the territory. Let's give him a
cheer," hollered Jack, half standing and giving Cotton a
bow. "Figured we'd just have to eat your share while you
lollygagged around the whole mornin', getting' tangled up
in them soft blankets."

The men laughed even louder, each raising his coffee
cup in Cotton's direction. Cotton could only smile and go
along with whatever joke Jack had planted in the minds of
the cowboys seated around the table. Jack was, it was plain
to see by his weaving back and forth, his slurred words,
and his glazed eyes, quite drunk. It was also obvious that
after Cotton had settled in for the night, Jack had done just
what he had tried to do the second they hit town: gone to
the saloon for an evening of drinking and gambling.

Cotton decided to eat in silence and let Jack continue
his playful antics. Perhaps he'd end up drinking enough
coffee to get sober before Cotton had to give him the bad
news that they were heading for Apache Springs right after
breakfast. Jack was unmoved by his sober friend's presence, and he just got louder as he spun outlandish tales of
his exploits after the war and bragged of his abilities with
a six-shooter. He patted his Remington to emphasize his
point. Cotton waited for him to draw the damned thing and
blow a hole in the coffeepot to prove he could be drunk as
a skunk and still hit his man.

Cotton seethed inside at Jack's behavior. He was contemplating what to do about it when they were all brought
to attention by the sound of gunfire from outside. Chairs

went scooting across the floor, some toppled by men in their haste to get in on whatever was happening. They all rushed the door at the same time, slamming into one another as they pushed through and ran down the long hall. Jack didn't budge. He busied himself stuffing his mouth with food, something he'd not had much of for the past few days. Cotton started to get up, thought better of it, and frowned at Jack as he sat back down. He forked a piece of meat and slapped it on his plate, poured some gravy across it, and began slicing it into bite-size chunks.

"Looks like you had yourself a pretty wild night, Jack. Did you forget we have a long way to ride today? After about a half hour in the blazing sun, your tongue will think it's been stomped on by a herd of longhorns. Yessir, you may soon be wishin' you were dead. But you can count on one thing, we damn well *are* going."

"Will you shut up, Cotton. Can't you see I'm eatin'? And don't get yourself all het up over me. I'll be ready to ride. Count on it."

Cotton's ire had risen to its peak. He half-stood, half-leaned across the table and grabbed Jack by his shirt collar, pulling him forward enough to scoot the table an inch or two.

"Listen, you–" was all Cotton got out of his mouth before one of the men came bolting back into the dining room, wheezing as if he was almost out of breath.

"Mister, if you really are a sheriff, you gotta come quick. Someone in that McMasters bunch just gunned down the town marshal. Things'll get ugly right quick if a cooler head don't jump in."

Cotton let go of Jack's collar and stood up straight. Jack went back to eating as if nothing had happened.

"I'm a sheriff, all right, but not in this county. I have no jurisdiction here. There ain't much I can do."

"Well, you got to try. Otherwise, there's goin' to be more killin'. Without the marshal around to put a stop to it, we'll be lookin' at a war. It'll tear this town apart. Please, you got to do somethin'."

Cotton frowned as he strapped on his Colt, grabbed his hat, and followed the cowboy out the door, looking back to see if Jack was going to follow. Jack remained at the table, eating and drinking with both hands.

As Cotton reached the porch, he stopped to survey the situation. It was plain that the man had not exaggerated. There was a mob of miners standing outside the saloon, and down the street was another group of men—townsfolk, shopkeepers, and the like—armed with rifles and shotguns. Both groups looked like they meant business.

Chapter 12

———✦———

"Damn, Virgil! You jus' knocked old man Brennan over the side of the cliff. No way he lived through that. What'll we do now? If the sheriff finds out we done it, he'll hang us for sure," Ben said, nervous and shaken by Virgil's compulsive actions. "And it won't help none that we got his lady friend tied up like a Christmas goose."

Virgil stood staring over the edge of the steep cliff. His face contorted into an evil sneer at what he saw. At the bottom he could make out the old man's horse twisted and broken. He ignored Ben's whining. He rubbed his whiskered chin and stared at Brennan's dead mount.

"Virgil, I think it'd be best if we sashayed on outta this place. Get as far away as possible. We could take some of the cattle with us and sell 'em in Arizona," said Blade.

"Will you two shut the hell up! Can't you see I'm thinkin' on it? An' I don't need two snivelin' cowards crawlin' up my spine."

"Virgil, it's our skins, too. We can't sit around until they

figure out who did it. That's what gets a man shot," said
Ben.

Virgil picked up a small stone and pitched it over the
edge. He grew increasingly nervous, realizing he might have
gone too far this time. When he returned to the others, he
mounted up and said, "We'll leave him right here, and we'll
go on into town just as we planned and have ourselves a few
beers. Act as if nothing happened. No one'll find him before daylight. They'll likely figure he wasn't watchin' close
enough, got too close to the edge, and got dashed to pieces
on them rocks down there due to his own carelessness."

"But what if they ask how come we wasn't with him
when it happened? Them other hands saw us leave together, you know," said Blade. "The boy, too."

"We'll tell 'em we split up before ol' Brennan took that
trail. We never saw him after that. That's how we tell it.
Now, do you two idjits know what to say if anyone asks
about the old buzzard?"

Blade and Ben looked at each other, then nodded.

"Reckon so, Virgil."

The three rode into Apache Springs, dismounted in front
of the saloon, and went inside. They walked over to an
empty table and called for the bartender to bring a bottle
and three glasses. They'd no sooner been served than a
voice from behind them startled Virgil.

"Well, well, look who the wind blew into town."

Not yet seated, Virgil spun around, his hand grappling
for his gun. When he saw who it was, he relaxed and turned
back to his companions, shaking his head.

"Mind if I join you gents?" the man said.

"Comin' up on a man like that is a good way to get your
brains scattered across the floor, Red. You should know
that," Virgil said, easing into a seat. "Boys, this here is Red
Carter, a nastier rattler you'll never see."

The man joined the three without an express invitation.
Virgil signaled for the bartender to bring another glass.

"What are you doin' here, Red? The last time I saw you was in Abilene, where some marshal was threatenin' to blow away your manhood. How'd you get outta that mess?"

"As luck would have it, a fair maiden came to my rescue just in the nick of time. Enabling me to slip out of town easy as you please."

"And this here maiden, what happened to her?"

"Well, sir, she and that marshal sorta took up with each other," said Red, who was now nearly doubled over with laughter. Ben and Blade joined in.

"Why are you here, Red?" said Virgil, puzzled by the whole conversation.

"Well, I have been wanderin' around just lookin' for an opportunity to come my way."

"What sorta opportunity you lookin' for?"

"Anything that will put some money in my pocket. Things have been tough lately. I was on my way to explore what this town had to offer when I saw you."

"I ain't seen no rare opportunities around here. How about you, Ben? Blade?" said Virgil.

The other men shook their heads.

"Well, as I was about to ride out of town, I heard about an old friend who might be figurin' on makin' a big strike hereabouts, and I thought I'd see if I could get in on the action."

"And what old friend might that be?"

"The only old friend I know around these parts is you, Virgil. So, what do you say, old friend, how about cuttin' me in? Don't tell me you couldn't use another gun."

"Where'd you hear such a bunch of nonsense? There ain't no strikes about to be made by me nor anyone else. This place is deader than a month-old corpse."

Red leaned forward on his elbows, narrowed his eyes, and looked at Virgil like a wolf eyeing his next meal. He glanced around closely to make sure no one was near enough to overhear the conversation.

"I heard you had brought in some of the best gunmen in the territory for some reason. And the onliest reason I can conjure up is that you must be fixin' to pull off some big haul, keepin' it all hush-hush, so the sheriff don't get wind of it. That's the way you operate. So, what is this big score?"

"Askin' too many questions could shorten a man's life if he wasn't careful," said Virgil.

"Reckon it could at that, if that man didn't have some talents that might fit with whatever the job is. If you're interested in another gun, I'm available."

"Why should I trust you, Red? The last time we met, you tried to slip out of town with some of my money. You do remember that, don't you?"

"I reckon it's comin' back to me, now, in bits and pieces. But that was quite a spell ago, and I've changed my ways. You can put your trust in ol' Red Carter from now on. So what do you say, can you use another hand?"

"Maybe. Just maybe. Dependin', of course, on what you deemed your share to be worth."

"I figure about twenty-five percent. Since I assume it's three of you and me. What do you say?"

"I'll cogitate upon it. Now, if you don't mind, I'd like to get back to my drinkin'."

Chapter 13

———❖———

Cotton stood beneath the small porch overhang of the boardinghouse in Silver City, rubbing his chin and trying to see a way out of an incendiary situation. He had no reason to get involved and little incentive. When men line up on two sides of a life-and-death issue, someone is bound to come out of it shot full of holes. He didn't want to be that someone.

He looked up to see a man running across the street toward him. The man was too heavy to be running in the building heat of morning and clothed in a wool sack suit at that.

"You the sheriff I been told about?" asked the man, as he drew up in front of Cotton, nearly out of breath from the exertion.

"I'm Sheriff Cotton Burke, from Catron County. I'm not sure what I can do. I have no jurisdiction here. Who are you?"

"Mayor Martin San Angelo. And I can assure you we don't intend to stand on jurisdictional formalities. We need help. We'd be obliged if you'd consider taking the situation in hand. Most obliged."

"First, tell me what happened."

"Well, them miners of McMasters's down in front of the saloon got drunk and started busting up the place. The bartender went for the town marshal to put a stop to it. When the marshal came and told them to break it up, someone got angry and pulled a gun. After that, I can't say for sure exactly what occurred. All I know is, we got a marshal lying dead in the saloon with a bullet in the heart, and the town's about to erupt into an all-out war."

"Have you had trouble with these miners before?"

"Not that much, just a little rowdiness, nothing like this, ever. Most of them miners are decent folk. They know the town needs their money to survive, and they let us know it. Lately, though, their boss man has made a mockery of the town's rules, such as totin' a gun in town. That McMasters is a snake, I'll tell you that."

"Tell me more about this McMasters fella."

"He's the new owner of the mine. Nasty fella. Even most of his men hate him."

Cotton said nothing for several minutes as he tried to weigh the consequences of his getting involved. In such situations, there were usually one or two individuals that set the fire. Cutting those individuals out of the herd usually poured enough water on the flames to put an end to it.

Behind him, Memphis Jack stepped onto the porch, wiping at his mouth with a checkered napkin. He walked up to Cotton and said, "Well, well, got yourself another chance to be a hero, Cotton."

"Go back to your breakfast, Jack, and stay out of this."

"Why, how could I ever forgive myself if I let you go gettin' yourself all shot up by a bunch of fool miners? Wouldn't look good for old Memphis Jack's reputation as a law-abidin' citizen, now, would it?"

"Stay out of it, Jack, and I mean it." Cotton stepped off the porch and into the street. He took off his gun belt and handed it to the mayor.

"Hold this," he said, and he started walking toward the miners.

As he walked, he drew a cigarillo out of the pocket of his vest, then shook out a sulfur from a brass box in his side pocket. He lit up and took a long draw on his smoke. By the time he got to within ten feet of the miners, he knew which one of them was the lead bull. Warren McMasters stood at the head of the bunch, his gun and holster slid around in front and his hand on the butt of a Remington .45.

"Who the hell are you?" said McMasters. "And what kind of fool faces down a force of men without a gun?"

"I'm here to try talking things out. The mayor of this fine town has asked if I would palaver with you folks, maybe see if we can't settle it peaceably. Maybe if you was to just hand over the man who shot the marshal, the town would agree to a trial, fair and square, and let justice be done."

McMasters squinted in the sun, trying his best to size up whether this man was a dreamer or just too dumb to figure what was about to happen to him.

"Ain't gonna be no trial, Mister whoever-the-hell-you-are. And for your information, it was *me* that plugged that loudmouthed law dog. Another thing, my boys have been propping up this filthy burg for years, and we weren't about to be bullied by no tin-badge marshal. Without the Mc-Masters mine, this here collection of firewood would have been a termite hill long ago. Now, go on back and tell that two-bit mayor what I've said. And if you come back, you better be armed."

"Tell you what, Mr. McMasters, how about we share a smoke and you can take a minute to it think over. Maybe you'll change your mind, see it their way. It *is* a fair offer."

Cotton didn't give McMasters a chance to object before he stuck his hand inside his vest, ostensibly to draw out a smoke. Instead, he pulled out a spur-trigger Colt .38 New Line pocket revolver and stuck it in McMasters's face. The mine owner blinked once as a look of disbelief flooded his reddening face. He started to sputter something, but Cotton

didn't give him the chance as he pulled the badge from his
vest pocket and pinned it on.

"Tell your boys to go on back to the mine while we
saunter over to the jail. If they refuse and decide to make
a fight of it, they'll be taking you back in a box. Now what
do you say?"

McMasters turned slightly as he called back over his
shoulder, "Don't let this fool bluff you. He's only one man
and you can cut him down before he can pull the trigger on
that toy pistol." McMasters was shaking with anger, and
obviously considering whether to draw his Remington.

Just then, Cotton saw a figure move forward out of the
shadows from behind the miners, closing the distance
between him and the men quickly before barking out his
order.

"Your boss likely just cut his own throat with his big
mouth and he'll probably be joined by about eight of you
if any of you decide to butt in," said Memphis Jack, as he
stood with a six-gun in one hand and a double-barreled
shotgun in the other, eyeing the restless bunch of dirty,
hungover miners. "Your call, boys."

Chapter 14

———◆◆◆———

Virgil Cruz warily eyed the man who'd interrupted his drinking with a surprise proposition. Red Carter's reputation for being a good hand with a gun was well known. Virgil watched him closely as Red quietly drank a whiskey, then refilled his glass and gulped down another. He was filling it up almost to the brim for the third time when Virgil spoke up.

"I don't recall invitin' you to sit down here and drink up all my whiskey, Red. How's about you just mosey on outta here and I'll get back to you on that proposition of yours. Where you stayin'?"

"When you're ready to talk, I'll be at the Hilltop Hotel. Don't chew on it too long, or I might have to find another opportunity. Time's a-wastin'."

"How do you know how much time I got?" said Virgil.

"Like I said, the town's got ears."

Red pushed back his chair, threw down his third drink, and muttered once more that it seemed like a man could make up his mind quicker than this. Virgil watched through gritted teeth as Red left the saloon. He'd known Carter from several years back when they'd both ridden with a bunch of raiders on the border between Kansas and Missouri. While they never were friends, Virgil learned early on that when Red got something in his head, it was likely to stay there until someone convinced him to change his mind, usually at the point of a gun. Right now, the latter was along the lines of Virgil's thinking.

When Red left the table, Virgil leaned over to Ben and said, "I never liked that rattler, and I like him less now that he's showed up here flat broke and desperate. I'm not about to let him hornswoggle his way into our business. Blade, you keep an eye on him. Ben and me will figure a way to get rid of him, permanent."

"How do you suppose he got wind of our scheme?" said Ben.

"I ain't sure he knows anything. He's been known to bluff. We'll get it out of him before he breathes his last. Bet on it."

Blade got up and followed Red out onto the street. The sun had set, and what little illumination there was came from the sun's afterglow and the coal oil lanterns that had been lit in the many shops and businesses up and down the way. Red had headed toward the gunsmith's shop. He paused in front of the window and then went inside. Blade crossed the street and sat on a bench in the shadows. He tried to see what was going on inside the shop, but the windows were filthy. He figured he'd just wait out the man. How long could he stand around talking about guns, anyway?

Fed up with waiting for Red to emerge, Blade crossed the street to get a closer look through the door. As he approached, the gunsmith came to the door, pulled a shade, and hung the closed sign in the window. Blade pushed his way in just before the gunsmith had a chance to lock the door.

"There was a gent come in here 'bout a half hour back. He didn't come out. Where'd he go?" Blade said.

"He left by the back door. Said something about too many folks interested in his whereabouts. He was only here for a couple of minutes."

"Damn! Virgil's sure gonna take my head off over this," muttered Blade, as he hurried from the gunsmith's shop to find Virgil and give him the bad news.

Hank Brennan's first movement was a twitch, fingers that tried to clench into a fist, then a groan, and the relaxing of his hand at the failure. His eyes slowly opened, then closed again from the pain that the simple effort had taken. He tried to take a deep breath but winced as a jolt of what felt like a red-hot branding iron shot through his chest. Where was he? What had happened? His breathing was shallow and the realization of his situation unclear. He could make out only that there was no light. He was either blind or it was night. A slight breeze and a chill in the air convinced him he was outside, even though he could not make out any of his surroundings. He felt exhaustion. The need for sleep gnawed at him. His senses were overwhelmed with a combination of throbbing pain, weariness, and the panic of not knowing where he was or what had happened to him. He tried with every muscle in his body to sit up, take an inventory of his situation, all to no avail. He called out but heard only the screech of an owl and a rustling in a nearby stand of pines. He came first to the assumption that he had somehow been killed and that this was what hell was like. He tried to accept this fate with a defeated suspicion that he could expect to remain in desperate pain, languishing in this dark, lonely place for all of eternity.

Every little movement he made sent messages to his brain that much more than a little discomfort was his lot. Stabbing bursts of pain ran up his leg. His arm, unmovable, was twisted awkwardly under him. The warm, sticky presence of blood on his face, trickles of which ran to his lips, sickened him. His mind was clearing sufficiently enough for him to realize he had several broken bones and that he was in serious condition with little hope of help. The cloud that filled his brain was slowly, but surely, beginning to evaporate; his senses would soon return, and he would devise a plan of survival. If, that is, he lived long enough to come up with a plan. Right now, no such plan came to mind. So, for the moment, the only thing he could think to do was to close his eyes and hope for blessed sleep to envelop him.

Chapter 15

—◦•◦—

As soon as he had Warren McMasters securely behind the heavy steel bars of a jail cell, Cotton angrily turned on Memphis Jack.

"What did you think you were doin' out there? You could have started a street war. I had it under control. Mc-Masters wasn't going to forfeit his life just to get me."

Jack rolled his eyes, giving out a deep sigh.

"You're welcome, Cotton. Anytime I can be of help, don't hesitate to call."

"Now I've got to figure what to do with McMasters. I can't sit around nursemaiding this hothead while I wait for some circuit-ridin' judge to float into town like a tumbleweed."

"You lookin' for a suggestion?"

"Not from you, Jack. I need a *legal* solution."

"I'd like to remind you, Cotton, that we *was* once lawmen together. Or have you forgotten those joyful times?"

"I haven't forgotten. But then I'm not the one that ripped that law six ways from Sunday, neither. In case you haven't

forgotten that little incident in Fort Worth." Cotton gave
Jack an incredulous look.

"Yeah, well it was a case of lettin' rotgut whiskey
take charge. It ain't happened since. That trouble cost
me my job as a deputy, and I ain't forgot you were the
one that buried my chance for a career behind a badge,"
said Jack.

"No, Jack, I wasn't the one that got stinkin' drunk and
shot up the town. An innocent man died from one of those
wild shots, remember? That's what killed your career as
a lawman. Not me. You need to think on what your own
addle-brained antics cost you. It's time to grow up."

Jack's reaction to the barrage of condemnations leveled
at him by Cotton was masked by his stone cold, straight-
ahead stare. The sheriff knew full well these comments
would be hard for Jack to hear, almost as hard as they were
for him to say. Jack made no reply.

"You screwed up, Jack. Then you hid behind the pity
that your whore Melody poured over you like maple syrup.
She took you in and cared for you. Gave you plenty of sympathy. You folded up like a tent in a tornado. Hell!"

The anger built slowly in Jack, an awakening volcano
on the verge of erupting. He sprang from his chair and dove
for Cotton with fire in his eyes.

"Damn you, Cotton Burke! You self-righteous son of a
coyote! I'll . . ."

Cotton had had a pretty good idea of what his words
might invoke. He slid aside easily as Jack's pent-up anger
exploded. Jack missed Cotton by inches and crashed awkwardly on the floor, sprawled facedown on his stomach,
beside where Cotton had been sitting. Twisting his body
and grabbing at the corner of the desk to pull himself up,
he lost his grip, slipped, and fell back hard, smashing his
head on the leg of the potbellied stove. He lay there for several minutes, breathing hard, rubbing his head, his energy
finally spent amid a flood of self-recrimination.

Cotton reached down, took Jack's wrist, and pulled him
to his feet.

"Feel better?" he said.

"I could use a drink," muttered Jack.

"That seems to always be the answer to your problems, doesn't it? How about some coffee, instead?"

"No, thanks. I'll go my own way," said Jack, as he stumbled out of the room. Not looking back, he made his way out into the dusty street, and headed for a saloon.

Cotton shook his head and wondered what he could do to get Jack to understand the importance of staying sober for the job he was about to give him. He was growing increasingly uncertain whether Memphis Jack Stump had been the right choice.

"Hey, lawman! You tryin' to starve me? When's some vittles comin' my way?"

The screeching from McMasters's cell brought Cotton back to the matter at hand: his prisoner and what to do with him.

"Hold on to your britches, McMasters. I'll get you something after a bit."

"Well, you damn well better hurry, or it'll be too late, and I think I deserve at least one meal on the town, before there ain't no town standing." McMasters laughed.

Cotton got up from the desk and walked to the door separating the marshal's office from the cells. He leaned in, scowled at the mouthy mine owner, and snorted.

"What is that supposed to mean? You bein' behind bars seems to cut down on the effectiveness of your loudmouth threats. As I said, you'll get fed when I'm good and ready. Not a second before." Cotton had turned to go back into the front room when McMasters jumped up, grabbed the bars, and started yelling.

"You just wait until my men get back here, and then we'll see who's sittin' in the catbird seat, you or me. I'm bettin' a dime to a dollar it'll come out with me lookin' at you facedown in the dirt," shouted McMasters. "There'll be a bullet or two in your sorry carcass, too."

"Your threats don't mean a thing to me, McMasters. I've come up against your kind for a long time now, and

I'm still standin'. So why don't you sit back and save your breath for the judge."

"Yeah, well you haven't come up against the likes of Santa Fe Bob before. He's meaner'n a snake, and I've seen him draw and fire before a man's had a chance to blink. My men'll have him here quicker than you can say 'uh-oh.'"

"Never heard of him," Cotton said and sighed as he leaned back in the marshal's creaky chair and began looking through the desk drawers for evidence of previous encounters with the McMasters bunch. In a stack of wanted dodgers, he stopped at one that caught his attention immediately.

"Well, I'll be . . ." He broke out in a laugh.

Chapter 16

———◆◆◆———

At the Silver City Saloon, Memphis Jack was on his third whiskey when a cowboy sidled up to him and introduced himself.

"Name's Shue. Ben Shue. You were with that sheriff fellow that took McMasters off to the pokey, weren't you?"

"Yeah. What of it?" Jack rolled the brown liquid around in his glass before downing the last gulp. He tapped the glass on the bar for the bartender to refill. He tried to take a step away from the foul-smelling cowboy but was followed step by step by the man.

"McMasters has some nasty acquaintances that owes him a favor. And he ain't shy about callin' in a marker when he's got a score to settle. I'd reckon by now one of his men has sent out the word. We could be seein' some dry-gulcher ridin' into town almost any day now."

"I reckon ol' Cotton Burke can handle himself all right. He ain't one to mess with, either."

Memphis Jack believed what he was saying, but then he hadn't seen Cotton for several years and didn't know what he'd been up to. In times past, he had seen gunfighters like Cotton Burke lose their touch over seemingly minor incidents. He had no idea whether Cotton had been faced down, or been wounded, or been forced to back down because of too many guns pointed his way. Come to think of it, he had to admit he really didn't know Cotton at all anymore. And he certainly didn't know why he'd been yanked out of his hotel room and dragged to this godforsaken hellhole.

The more Jack thought about it, the more the whole thing began to sour him on even listening to whatever tale of woe he was certain was headed his way. Cotton claimed to need his help, but he hadn't really explained what that help would involve, nor did he seem in any great hurry to do so.

"And it's damn well time he did just that," mumbled Jack as he turned and started for the swinging doors.

"What was that, friend?" said the cowboy.

"Uh, nothin', just a little problem that needs solving."

Jack brushed past the man, slammed through the doors, and stalked straight for the jail, where he found Cotton intently studying a stack of papers, some brown with age. Jack wasn't exactly drunk, but he wasn't all that sober, either. He let the door slam behind him and quickly plopped into a chair across the room. He knew that standing, in his present condition, was inadvisable, since he needed to look rock steady when he hit Cotton up for some answers. And he wanted to avoid the contempt he knew he'd get from Cotton if his demeanor showed he'd bent his elbow too many times. He also wasn't certain what he'd do if the answers he got—assuming Cotton even acknowledged him—weren't to his liking. But he was damned sure going to try, or get on his horse and head back to Melody. And if Cotton Burke didn't like it, well, that was just too bad. Jack wasted no time in beginning his rant.

"Cotton, I need some answers and I need them now. You understand? I didn't ride all this way to have you treat me like some stable boy, you barkin' out orders, and me bein' told to sit in the corner because I did somethin' you didn't like. So what's it goin' to be, straight talk or do I walk out of here and leave you to solve your little problem by yourself?"

Cotton didn't look up at the sound of Jack's belligerence. His expression was hard and his gaze was distant, as if he was lost in something that was most troubling. Jack was hesitant to push further, but he had made up his mind and he wasn't going to be sidetracked by Cotton's foul mood. Jack cleared his throat and raised his voice, again.

"Cotton, you consarned coyote, you listenin' to me? I asked you a civil question and I deserve a civil answer. Now, what's it goin' to be?"

Cotton still didn't respond to Jack. *That's the last straw*, thought Jack, and he drew his Colt, cocked it, and fired it into the ceiling. The blast instantly filled the small room with gray smoke and the smell of cordite. A breeze wafting through the open window swirled the smoke into an eddying haze that undulated for a minute in its tight confines before thinning out enough to see across the room.

"Now you goin' to speak up?"

As the smoke slowly cleared, Cotton raised his eyes to Jack. He made no move to react to Jack's still-smoking gun, or to his outburst, or to the hole in the ceiling. Cotton rubbed his chin for a second, then eased back in his chair. A smile crossed his lips as he tossed a wanted dodger on the desk with the words "Killed in Santa Fe, July 8, 1880" written across the face of Santa Fe Bob. The date was two weeks before he and Jack had arrived in town, and had been written by the town marshal.

Finally, the smile left his lips, and he looked up at Jack.

"If you're through acting like some drunken cowboy hurrahin' the town, I reckon we can palaver a spell. But I can guarantee you aren't goin' to like what I have to say. So if you're ready, put that fool gun away and we'll go get a steak and you can listen to my story. And then you'll find out what your future may well hold." Cotton stood up and headed for the door; Jack followed suit with an expression of complete confusion.

The two of them went across the street to the hotel dining room. Cotton steered Jack toward a table in the back where they could talk without interruption. A lady brought over a pot of coffee and two cups then left to get their food.

"Okay, Cotton, time to let me in on this big secret you've wrangled me into, and I want it straight. Keep holdin' out and I'm on my way back to my sweet Melody."

"You may want to hold back on that threat until you've read a little something I've brought along," said Cotton, as he patted his shirt pocket.

Chapter 17

———◆◆◆———

"Virgil, what're we goin' to do about that Red Carter fella? I lost him when he cut through a store and slipped out the back. Musta knowed there was someone on his trail," said Blade Coffman.

"You lost him! You couldn't track a mule pullin' a plow. You're just plain worthless! I shoulda done it myself."

"I'm sorry he got away, but that still don't answer my question: What're we goin' to do about his deal?"

Virgil Cruz leaned back in his chair, gulped the last of his whiskey, and held the glass in his lap, turning it around and around as his expression turned from dour to surprised. A slight grin crept across his mouth and he broke out in a laugh.

"Why, boys, I figure we'll send him off on an opossum chase, that's what. Matter of fact, I think we can put ol' Red onto another trail altogether." He leaned forward and poured his glass to near overflowing.

"Uh, how we gonna do that?" asked Ben Patch.

"You just watch and listen as I tell him about a bank

over in Santa Fe that needs some attendin' to. Maybe you two will learn a valuable lesson on the fine art of deceit." The look on Virgil's face even made a hard case like Ben Patch cringe.

Ben was about to ask Virgil something when he stopped mid-word, staring at the figure coming through the swinging doors. It was Red Carter. He walked straight to the table where the three were. He stopped short, making no attempt to sit.

"I've changed my mind about joinin' your deal, Cruz. No hard feelings, but I've decided to take my chances alone. No point in sharing all that loot." Red kept his hand on the butt of his Remington, turned and walked away. He leaned on the bar and ordered a whiskey, drank it, and left the establishment just as the piano player started playing "The Lady from Abilene."

Virgil's jaw dropped at what had just happened. His gaze followed Red all the way out the door. He was silent as he stared after him.

"Was that the valuable lesson we was s'posed to learn, Virgil?" asked Blade.

Virgil's face turned red as he grabbed his hat by the brim and slapped Blade across the face. In an attempt to duck, Blade fell backwards, his chair crashing to the floor. As he struggled to get to his feet, he was suddenly staring down the barrel of Virgil's Colt. He stopped cold.

"If that was supposed to be funny, it wasn't. If it was meant to mock me, it worked, and that don't make me happy. If I was you, I'd find it in my heart to offer an apology and maybe beg for forgiveness. Of course, your other choice is to get a whiff of one last puff of smoke just before your head goes flying off your shoulders. That clear?"

"Clear! Oh, yeah, clear as water, Virgil. Didn't mean nothin' by it. I wasn't thinking, that's all. Please accept my humble apology," muttered Blade, a bead of perspiration beginning to trickle down his nose.

Virgil replaced his six-shooter in his holster and sat back down. He glanced around the room to see how much attention he had attracted by his loud reaction to Blade's comment. Not one person was looking his way. He liked it when men feared his reprisals, none wishing to curry his ire by staring. He enjoyed being a man others were afraid of, and he played it for all it was worth.

"Now, that's more like it, boys."

"Uh, Virgil, what about what Red was talkin' about? Do you suppose he's figured out what we're up to?" said Ben. "How we goin' to find out what he knows?"

"Won't be hard. Not hard at all. Did either of you notice what was stickin' outta Red's hip pocket when he left?" said Virgil.

"Nope," said Ben. Blade just shook his head.

"A folded up newspaper."

"What's that got to do with Red's scheme?" said Blade, a little sheepishly, still shaken by his confrontation with Virgil.

"Don't know yet, but I figure we will soon enough. Blade, you run over and see if that newspaperman, Birney, has had anyone come in askin' questions about the sixteenth, and did he give a fella answerin' to the name of Red Carter an old edition of the paper. Then hustle on back here without delay."

Blade almost tipped his chair over again in his haste to get as far away from Virgil as possible, at least until he knew he'd cooled down. Blade had seen Virgil at his meanest on more than one occasion, but his wrath had never been aimed at either him or Ben before. It was unnerving.

After Blade left, Ben asked, "You wasn't expectin' Red to change his mind voluntarily, were you?"

Virgil scowled at the words, but then shook his head. "No, I reckon I wasn't. It came as a surprise. Of course, I reckon I never did know what Red was up to in all the years I've knowed him." Virgil kept shaking his head.

"Course, there is one thing I know: that Red Carter can't be trusted. So if he somehow escapes runnin' afoul of Cotton Burke, I figure to pull the rug out from under him and maybe get the blame placed on him for what we're plannin'."

"Is that how you plan to finish him?"

"If that's the only way. Red Carter's remainin' days on this earth can be counted on one hand. And I aim to be responsible for endin' his miserable life, one way or another," Virgil said.

Just then Blade came hurrying back through the swinging doors. He dropped into his chair and tossed down the last drops of whiskey in his glass.

"Birney said a man came in yesterday askin' about what might have been in the paper concernin' somethin' happenin' on the sixteenth, a date he said he'd heard on the street. He said the man pushed pretty hard until he broke down and gave him an old copy of the newspaper," said Blade.

"Well, boys, I reckon we know where ol' Red got his information. We go ahead with our plans, and make sure he gets what's comin' to him in the process."

"What is it you figure he's up to?" said Blade.

"As usual, no good. But this time him tryin' to cut in on our deal will blow up in his face. We'll still be the ones who'll be puttin' money in our pockets, and lots of it," said Virgil. "Red Carter will be takin' up space in boot hill."

Chapter 18

———◆◆◆———

Hank Brennan groaned as he tried to roll over enough to get a better idea of his situation. His battered body was jammed in between three jagged boulders and even the slightest movement sent a wave of agony throughout his body. He had slept fitfully, but the dawn brought with it hope that someone might ride by and hear his call for help. His right hand and arm were twisted beneath him in such a way as to keep him from freeing his gun and firing a shot to attract attention. Hank was helpless, and he knew it. He wasn't certain he would last another night if the temperature dropped any more than it had last night. His mind wandered between hope that Cappy would miss him and come looking and hopelessness that he was doomed to end his days in this broken condition lodged in a crevice on the side of a cliff.

His mind slowly cleared as to how he happened to get where he was. He had a foggy image of riding with Virgil Cruz, Ben Patch, and Blade Coffman, three of the most despicable types he had ever been cursed with hiring. But then, had he known what he was getting into, he wouldn't have employed them. Instead, he would have tried to have them tossed in jail for something, anything. That's certainly where they belonged. But when a ranch needs hands, sometimes any man will do.

The fog in his brain was lifting sufficiently to remember Virgil's horse crowding him too near the edge of the path along the rim of Crazy Horse Pass. That's where he was, jammed into an outcropping on the sheer cliff that rimmed the pass. Now it was all coming back. Virgil Cruz had tried to kill him. In fact, he probably thought he'd been successful.

Off in the distance, Hank heard what sounded like hoofbeats echoing in the canyon. His voice was weak from being unable to gather much air into his lungs without terrible pain. But if they came closer, he'd try his best to yell out. Maybe someone would hear him. It looked like the only way out of his nearly impossible situation. But after a few minutes, the sounds of the horses died away, having never come close to where he lay trapped and badly injured. Probably just a herd of wild mustangs, he thought. *Why didn't I just die in the fall instead of this? Having your life drained from you by inches is no way to go.*

Cappy Brennan strolled over to the bunkhouse. He had been unable to find his father and was getting concerned. He went inside to find two of the ranch's wranglers stretched out on their bunks.

"Either of you seen my father?"

They shook their heads.

"The last I seen of him was when he headed out yesterday with Virgil, Ben, and Blade. A little after noon," said one of them.

"So neither of you has seen my father since then?"

"Nope. Last thing he said was he didn't know when he'd be back."

"Where's Virgil?"

"Got no notion. Ain't seen him this mornin'. Can't say I care, neither," said one. The other nodded in agreement.

"Well, you ought to care. He *is* the foreman, you know. You need to have respect for the man in charge," said Cappy, even though he had no respect for Virgil himself. In fact, he had nothing but contempt for a man who seemed to have no redeeming virtue other than being good with a gun, even though that was worth its weight in gold in this part of New Mexico Territory. And his father certainly needed help if he was to get a handle on all the rustling going on in the county. Cappy turned and walked out. Then, as if a puzzle was forming in his head, he stopped and went back inside.

"Which way did my father and the others go? Did they take bedrolls?"

One of the men got up, walked to the door, and pointed to the hills off to the west.

"I overheard Virgil sayin' something about havin' trouble with the herd up there in Saucer Valley. They rode off in that direction. Don't recall hearin' anything about stayin' out."

"Get saddled. We're goin' out for a look-see. Maybe somethin's happened to them," said Cappy. The other two groaned. They'd just come in from riding herd most of the night, and they were tired and hungry. Breakfast was about to be served up at the big house.

"Uh, Cappy, how about we get a bite to eat first. We been up all night and we ain't et since last evenin'. My belly's growling something awful. Wouldn't want me to grow faint and fall outta the saddle and bust my head, would you?"

Cappy Brennan was torn between doing the decent thing, feeding his men, or going out to look for his father. He didn't like it that his father had been gone for so long. It wasn't like him at all. Everyone knew Hank Brennan wasn't one for sleeping on the ground, anyway, ever since he'd taken a bad fall during a cattle drive four years ago and suffered a broken leg that hadn't healed properly. But Cappy wasn't the hard-nosed boss his father was. Finally, he just shrugged.

"Okay, boys. But as soon as you're done, we'll need to get a move on if we're going to locate them before another nightfall. There's a lot of territory out there to cover."

The two cowboys hightailed it straight for the cook shack before Cappy changed his mind. If it had been Hank giving the orders, they'd be going hungry. Hank was tough as nails and not easily swayed by the needs or wants of others. Everybody liked Cappy, but they also knew he wasn't the tough, no-nonsense rancher his father was. And they all took advantage of his basic good nature, which they perceived as a weakness.

Cappy followed the two men to the cook shack in back of the ranch house. Hank had found the cook, a Chinaman named Wu Chang, while on a trip to San Francisco before Cappy was born. Wu Chang had been cooking at a run-down restaurant near the waterfront and forced to sleep in a lean-to in the alley. Hank liked Wu's cooking but didn't like the way he was being treated, so he offered him a job and brought him back to Apache Springs.

"Where Mr. Hank? He no come home to eat special meal Wu Chang fix him. I have bad feeling 'bout this, Cappy-san."

Cappy grew anxious at Wu's words. The Chinaman seemed to have a knack for knowing when something bad had happened or was about to happen. Cappy ate hurriedly and left the room before the others were finished. His stomach was churning. *Forget those lazy fools*, he thought, *I'll go out looking for Dad myself.* He started to saddle his roan, then changed his mind and went up to the house to wait for the others. He was nervously pacing the floor, contemplating what could have happened to his father, when he grew too impatient for the men to come get him. He went to the cook shack to see what was holding them up.

When he got there, Wu Chang said they had slipped out the back door earlier.

"I should have gone myself instead of waiting for that bunch of lazy bums," Cappy said through gritted teeth. He spun around and stormed out.

Wu Chang clapped as he left. "Now you talk like man! Hank be proud."

Chapter 19

———◆———

"I haven't told you what you're doin' here because I wasn't sure myself," said Cotton, taking a slurp of hot coffee.

"You drag me outta bed at gunpoint and you ain't sure why? What's the matter with you, Cotton? You gone loco?"

"No. I wasn't sure because I had to find out if I could trust you before I spilled what's been goin' on in Apache Springs. Now I'm stuck here in this one-horse town, and things are goin' from bad to worse. And I don't know any more about where you fit into my problem than I did when we got here."

"Well, here's how it is. You either tell me what you want of me or I'm getting' on my horse and ridin' outta here. You can accept that or you can shoot me in the back. One way or another, I'm free of your dad-blamed nonsense," said Jack. He finished his coffee and started to get up. Cotton grabbed his arm and tugged him back in his chair.

"You're right, Jack, I have been a little hornswoggled. I reckon I owe you an explanation. Whether you stay or go oughta be your decision, not mine, because what I'm about to ask you is damned dangerous. What say we order a couple steaks and I'll get to it?" said Cotton.

"Now you're talkin' sense."

Jack sat up with a wide-eyed grin when the cook came out with two rare steaks. Though Jack's looked a little like someone had dropped it on the floor then scooped it back onto the plate. He didn't complain because, as suspicious as it looked, he was hungry enough to have gone out and gnawed a chunk out of the hindquarters of the cow itself.

The two of them tore into their food like they'd neither one eaten for a month. The steaks disappeared in a flurry of knives and forks, along with bread sliced thick as a fist and fresh-churned butter slathered on like plaster. Their coffee cups had to be refilled three times, and the pot of beans was scraped so clean it could have been used again without washing. When they were finished, they sat back with satisfied grins and groans.

"That was good, but I'm waitin' to hear this bucket of hogwash you're about to splash my way. So have at it. I'm all ears, especially since the tab's on you," said Jack. "Oh, and by the way, a whiskey would go down nicely, as well."

"If you're still here after what I'm about to tell you, Jack, we'll go have that whiskey together."

Jack lifted his last cup of coffee in toast to Cotton's offer.

"I'm the sheriff of a little town in the middle of Catron County called Apache Springs. It's been a quiet place, for the most part. I haven't had to shoot anybody for over a year, and that's an improvement over my last town. But things have changed since a bunch of gun sharks started driftin' in about a month ago. I didn't think too much about it until things started happenin' that got me to lookin' into the history of a couple of them."

"I take it you didn't like what you found," said Jack.

"The number of cattle disappearing went up considerable. Then, petty thefts turned into major thefts. Last month, a rancher got himself killed when he caught some-one breaking into his house."

"Well, where the hell were you when all this was hap-pening?"

"It's a big county and I only have one deputy, and he's not worth much. I don't have a handle on who's behind the crime increase. I have my notions, but I don't have enough solid evidence to go after anyone."

Jack let out a loud burp and patted his full stomach. "But you got someone in mind, right?"

"Yeah. Virgil Cruz, a lowlife workin' for the Brennan ranch. He's been around for a while, but lately he's been gatherin' a bunch of saddle bums around him that look like honest work don't suit them, neither."

"So you're lookin' for someone to back you up? That what you're thinkin'? An extra gun?"

"Not exactly."

"Then *what*, exactly?"

"I want you to ride in a day ahead of me and look around. Tell folks you're drifting and looking for work—the kind a fast gun might get you. Then, if the opportunity arises, try to get inside Cruz's bunch. He works out of the Double-B, Hank Brennan's spread. With you on the inside, maybe I can get ahead of these owlhoots and catch them in the act before someone else gets killed."

"That's all you want me to do? I'm supposed to saunter into a hornet's nest, sidle up to a bunch of thieves and cut-throats, somehow avoid getting shot in the back, and then just walk out with details of all their nefarious plans—that all you want? How about I shoot myself right now and save Catron County the cost of burying me later?"

"Look, I know what I'm asking is dangerous. If I could do it myself, I would. But you're my only chance to put a stop to whatever this bunch is up to." Cotton knew how the whole thing sounded. Not only dangerous but downright foolish for anyone with a speck of common sense to agree to. "And that's not the whole story, neither."

"There's more? How the devil could it get much worse?"

Jack sat up in his chair, leaning forward with obvious curiosity.

"Two days before I rode to Gonzales, I received this note. It was nailed to the front door of my office." Cotton reached across the table and handed the folded paper to Jack. Jack opened it and spread it out on the table. Jack's eyes followed the writing back and forth. Occasionally, he'd wince at the poor handwriting as he struggled to decipher the message.

Sheriff. We got Otis Wagners widder. Shes gonna be safe and sound as long as you do what this writin says. First off, you best stay away from the Dubble–B. If we see you ridin out that way, we'll up and shoot the lady. Thats fer surre.

You stay away from the Brennan place until after the 16th, and the Wagner wumin lives. An we'll be gone.

Jack folded the paper and handed it back to Cotton. He stared at the table for a minute before responding to what he'd read.

"What do you figure they got in mind? And what does the sixteenth have to do with all this?"

"Up to now, except for the rustling, most of the crimes have netted these leather slappers little more than petty cash. Then a man gets killed defending his own home for a few dollars. They're getting more and more desperate. The only thing that I can think of around the sixteenth is that's about the time the Southern Pacific is due to pass about five miles north of Apache Springs with what's rumored to be a lot of gold. If this bunch were to hit that train successfully, they'd stand to ride off with maybe a million dollars, if past shipments are any indication." Cotton leaned back in his chair and folded his hands on the table. "That's the story, Jack. I can't prove a damned thing. The robbery is only a theory. And the sixteenth is the only thing that ties it together in my mind. I have to stop *whatever* Cruz has planned, and I can't let anything happen to Emily Wagner. While I'm alive, she'll not die at the hands of a bunch of greedy gunslingers."

"You say her name like there's more to it than her bein' someone's widow."

Cotton flushed at Jack's suggestion. "I won't let anything happen to her, that's all. She's a fine lady, and that's all that needs to be said."

Jack grinned and then whistled. "A million dollars, you say?"

Chapter 20

———◆———

Emily Wagner wasn't certain how long she'd been left alone in the musty cabin. Each time Scat slipped out, she would twist and turn, pulling at the ropes binding her wrists and ankles. Her fingernails were bleeding from trying to pick apart the rope's fibers, to loosen the bindings. Her circulation was being slowly cut off from the tight knots and her inability to move about. She was stiff and sore and hungry. It would be a cold day in hell, though, before she gave in to the thinly veiled overtures suggested by Scat Crenshaw. *Where is Cotton?* That thought ran through her head, turning over and over, a soundless scream for help. She wished now she'd pulled the trigger on Cruz when she first saw him sitting there, astride his roan mare like some smug, filthy outlaw general. Her hatred for him rose in her throat, a choking, clawing hatred.

Scat stomped up the steps, shoved open the plank door, and entered the darkened room. He looked down at Emily with a licentious smile. He liked to look at her. It gave him a feeling of power to see her lying there, unable to get away, her life completely in his hands.

"Well, Miz Wagner, having second thoughts about my offer? A nice cut of beef cooked over a hot fire, maybe some beans, and coffee, how does that sound in exchange for a little friendly attention for ol' Scat?"

"Not on your life, you filthy animal. I'd rather die than have you touch me." Her eyes blazed with contempt for the evil that stood before her.

Scat unbuttoned his shirt, pulled it open, then began unbuttoning his pants.

"I don't think you're in much of a position to stop me, missy," he said with a sneer. He took Emily by the shoulders and rolled her onto her back. She began squirming in an effort to get her knees up to defend against his next move.

Emily was aware that she was in no position to save herself from the advances of this man. But she would try with her last breath to stave off any such attempt to overcome her strongest defenses. She was quite literal in her admonition that she would die fighting him off.

Just as Scat began untying the ropes that bound her ankles together, sounds approached of a horse being reined in right outside and then the stomping of boots on the porch, just before the door burst open and Dogman, Scat's brother, stormed in. Scat struggled to keep his pants from falling down around his ankles as he straightened at Dogman's inopportune entry.

"Scat, there's some riders coming. Whatever you're fixin' to do, I'd advise against."

Scat struggled to get all his buttons buttoned and his suspenders pulled up. Before he could get his gun belt back on, Virgil Cruz burst through the open door. He took one look at Scat and his face grew red with rage.

"What the hell do you think you're doin'? I told you if you laid a hand on this woman, I'd kill you myself. And here you are a-fixin' to do just that." Virgil drew his six-shooter and jammed it into Scat's belly. He cocked the hammer as Scat tried backing away.

"Virgil, I wasn't goin' to do nothing. I was just seein' if she needed some food or to take a trip to the outhouse. That's all, I swear." Scat's face was bursting with moisture, the perspiration pouring down like a waterfall.

"I see. And I suppose them buttons got themselves all mixed up." Virgil pushed harder, until Scat was backed completely against the wall.

Scat glanced down to see where he'd missed a couple of buttons, and his left suspender had come loose. He swallowed hard before he spoke.

"All right, all right, Virgil. I admit I was almost carried off with desire for this little lady. It won't happen again, I swear." Scat was shaking.

Virgil released his pressure against Scat's belly slightly.

"You can bet it won't. If you doubt my word, you better do some thinkin' on what it's like to take a bullet in the gut. You bleed to death. I hear it can take a while, and the pain is terrible. Do you understand me?"

"I do, I swear. It'll never happen again, Virgil," Scat whined.

Virgil released the hammer and slipped his gun back into its holster. He turned to Emily, who was cowering as far back on the bed as she could scoot.

"Did he touch you, Miz Emily?"

"No. But he was only a minute away. He'd have had to kill me first, though," she said, her voice high-pitched and shaky.

Virgil grinned at her answer. Then he turned to Scat and Dogman.

"Your last chance to follow orders has come. There'll not be another. Don't give me a reason to doubt either of you. Now, get the lady some food and do it pronto. And if she needs to go out back, watch from the cabin to see she don't get away. Any questions?"

"No, sir, Virgil," said Dogman. "I'll stay right here and make sure personal-like that the lady is safe and sound."

"And she don't need to be hog-tied, neither. You can watch her with nothing but her wrists tied. Now, the plan is still on as we discussed. I ain't heard a word from Sheriff Burke, so I figure he took seriously what I told him about stayin' clear of us if he wants the lady kept in one piece." Virgil walked to the door, turned to looks at Emily, and said, "It appears Cotton Burke thinks a lot of you, missy. Let's hope he keeps on thinkin' that way."

Ben and Virgil mounted up and rode out as hard as they had ridden in. When they were out of sight, Dogman squinted at his brother and said, "I wouldn't mess around with that hombre, Scat. He's as mean as any I've come across. You better keep your pants buttoned up, too. I don't aim to take a bullet for you."

Scat stood staring after his brother as Dogman went outside to sit on the porch. Scat swallowed hard, then turned to Emily.

"Don't think this finishes it between us, lady. I aim to have my way with you before it's all over. For now, I reckon I can get you a bite to eat."

"While you're fetchin', consider this: Cotton Burke won't pay no mind to some idle warning from the likes of Virgil Cruz, or you, either. Mark my words, you'll be dead before this big deal of yours takes place, whatever it is."

Emily spat at him as he stomped out the door.

Chapter 21

———————

Cotton and Memphis Jack each tried to stare the other down. Finally, Cotton lifted his cup and drank the last few drops of coffee.

"Well, that's my story. Are you in or out?" he said.

"I haven't heard you say 'please.'" Jack grinned as he scooted down in his chair.

The satisfied smirk on Jack's face told Cotton he'd better acquiesce on this one, if he wanted his help. Cotton shook his head and mumbled something under his breath.

"What was that, Cotton? I didn't quite hear you."

"Please! I said, please, dammit. There, you happy, now?"

"Yep. Reckon I am. Now, how about givin' me the particulars on this crowd of misfits. I don't want to go ridin' into a nest of vipers without knowin' all there is to know about 'em."

Cotton sat up, pulled a piece of paper out of his shirt pocket, and spread it out on the table.

"Here's a list of the rannies that had drifted into town

before I found you. I jotted down what little I know about each one. You ever met up with any of them?"

Jack perused the list, then shook his head. "Nope."

"Good. Now, here's a layout of Apache Springs—the important buildings and a little of the surrounds—which could come in handy."

"What's my excuse for driftin' into town?"

"I reckon you could be lookin' for work or maybe you heard Cruz was sizin' up men with a gun hand," said Cotton.

"Ain't that gonna make it look like I already know more'n I should?"

"Hmm, maybe you're right. An out-of-work cowpoke probably makes more sense. Maybe you should start at the Brennan spread."

"I'll just ride into town, let someone point me in that direction after a little prodding. How's that sound?" Jack pulled his Remington from its holster, half-cocked it, and rolled the cylinder through. Fully loaded. He started to scoot his chair back and stand up. He downed a last sip of coffee, making a face that suggested it was stronger than he liked.

"Sounds fine. The time it takes for me to straighten out this McMasters thing will give you some breathing room in Apache Springs." Cotton stood, stuck out his hand.

"What do you figure to do with McMasters?"

"Don't have an answer for that just yet. But something has to be done right quick. This town's fixin' for a fight, and I don't want to be in the middle of it."

"Well, you better watch your backside. If something happens to you before you get to Apache Springs, I could be in a heap of trouble."

"I'll try my best not to let that happen," Cotton said.

Jack gave Cotton a salute as he left, then went to the boardinghouse to gather his things. He wasn't all that anxious to be heading for who-knew-what in a town that seemed to be filling up with undesirable gunslingers, but he had agreed. His word was good, and he'd live up to it, even if it could put his life in danger. Truth be told, he had always admired Cotton Burke, rough exterior and all. Cotton was too damned strict for Jack's taste, but a fellow always knew where Cotton stood on any issue. And he stuck up for his friends. That was good enough for Memphis Jack Stump.

As the noon sun began its slow crawl down the side of the mountain, the air grew unbearably hot and Hank Brennan knew he couldn't hold out much longer without help. He had lost all feeling in his legs and could only move one arm, and then he couldn't seem to get any purchase on anything that would help him move from his tenuous position. He could hear the critters setting out on their quest for a meal, stirring about, sniffing the ground for signs of prey. If he could only free his gun from its holster, maybe he could fire off a couple of rounds, possibly attract a nearby rider, although that didn't seem likely, since the trail he'd been pushed into the ravine from was seldom traveled by any except his own men. None had reason to be there any time soon.

He struggled to bring his one good arm around to free his gun from his holster, which was wedged beneath him and his twisted, broken arm. Slowly, he tried stretching his fingers between his broken body and the granite boulder that trapped him. Nearly unbearable pain shot through his back. He cried out with each attempt to move.

With each breath, Hank nearly passed out from the agony of stretching badly bruised muscle over broken bones. He knew there was little hope of anyone being close enough to hear a shot even if he could reach the revolver. If he didn't get it clear of the holster, he wouldn't dare cock it and pull the trigger. The way his leg was twisted, the .45 would surely blow his leg off. If he wasn't rescued almost immediately after such a wound, he would surely bleed to death. The odds were slowly building against him. He was already getting light-headed from loss of blood, and the

day's blistering temperature had nearly sapped what little
energy he had. Could he last until evening when cooler
temperatures would bring relief? If anyone *was* out looking for him, they wouldn't consider coming anywhere near
the cliffs at dusk or later, for fear of slipping off the trail
themselves and falling to an almost certain death, dashed
on the rocks below. Hank couldn't understand why he
wasn't dead.

As he began to slip into unconsciousness, both from
the heat and the sheer exhaustion of struggling to reach
his gun, he kept bringing himself back by sheer stubborn,
tough-minded willpower. Nightfall would be on him before he knew it, and with it, he figured, his last chance. He
pushed himself beyond the pain with one last, agonizing
thrust at the butt of his revolver. Digging at the wooden
grips with little more than his fingernails, he finally found
purchase on the walnut handle of the six-shooter. With his
bruised and bloody fingers, he slowly began to drag it from
the Mexican-style holster. Suddenly, when it looked like
he might succeed, the revolver slipped from his tenuous
grip. At first, his heart sank at the prospect of all hope having disappeared, but as his strength began to fail him, and
his hand dropped to his side, he felt the cold steel of the
cylinder still within reach. He latched on to it, tugging at
the gun until it was clear. He smiled wearily at his good
fortune. Hank Brennan held his only real possibility of survival in his weak, shaking grip. Now all he could do was
wait.

Chapter 22

———◆———

Cotton stood in the street, watching Jack's back as he rode out of town, dust swirling from his horse's trail. Alone now, Cotton began to feel the strain of what to do about the man he had behind bars. As he turned to go back inside the jail, he saw the mayor walking toward him from a half block down. The man had a scowl on his face that could have scared away a bear. Cotton walked back inside the jail, knowing the mayor would follow and that the conversation wasn't likely to be a pleasant one.

"Howdy, Mayor, what can I do for you?"

"Sheriff, our problem is growing by the minute. McMasters's men are getting pretty liquored up over at the saloon. I figure they must be talkin' of breaking him out, and I'm sure you know what that will lead to."

"I'd say some townsfolk are workin' themselves up to form a vigilante gang, break McMasters out of jail, and get to hanging him. Am I close?"

"You hit 'er right on the head. So what can we do about it?"

Cotton sighed and turned to stare out the dust-encrusted window. Considering the explosive nature of the situation, he saw but one way to solve it. He couldn't let the mine boss get strung up without a trial, and he sure as hell wasn't about to let McMasters's men free him; his options had narrowed down to hauling the gun-happy rattler out of jail and dragging him to Apache Springs, Cotton's jurisdiction, to await a circuit judge. It wasn't such a far-fetched idea on the face of it. There were plenty of times lawmen had resorted to such tactics in order to keep a man alive long enough to receive a fair trial. The problem lay with the many miles of hard riding and twisting trail between Silver City and Apache Springs, with plenty of places for a handful of gunmen to overwhelm him—miners or townsfolk. He clearly understood the risks involved. But it seemed the only option.

"Mayor, the best solution is to take McMasters to Apache Springs for trial. I'd better get started right away, before some up-righteous citizens decide to take matters into their own hands."

The mayor frowned at his words. Cotton figured the man was concerned about the dangers involved and the prospect that McMasters might escape, maybe to return for revenge.

"Don't that make things even more dangerous for you?" the mayor asked.

"Reckon it does, but what choice do I have? I can't ride out of town, leaving you to the prospect of McMasters's men trying to free him by force. You can't expect shop owners to risk their lives to keep him jailed until a judge comes. Or until you can appoint a new marshal. And I got important affairs to attend to back in my own county."

With a hesitant nod, the mayor silently agreed to Cotton's premise. Then he brightened up as a thought came to him.

"Sheriff, how about I send our blacksmith along to help get you there in one piece? He's a damned fine shot with a rifle. I'll bet he'd do it if I asked him to."

"If he's willing, I won't refuse the help. Tell him to be out back in two hours and to bring along plenty of ammunition. I figure we'll need it before too long. Oh, and be sure he understands we're to get McMasters there alive. That's just in case he was of a mind to have been a part of the vigilante justice you say is bein' talked about."

"Sheriff, there ain't a straighter-shooting man on the frontier than Bear Hollow Wilson. I'll swear to it on the Good Book. I'll see to it he's where you want him."

With that, the mayor hurried out of the jail with a look of relief on his weather-beaten face and a spring in his step.

On the face of it, the idea wasn't as implausible as Cotton had first thought. He took a deep breath and stepped outside to look the town over once more. *Not a bad town*, he thought. *It'd be a damned shame for it to allow vigilantes to become the rule of law.*

His memory wandered back to a time about ten years ago, in Kansas, when he had stopped over in a town that got carried away with seeking revenge on a couple of fools who'd somehow gotten it into their minds that holding up the bank would be the solution to all of their problems. They had been too young, too drunk, and too stupid to stop and think before barging into the bank with guns drawn, making loud demands to the teller to stuff all the money he could get his hands on into a canvas bag they'd brought along.

When the teller stood stunned at the request, one of the young men jammed his gun in the frightened man's face, screaming for him to get to it or else. Unfortunately, the gunman was a little too nervous, his trigger finger a little too itchy, and the gun went off, killing the teller, who was also the sheriff's son, on the spot. The men got away with twelve dollars snatched from the hands of a man waiting to make a deposit, and hightailed it out of town.

The sheriff had a posse gathered within ten minutes, and the chase was on. The gunmen were cornered no more than three miles from town, mainly because they didn't know the territory and had no way of realizing they were riding into a blind canyon. When it became clear that the posse had no intention of awaiting a trial, the sheriff's own loss overcame his sense of legal propriety, and he looked the other way as the two men were strung up on the nearest tree.

Crying for their mothers, both men met their maker after several minutes of kicking and gagging, their faces turning blue as they choked to death. The bodies were left for the buzzards as a warning to others who might be tempted to follow these men's ways.

Disgusted with himself for allowing vengeance to overcome his better judgment, the sheriff became morose. Not a word was spoken between the men on the way back. Soon after he returned to town, the sheriff threw his badge into the street, announcing his retirement. He retreated to the nearest saloon, where he became a regular. He drank himself to death within a year.

The town never recovered, either. The sheriff's guilt became the town's guilt. Travelers seemed to give the town a wide berth, and businesses soon began moving out in favor of a location where the climate was more favorable. The last Cotton remembered hearing, even the railroad had chosen to swing farther north. It was claimed that the town became inhabited only by ghosts, with some claiming they had heard the sorrowful moans of the two unlucky robbers and the sobs of a father still mourning the loss of his son.

Chapter 23

———✦◆✦———

Cappy Brennan was feeling guilty that he had waited for help to ride out to find his father. By the time he had decided to look for Hank by himself, it was already nearing noon. He knew it would take time to search all the possible routes he could have taken. If darkness should come before he located his father, no one could expect him to be out on those treacherous trails leading up to Saucer Valley. *A man would have to be plumb tetched in the head to venture up there in the pitch-black*, he thought. He had justified his wait with the hope that other wranglers would ride out with him. But by the time his patience had run out waiting for them and he went looking for some of the others, they were already gone. He was muttering to himself as he swayed back and forth on the sorrel's back.

As he came to the spot where the trail narrowed and came close to the edge of a drop-off that could land an unwary man at the bottom of the steep ravine, dashed to pieces on jagged rocks, he reined in his horse, stopping to listen to the sounds of birds or other critters that might go silent if anything was amiss. From boyhood, Cappy had been taught that animals could give a man a good sense of whether danger lurked nearby, or if all was normal and safe enough to venture on. And if Cappy did one thing right, he listened to his pappy.

Unseen but close by, Hank lay still, nearly hidden by the shadow cast from the crevice in which he was imprisoned, when a familiar sound came from near the top of the bluff. The unmistakable clatter a horse makes on rock and gravel. The sound came closer. Someone was riding nearby. But who? Could it be Cruz and his cutthroats coming back to make certain he was dead? Hank prayed he was making the right decision as he raised the gun as high as he could and squeezed the trigger.

Cappy was leaning quietly on the saddle horn, one hand on top of the other, hearing little more than his horse's occasional nicker and the sound of a hawk as it screeched from the safety of a cottonwood. Suddenly his horse reared at the explosion that seemed to erupt out of nowhere: a gunshot—no, two gunshots, and they sounded like they had come from over the edge of the cliff.

Cappy sprang from the saddle, dropping heavily to the ground. He drew his revolver and edged closer to the rim, near where the trail almost dropped off itself. He peered cautiously over the side and was instantly shocked at what he saw. There below, a sudden splash of sunlight showed his father lying in a broken heap, jammed in between two large boulders that jutted out from the cliff. Beyond, he could make out the battered remains of his father's horse, dashed on the rocks far below.

"Dad! What happened? Are you able to move?" Cappy shouted.

Hank tried to speak, but his voice was weak. He could only move his head slightly from side to side. Cappy could see that the old man was too badly injured to speak. It would be up to the son to save the father, a complete reversal of their life together thus far.

Cappy saw no easy way to reach the old man. Then,

just over the side of the cliff, he spied some smaller rocks and juniper limbs sticking out sufficiently to give him a platform from which to make his way down on a rope. He figured to attach one end of it to his saddle horn and the other around his waist. As long as his horse didn't move or get frightened and try to run away, perhaps he could get down the cliff far enough to free his father or figure out what to do next.

He draped his canteen over his shoulder, then tied off the rope, patting his horse and talking lowly to keep the animal from getting skittish as he pushed off over the side. As he found his footing on the rock below, he began to ease out the rope, and with his feet nearly straight out in front of him, he rappelled cautiously down the rocky cliff.

Cappy was a healthy young man of nineteen, lanky and raw-boned. He knew he would never be the rough-and-tumble cowboy one might expect of a lad who'd grown up on a ranch. He'd always been quiet, a reader and a studier of his surroundings, seldom loud and boisterous like the rest of the men at the ranch. But he could see his life was about to change. He'd need to find some real grit and something he'd not anticipated: unselfish bravery and strength gathered from deep inside. He was about to be tested far beyond his wildest dreams.

Cappy dropped to the ground beside Hank. He could see by the way the old man lay twisted that many bones were broken. Moving him would be an arduous and tricky task, one that could easily end a man's life if not done carefully. In a book he'd read in the library at home, Cappy had learned how some men had made a sling of sorts out of blankets and pulled a calf from where it had slipped off a hillside into a muddy pond. The same sort of rig might work here, he thought.

"Dad, can you talk? How bad are you hurt?"

Hank could only whisper, but his expression at having Cappy by his side showed his relief. "It's bad, son. I can't move either leg, and my left arm's busted up good. I think I may have some ribs stove in, too."

"Here, take a drink of water," he said, holding the canteen to his father's lips. "How'd this happen? You're always so careful up here on these narrow trails."

"It weren't no accident. That rattler Virgil Cruz drove me over the side on purpose with his horse. I reckon he figured I was gettin' too curious about what he done to the Tulip boys. I think it was Cruz that shot them. The sooner that owlhoot starts burnin' in hell, the better." Hank spit out the words with such venom, Cappy thought he saw a spark of determination in his father that might just help him come out of this alive.

"Okay, Dad, I'm going back up and bring some help. I'll ride to the ranch and try to find some of the others. With several ropes and some blankets, we'll try to get the horses to pull you up. You just rest until I get back. Here, take my canteen. I'll unscrew the top so you can get to it with your good hand."

"Thanks, son. Reckon I'll be here when you get back. Be careful not to let on to any of Virgil's men I'm still alive, or he's sure to come back and finish the job," Hank reminded him, forcing a painful grin. Cappy nodded with a grimace.

When Cappy scrambled to the top of the hill, he mounted up and urged his horse to follow the trail back to the ranch house at a dead run. As he approached the main house, Wu Chang came out. Cappy jumped from his horse and ran to the cook.

Keeping his voice low, he said, "Wu Chang, are any of the boys around? None of those that Cruz hired, mind you. Only some of 'em we can trust."

"They no here, Cappy-san. They either out with cattle or they go to town with Virgil. No come back till dinna."

"Then it's up to you and me. Get your mule, some ropes, and blankets. We have to haul my dad off a ledge. He's busted up real bad. I'll hitch up the wagon. I'll gather some strips of leather and several pieces of split wood. We'll have to put splints on his legs and one arm."

"You know how do that?"

"No, but I can learn. I can't let Dad down. He's countin' on me."

Wu Chang turned and ran back inside to comply with Cappy's orders. The urgency in the young man's voice had left no doubt that this was a matter of life and death.

Chapter 24

Memphis Jack reined in atop a rise that looked down on the town of Apache Springs. It looked peaceful enough, no gunfire or assemblage of rowdies running amok in the streets. He remembered what Cotton had said about not going near the sheriff's office. The town's one and only deputy might not take kindly to another gunslinger riding in, and Jack wasn't about to let on to anybody what his mission was, or that he even knew Cotton Burke.

He pulled his Remington, checked again to be sure it was fully loaded, and started down the road to town. The main street was wide and desolate, only a half dozen horses were tied to hitching rails, most of them in front of the town's only saloon. A wagon rumbled down the street, stopping at the side of the general merchandise store to unload some crates. A woman was sweeping dirt from the wooden sidewalk in front of a dress shop, and the clanking of the blacksmith's hammer echoed between buildings.

Jack draped his horse's reins over a rail, stomped his boots on the boardwalk out front, and entered the saloon, taking a quick look around, ready for whatever might come. He strode up to the bar. The bartender, One-Eyed Billy Black, was at the other end of the long, polished bar with an impressive mirror and stacks of glasses at his back. Billy noticed Jack, tossed aside a rag with which he had been shining some coffee cups, and approached him like a long lost friend.

"Howdy, neighbor, what'll you have?"

"Well, let's see, how watered down is your whiskey?"

The bartender looked embarrassed, then swallowed hard and answered with a sheepish grin, "Not too bad, considerin' we're out here in the middle of nowhere. 'Bout ten percent, that's all."

"Fair enough. I'll have a double, Mr. uh—"

"Billy Black. Most folks call me One-Eyed Billy. I reckon you can figure out why."

"The patch does sorta give it away. Accident?" said Jack.

"If you can call a sidewinder with a forty-four an accident, then I reckon that's what it was. Course, since he was aimin' at my heart when he pulled the trigger, I consider myself lucky he was too drunk to shoot straight. His shot went wild and hit a stack of glasses. Ricochet got me."

Jack took a sip of whiskey, made a face, and turned it slowly in his hands. He looked around the nearly empty saloon. Five cowboys were the only patrons, and they seemed content to watch a man shuffle and reshuffle a deck of cards, never dealing a single one. Talk seemed the game of the day. No money was changing hands.

"Must be too early for any serious gambling, huh, Billy?"

"Well, I'll tell you, mister, ever since Virgil Cruz and his bunch of rowdies rode into town last fall, ain't been too many of these rannies willin' to stake their lives on turnin' up a winnin' card. Cruz seems to take most all the pots."

"No one ever calls him out?"

"One feller did. He's buried up on the hill back of town. The only other one that had the guts to suggest something smelled mighty peculiar left town with a bullet in his gun arm and not a penny to his name."

"Sounds like a rough bunch."

"More to it than just sound, mister. Uh, I didn't catch your name."

"Memphis Jack Stump."

"You ain't from around here, are you?"

"Nope."

"You in Apache Springs for a reason?" said Billy.

"I don't suppose you know of anyone lookin' to put on an extra hand, would you?"

Billy glanced down at the hand-tooled gun belt with the silver conchos and twelve cartridges, and the well-oiled Remington jutting from a holster suggesting it got a fair amount of use.

"What kind of work you lookin' for?"

"I'm not particular, just so it pays enough to keep me in bullets, a dry place to bed down, and three meals a day. Maybe a friendly game now and then."

"Hank Brennan is always lookin' to hire anyone who can use a gun. They seem to have more than their share of rustlin'."

"How do I find this Brennan ranch?"

"Straight out Southtown Road for about five miles, then angle off into the hills at a fork. There'll be a sign on the left. Can't miss it."

Jack threw down two bits and tipped his Stetson in thanks. He ambled out the door, stopped, looked around for a moment, and then mounted up for the ride out to Brennan's.

As he topped a shallow rise after the turnoff that Billy had told him to take, Jack saw two riders coming on hard. One was a Chinaman clinging for dear life to the reins of a bald-faced mule. The other, a slender young white man, was driving a two-horse buckboard. They were closing the distance rapidly. Jack wasn't certain whether to take cover until they passed or stay and greet them, since they were probably from the Brennan spread anyway.

The younger man brought the wagon to a dusty stop five yards from Jack. He held up his hand as he called out, "Hey, mister, where you headed? We could use some help if you could use a couple dollars," said Cappy.

"What kind of help?"

"My pa was knocked off his horse and he fell down a steep cliff. He's hurt bad. Wu Chang here was the only help I could round up. I know my pa would appreciate you comin' along. It'll take some strong arms to get him pulled up that cliff face."

"Who's your pa, son?"

"Hank Brennan. The owner of the Double-B ranch. You're standin' on our land right now. If you're comin', fall in. The trail up ahead is mighty narrow; two ridin' side-by-side couldn't make it. Reckon my pa found that out the hard way." Cappy whipped the horses into a run as soon as the words had left his mouth.

Luck seemed to be riding with Jack as he wheeled his roan around and caught up with others. He couldn't have found a better way into the Brennans' confidence than lending a helping hand to save the boss man. He smiled at his good fortune.

"I'm right behind you, son. Lead on," Jack shouted.

Chapter 25

———◆———

Cotton rummaged around for a set of shackles to keep McMasters in line. It would be tough enough keeping him out of the line of fire if any of the townsfolk took it into their mind to keep him from getting to trial. And it was a sure bet some of McMasters's own men would track them and try to free their leader by any means necessary. Cotton knew his situation could easily turn sour.

He located a pair of short-chain shackles and tossed them into McMasters's cell.

"What the hell are these for? You ain't takin' me outta here, you bastard. I won't go." McMasters, beet red, was spitting mad as he gripped the bars and tried to shake them into setting him free.

"I'm takin' you to Apache Springs for trial. It's the only way I can see you makin' it into a courtroom in one piece. The town's a mite upset about you gunnin' down the town marshal, and they don't seem to be growin' in sympathy for you. So put the damned things on or I'll do it for you. And you won't like that one bit," snarled Cotton, whose patience with the whole situation was clearly running out.

McMasters grumbled loudly as he closed the cold steel on his wrists. "I'm goin' to feel real bad about you breathin' your last out there in them hot, dusty hills between here and Apache Springs, Sheriff. I figure Santa Fe Bob is already on his way. It ain't too late to change your mind and just turn me loose, no hard feelings."

Cotton smiled at the mention of Santa Fe Bob and was about to give his prisoner an idea of what he could do with his suggestion, when the sound of heavy boots approaching the jail filled the room like distant cannon fire. Just then, a man the size of a bear pushed through the door, dropped his pack and rifle on the floor, and leaned on the desk with beefy arms stretching his rolled up sleeves.

"Name's Bear Hollow Wilson. Mayor says you could use some help draggin' this varmint up north where they can try him quick and hang the son of a bitch. Well here I am, ready to travel and able to give a fair day's work in the process. Ain't had a day off in five years. Lookin' forward to a little change. This job pay anythin'?"

Cotton's jaw dropped at the sight of the blacksmith. Broad in the shoulders, bald headed, with a full beard and thick eyebrows, Bear Hollow lived up to his name and more. Cotton figured this mountain of a man could lift his weight in iron bars and have plenty of strength left to wrestle a couple of cowpunchers at the same time.

"I expect the town could see its way to two dollars a day and grub. Glad to have you along, Mr. Wilson."

"Don't go getting' formal on me, Sheriff. I go by Bear, plain and simple. Your offer sounds fair. I reckon I'm ready to go anytime you are," said Wilson.

"As soon as I get McMasters trussed up proper and find his mount, I'll get some ammunition, grab some blankets, and we'll be set. The sooner we get on the trail, the less chance of anyone followin'," said Cotton.

Bear Hollow nodded his acceptance, then said, "Tell you what, Sheriff, I know McMasters's horse well enough, what say I go round the critter up? Might save a little time."

"Thanks, Bear. Oh, and don't say anything to anyone about where you're going."

"No need to concern yourself about that. I wouldn't look kindly on one of my own townsfolk drawin' down on me just to get at this rattler." Bear Hollow lumbered out the door like a boulder rolling downhill. Cotton shot McMasters a glance and saw fear in the man's eyes.

"Somethin' got you worried, McMasters?"

"Uh-huh. That man's one of them that swore to nail me to a wall if he ever got the chance. Looks like you just gave it to him. I'll never see Apache Springs alive. You can bet on that."

"Oh, you'll get there alive, mister, but I can't promise how long you'll stay that way after a jury hears your case."

Minutes later, Cotton heard a pounding on the back door to the jail. He opened it to see Bear standing between the jail and the outhouse holding the reins of three horses.

"Figured it would be best if I was to come around back," he said. His pack, rifle, and bedroll were already loaded on a big, gray mare.

Cotton unlocked the cell and yanked McMasters out. He pushed his prisoner through the door and toward the awaiting horses. He asked Bear to help McMasters up on his horse, then turned to retrieve a shotgun and ammunition. While he was doing this, McMasters's words to him, about Bear's possible hidden plan to make sure the mine boss didn't make it to trial, haunted him. Was he starting off on a journey with not one, but two, dangerous men?

As he was about to leave through the back door, the mayor came through the front.

"Sheriff Burke, what shall I tell anyone who asks about our prisoner?"

"You'll think of something. But whatever it is, don't let the truth get out. Now, remember, as soon as I get him to Apache Springs, I'll telegraph you to gather up witnesses to the shooting and get them up there for a trial."

"Yes, sir, I'll do that. I'll tell everyone you're handling the situation and that I'll let them know when the trial is to be, but, of course, I won't let on that you've left town with McMasters."

"I hope your townsfolk are of a mind to listen to you, Mayor; I don't favor havin' to shoot my way out of any ambushes set up by angry citizens. Also, you might remember to remain real tight-lipped whenever any of the miners are around." Cotton went out back, quickly swung into the saddle, spun his horse around, and led the trio out of town, staying out of sight as much as possible by keeping to the alleys. He could feel the hair on his neck stand up as he turned his back on this dusty little village. A whole lot of hatred seemed to be building up fast, more than a little of it aimed straight at him. His confidence in the mayor's promise to keep the whole matter confidential was fading, as well.

Then Cotton heard a couple of gunshots echo in the streets behind them.

Chapter 26

———◆◆◆———

Virgil Cruz paced back and forth in front of the saloon. He didn't like the idea of leaving Scat Crenshaw alone with Emily Wagner at the line cabin. He knew that if anything happened to her, Cotton Burke would spend the rest of his days settling the score. He wasn't really afraid of the sheriff, but a man in love could be doubly deadly. And now that he'd committed to the kidnapping of Emily as his ace in the hole, he was uncertain that any of his hired gunmen could be trusted alone with an attractive woman any more than Scat. In fact, he wasn't really convinced he could even trust himself. She was too damned pretty. He was silently wishing he could have come up with some other way to keep the sheriff off his trail until he and his men had pulled off the biggest train robbery in history. The sheriff with the fast gun was the only thing standing between him and a fortune. That's why, against his better judgment, he'd decided to take such a chance by grabbing Emily Wagner. It was a decidedly risky move.

For now, it appeared Cotton Burke was heeding Cruz's

warning to stay clear if he wanted to see Emily alive again. The message Cruz had sent was blunt. But it was also a little disconcerting that while Cotton Burke seemed to be obeying the warning, he hadn't been seen anywhere in the vicinity for a week. *Where the hell is he? And what the hell is he up to?* Cruz kept running these questions over and over in his mind.

The batwing doors flew open and Blade Coffman lurched outside.

"Hey, Virgil, come on back inside and have a drink with me and the boys. We're celebrating the demise of old man Brennan and the disappearance of that sheriff."

Cruz grabbed a handful of Blade's shirt and pulled him close and slapped him across the mouth. "Listen, you loudmouth fool, there *is* still a deputy in town, and while he ain't much, he has ears. And he knows where to find a deputy U.S. marshal no more'n a day's ride into Arizona. That whiskey is loosening up your mouth. So, before you all take leave of your senses, I think it's time you and the boys saddle up and head on out to the ranch rather than say somethin' that could hang us. Do you understand, you addle-brained son of a mule?"

Blade glared at Virgil then pulled away from his grip, stumbled back against the whipsaw siding, and wobbled back inside. After a couple minutes, he reappeared with Ben Patch in tow. They silently walked past Virgil and went straight to where their mounts were tied. Virgil followed, mounted up, and led his besotted crew out of town. Cruz figured that with Hank Brennan out of the way, he'd have the run of the ranch, as there was no one there who dared stand against him, certainly not Cappy Brennan, who Cruz knew had the bravery of a mouse.

"Virgil, you figure anyone has found that old fool at the bottom of the ravine?" said Ben, the first to break the silence.

"I don't know. If they have, they'll figure he just got too close and toppled over. He ain't been too sure of his footing ever since he got that leg broke," snorted Cruz. "It don't make a heap of difference, anyway, 'cause it's time we took over that operation."

"How about them that saw us ride out together? Ain't they gonna think it's strange when we come back and he don't?" said Blade.

Virgil rubbed his chin for a moment. He reined in and took out the makings from his shirt pocket. He frowned as he tapped tobacco onto the paper, ran his tongue across the edge, rolled it, then struck a lucifer on his jeans and lit the cigarette. He blew out a stream of white smoke, staring off into the distance. Blade was right. If folks did make a connection between the three of them and Brennan's "accident," that deputy might start thinking things he shouldn't. There *were* a couple of boys back at the ranch when they all rode out together. And there was Wu Chang. Maybe someone overheard Brennan order Virgil and his men to ride with him up to Saucer Valley to see where the Tulip boys were buried. Things weren't shaping up to be as simple as Cruz would have liked. Complications were setting in. Unsavory complications.

"Ben, you ride back to town and keep an eye on that deputy. See if anyone comes around asking questions about Brennan. With Dogman stayin' at the line shack and keeping an eye on his brother, I feel better about leavin' the widow woman there. If I find Scat's laid a hand on her, I'll skin them both. Dogman had better keep that demented rattler in line.

"Blade, you and me will ride on in like everything is fine. We'll tell Wu Chang, Cappy, and anyone else that might ask that Brennan decided to ride on alone and sent us out to check on the south herd. Any questions?"

The other men shook their heads. Ben rode off to do as Cruz had ordered.

"Blade, what say you and me take the shortcut back by way of the rim to Saucer Valley. We'll have a look-see down on old Hank's remains, maybe even do him the honor of givin' him a Christian burial."

Blade Coffman, still chafing from Virgil's rough ad-

monishment right out front of the saloon, where the townsfolk could see, merely nodded and prodded his horse to
follow in behind Cruz's.

Cruz was no fool; he knew that Blade would love nothing better than to get even, to plug him in the back the first
chance he got. But he wouldn't, at least not until he got his
hands on his share of what could be millions. Cruz would
need to toss this mad-dog killer a bone to take his mind
off getting even with him. Set him on another course altogether. A course that might even make him forget all about
the incident in town.

"Blade, tell you what. I think you deserve to set some
things right, things you maybe ain't even thought about for
a while. As soon as we hit that train, and you get your share
of the bounty, Sheriff Cotton Burke is all yours. I won't
touch a hair on his head. In fact, that knoll overlooking the
line shack would be a perfect spot for an ambush after I
tell him where he can find his little lady. What d'ya think?"

Blade's face brightened at Cruz's words. "I think that's
a mighty fine idee. Yup, mighty fine."

Chapter 27

———◆———

Memphis Jack eased near the edge of the precipice where Hank Brennan and his horse had gone over, while Cappy and Wu Chang gathered the ropes and blankets.

"This ain't gonna be easy, gents. That's a long way down there. You got a plan?" Jack asked.

"Well, I figured to tie off one of these ropes to that boulder yonder, and the other ones to the mule. I'll go down, wrap my father in blankets and tie the ropes around him. One of you can coax the mule to pull him up while I pull out so he don't slam against the side of the cliff."

"Might work. But I got a different take, that is if you don't mind me buttin' in," said Jack.

"Go ahead, mister, but don't take too long at it. Dad's close to cashin' in his chips, and I don't intend to see that happen without me doin' all I can to save him." Cappy put his hands on his hips, his determination seeming to grow with each heaving breath.

"How about Wu Chang takin' the reins of the horses

and the mule? The mule can haul up your father, and each of our horses will pull us up. That way, we can all come up at the same time. You can be at his head; I'll be at his feet. Ought to cut down on any chance of him getting twisted up in the ropes or being bashed on some of them jagged rocks juttin' out along the way."

"Mr. Stump, I think that's a fine idea. Let's get to it." Cappy seemed somewhat relieved as he commenced to tying off the ropes and instructing Wu Chang as to his part.

Hank Brennan winced when dirt and debris came raining down on him, as Cappy and Jack struggled down the ropes to get to his side. Each of them had a blanket tied to his back, and the loose end of another rope was wrapped around Cappy's shoulder. When they reached the stricken victim, Hank blinked in disbelief that he was actually looking at the possibility of being rescued. He tried to smile, but pain shot through him with the slightest move. Content to let nature take its course, he merely whispered, "Take her easy, boys, I ain't much more'n a skin bag full of busted bones."

"Hang on, Dad. We'll have you outta here in no time," Cappy said. He knew there was only about one chance in twenty that Hank Brennan would live to see another sunrise. The old man had been right; he was busted up bad. Real bad.

"Who's this hombre with you, son?"

"Calls hisself Memphis Jack Stump. We met on the trail. He volunteered to help when I told him about your predicament."

"Thanks, mister," whispered Hank, trying to force a smile.

"Glad to help, Mr. Brennan. Now, you just lie quiet while we get you ready for a ride to the top," said Jack.

With Cappy at his father's shoulders, Jack began to slowly wrap the blankets around Brennan's body, even covering his head to protect him from making contact with the rock face, taking care not to jostle him any more than necessary. Hank groaned with each move, as Jack began wrapping one end of the rope and tying it off, creating a sort of package like he'd seen storekeepers do.

"I'm right sorry if I got the ropes a tad tight, sir."

"Don't think nothin' of it. All I want is to get off this godforsaken rock."

When Jack was finished wrapping Hank up like store-bought goods, he looked at Cappy. "He's as ready to go as I can get him. Signal Wu Chang to start the mule and horses to backin' up."

Cappy cupped his hand and hollered up. They were quickly greeted by a gradual tightening of the ropes. The weight caused the ropes to squeak as the slack became taught. They were all three eased up off the ledge where Hank Brennan had spent the past day and a half. Cappy and Jack each had a hand on one end of the blanketed package that held their human cargo. Boots slipping and banging against the rock face of the cliff made for a rough trip to the top for the two of them, since they took all the bumps and bruises in order to keep Hank from further injury. Cappy lost his footing once and slammed his knee into a sharp rock that jutted out. He made no sound, though, despite the tear in his jeans and the blood that oozed from the gouge in his skin.

Once they were all safely on top, Cappy hastily began to throw off the rope that was secured around his waist and scramble to start untying his father. He tugged furiously at the stubborn knot.

"Hold on there, son!" Jack hollered. "Be damned careful you don't get in such a hurry you bust him up worse than he already is."

"Yeah, you're right. Thanks." Cappy let go of the rope, sat back and took a breath, then returned to the task with more deliberate care. "If you'll kindly help me get him into the wagon, Mr. Jack, Wu Chang and I can get him to Doc Winters in town."

Hank began trying to speak. Cappy pulled the blanket

back in order to hear his father's raspy whisper, "Listen, son, you'll have to bring the doc out to the ranch. If Cruz is in town, he'll know I ain't dead like he intended and he'll sure as hell try to finish the job. That man is the devil hisself, and he'll stop at nothin' to get what he wants. Whatever that is."

"We'll see to it he don't get nothin' but a rope for what he's done," said Cappy, turning to Jack. "Mr. Stump, I'm obliged for all you've done, but I got to ask one more favor, if you've a mind to stick around a mite longer."

"Ask away. I got no place to go in particular. In fact, I was on my way out to your ranch lookin' for a job when I run onto you."

"If you would go into town and bring Doc Winters out, I'm sure we can oblige you with a job. We need a dependable, honest man out here. They're hard to find nowadays."

"I'll bring the doc. And I'll keep my mouth shut about what he's bein' asked to do."

"Thanks, Mr. Stump. And here's that two dollars I promised you," said Cappy, reaching into his shirt pocket for two worn paper bills.

"Son, if you'll drop that 'mister' crap, you can keep your money. I go by Jack. I'll be back as soon as possible. Take it easy over them ruts, too. Your old man ain't gonna feel too kindly about his rescue if you bust him up some more on the way to the ranch."

After helping the other two get Hank loaded onto the back of the buckboard, Jack mounted up and rode as fast as he could back the way he'd come from Apache Springs. His stroke of luck—helping save the life of the very man he'd hoped would give him a job and an opening into whatever it was that Virgil Cruz and his gang of owlhoots was up to—was turning out even better than hoped for. He spurred his horse on.

Just outside of town, he saw three men sitting along the road. He pulled off into a stand of trees and watched as they talked for a minute, then split up. Two continued on the way he'd just come. The other turned back toward town.

It crossed his mind that he may have just run onto Virgil Cruz and his men. He waited until the two passed by and then continued on to find the doctor, with a wide grin on his face.

Chapter 28

————————⋄————————

Scat Crenshaw watched Emily struggle to scoot as far back toward the wall as she could. The dirty blanket gathered in wrinkles beneath her as she squirmed awkwardly with hands bound. He edged toward her with a predatory glint in his eye that was unmistakable. He planned to have her whether Virgil Cruz wanted him to or not. And he damned well wasn't going to wait any longer to taste the fruits of this forbidden tree. This woman excited Scat. Oh, yeah, she most certainly did.

Her increasing alarm made Scat even more excited. He got a thrill when people's fear of him showed in their eyes. He thrived on intimidation, always pushing the very limits of others' trepidation. When he could see terror on the face of a woman, even better. An almost fiendish exhilaration surged through his body as he watched Emily try to escape, knowing full well that it was impossible. He waited for her to accept the inevitable, which would lift his spirits to new heights and make her subjugation even more pleasurable. He would have been even more buoyed by a change in her attitude toward him, but there was clearly no sign of any acceptance in her beautiful eyes, only hatred and loathing. He was about to grab her and force her to bend to his will when the door to the line cabin flew open and Dogman stomped inside.

"Dammit, little brother, didn't Cruz warn you about that woman? Didn't he say he'd skin you himself if anything happened to her? Now you're puttin' this whole opportunity for us to strike it rich in jeopardy, and all because of your overwhelmin' desire for a woman. Sometimes I think you ain't got enough brains to wipe your own ass," said Dogman. "When we pull this robbery off, you can go into town and buy twenty women, take 'em home with you if you've a mind." Dogman placed his hand on his revolver in case Scat was past reasoning with.

Scat's pockmarked face was ablaze with the fury that accompanies despotism, especially in a man with such few scruples and a multitude of cravings. He started to reach for his gun, stopped and thought better of it, then slumped heavily into the chair on the other side of the table.

"I can't take this no more. You gotta get me outta this godforsaken dump. I want to have a whiskey, deal a few hands of poker, anything to get my mind off this lady. You have to help me."

"Why don't you ride into town, find yourself a fallen angel. I'll stay and cover for you with this one, see that nothin' happens to her. Go on. I'll explain to Virgil," said Dogman.

"I better not go into town. I'll just take a short ride. I'll be back. But I won't be comin' inside no more. I can't take it, her lookin' so good and all," said Scat.

He couldn't help glancing back at Emily one more time as he stormed out of the musty cabin, mounted his horse, and galloped off without another word. Dogman switched his glance to Emily and said, "Missy, that was a close one. Don't worry, I'll see to it you're safe until the sixteenth. After that—well I can't say one way or another."

"W-what's going to happen on the sixteenth?" she said, barely above a whisper.

"Now, never you mind about that, missy, reckon you'll find out when the day comes. Hope you ain't got no plans with that sheriff, though." Dogman chuckled and took out a deck of cards and began shuffling to play poker with himself. Not a very profitable pastime, but at least he couldn't *lose* any money that way, either.

Cotton and Bear Hollow Wilson had come about fifteen miles from Silver City with their prisoner when the trouble that had started in town finally caught up with them. Off to their right, well up in the foothills, Cotton had caught sight of a group of men who seemed to be shadowing them, keeping just out of rifle range. Cotton's confidence in the mayor's word had dropped a notch. Bear appeared anxious about the men, too, since neither he nor Cotton could make out whether they were miners or townsfolk. Cotton was betting townsfolk wouldn't put one of their own in the line of fire. The town had a legitimate grudge against McMasters, but it couldn't do without a blacksmith. That might be why they were keeping their distance. The same could be said for the miners. They'd want to plan their attack to free their boss when they could guarantee his safety. The trail Cotton had chosen didn't give him much cover. But any attackers would find themselves in the same situation—too much open ground between them and the sheriff. That would change eventually, though, and everybody knew it. As they rode into rough terrain south of Apache Springs, Cotton, Bear, and McMasters would have to stick to the trail, which led through narrow gulches with high cliffs on either side and wooded hills, all of which made good cover for an ambush.

"Sheriff, I don't know this country very well, but I seem to remember this road being used by road agents. I don't suppose there's a better way, is there?" Bear was nervously glancing about as he saw the potential for ambush increasing.

"If those riders stay in the foothills, they'll find the land rising until they come to a sheer cliff that overlooks a valley. That's about a thousand-foot drop. They'll have to come down well before then to get at us. I'm counting on that."

"My guess is they outnumber us about four-to-one. We can't outlast them kinda odds."

"Maybe, maybe not. If you're any good with that Sharps buffalo gun you brought along, we might even those odds up a bit. I expect that reminds you of times past, don't it? I brought the Greeners in case they got a mite too close."

"How'd you know I once hunted buffalo?"

"Just a hunch, that and those two buffalo hides you got hanging on your back wall."

"Then I reckon you can guess I'm fair to middlin' with the Sharps."

"Yep."

As the trail began a slow descent into a winding valley with a stream running down the middle, Cotton was keeping a close eye on what the riders shadowing them were up to. But as the trees—mostly pines, cedars, and cottonwoods—grew larger and denser, his view of the riders became more restricted. Not knowing what the enemy was doing could get a man killed.

"We'll pull up here and rest for a spell. Bear, pull out that Sharps of yours and drop in a cartridge. Keep a keen lookout for the sun glinting off a rifle barrel, a blur of color, sudden movement—anything that seems out of place. We're on the edge of some dangerous country."

"Don't worry none about me, Sheriff, I'm plenty wide awake. And if my insides don't burst outta my skin, I might just be able to get off a shot or two."

Cotton was still snickering when the first bullets whizzed past his head, causing all three of them to dive for cover.

Chapter 29

———◆———

Memphis Jack knocked on the door to the doctor's office. The door opened, and before him stood a tall, thin man with a two-day growth of beard, wearing wrinkled pants and suspenders that hung down to his knees. The smell of whiskey hit Jack in the face like a foul wind.

"Doc Winters, Hank Brennan's son sent me to fetch you. Hank's been badly injured in a fall. You need to come quick. I'm not sure he's goin' to make it, but I figure you gotta try."

"I'll drop by tomorrow sometime. If he's still alive, I'll take a look and see what I can do then. Good day to you, sir." The doctor started to close the door in Jack's face.

Jack jammed the toe of his boot in the door and gave it a hard push. The doctor was almost bowled over by Jack's insistent shove. He stepped back awkwardly and to steady himself grabbed the edge of his desk, where an open bottle of whiskey sat beside a half-filled glass.

"Sorry to interrupt your drinking, Doc, but this is an emergency. And you damned well *are* coming."

The startled look on the doctor's face showed he was inebriated enough that Jack's words needed some time to register. When Jack rested his hand on the butt of his Remington, the doctor seemed to understand more quickly. He reached up on a shelf to get his bag and stumbled out the door in front of Jack.

"Where's your horse?"

"I have a buggy around back, sir. I am not an equestrian, nor do I wish to become one. Now, where is this man?"

"Out at the Double-B ranch. About ten miles out of town."

The doctor looked bewildered. "You don't expect me to travel that far without libation, do you, sir? Bring along my bottle and glass. And one for yourself if you've a mind."

At that point, Jack had listened to enough of the drunken doctor's fancy words and slurred excuses. He pulled his gun, stuck it in the man's belly, and said, "Listen carefully. You'll need to be cold sober for this one, Doc. And I aim for that to be by the time we get there. Now, move."

Jack harnessed the doctor's horse and backed it into the traces. He held the horse by the bit and waited for the doctor to struggle aboard. With some difficulty, Doc Winters was finally settled in the buggy, as ready as he'd ever be for the rough trip to the Brennan ranch. Since the doctor was in no shape to drive the buggy himself, Jack tied his gelding to the back and climbed in. He snapped the reins, urging the animal forward. The mare jumped at the sound.

Jack figured it would take a couple of hours to get to Brennan place, considering the condition of the crude road, which was more like a barely improved deer trail, full of sizable ruts, twists and turns, and places where it narrowed to an opening between rocks that getting the buggy through could be a challenge. He also couldn't help worrying if he would be able to get back to the ranch before Cruz and his men discovered that Hank Brennan was alive and lying in his own bed waiting for help to arrive. What would happen when Jack wheeled the buggy through the gate and up to the main house with a doctor on board was anybody's guess. It was certainly not a situation Jack welcomed facing. He snapped the reins to get the horse to understand the urgency of the situation; failing that, he reached for the buggy whip. The cracking sound of it urged the horse to a trot.

Jack became more and more tense the closer they came to the ranch boundary.

When Virgil and Blade came to the precipice where Virgil had bumped Hank's horse over, they dismounted and eased up to the edge to look over. Blade was the first to notice that something was amiss.

"Virgil, I see the horse down there at the bottom. She's a goner. But I don't see Brennan's body anywhere. You suppose he could have survived that fall and walked outta there?"

"Don't be a fool. No man could survive a drop like that. Why, it must be near five hundred feet to the bottom. Maybe we should ride back to where the trail splits and come up through the gorge to where his horse is lying. Then we'll know where that old fool is," said Cruz, as he got back on his horse and turned around to retrace their steps for about a mile, to where they would find a mule deer trail that led to the bottom. Blade Coffman followed closely, with fear growing in the pit of his stomach.

"Virgil, I don't like this, not one bit. What if Hank's still alive? What do we do then, huh? He could get us hanged if anyone found out what you done."

Virgil turned in his saddle, fury on his reddened face. "Dammit, I'm tellin' you he didn't survive. Nobody could, 'specially not some beat-up old coot standin' closer to the grave than them Tulip brothers was two days ago. Now, settle down and let me handle this."

"All right, Virgil, I'll shut up. But if we can't find his body, I say we pack up and skedaddle for the border, pronto. Leastwise, that's what I'm aimin' to do. You can keep my share of the loot, if there *is* any loot."

"There's loot, you dummy, and I know because the fella that told me swore on his life. Could be a million dollars on that train, and I aim to have me that money. And you'll not be backin' out, neither; 'cause if you do, you'll be restin' alongside the Tulip brothers, do you hear me?"

"I hear you, Virgil."

As the two got to the bottom of the narrow, winding gorge, they dismounted and began looking around for Hank Brennan's body. They searched fifty feet in both directions from the dead horse. There was no sign of Brennan anywhere. Virgil looked up and saw a jagged ledge about halfway up the side of the steep cliff.

"I'll bet he's up there, wedged in between them rocks. If that's where he hit, you can bet your ass he's busted up so badly he couldn't be walkin' around ever again."

"How do we find out for sure?"

"No need to. His horse is down here, dead. We saw them go over the edge together. There'd be no way for him to climb up the side of that damned mountain, so he's gotta be where I said. He sure as hell is dead. Let it go. We'll just ride back to the ranch like nothin's amiss. When they ask where Hank got to, we'll say he insisted on going off on his own. Told us to go to town for a few beers."

"Whatever you say, Virgil, but that don't mean I like it. Havin' a man's ghost followin' a body around ain't right. And I feel something, all right, and it ain't a breeze comin' up."

Chapter 30

———◆◆———

Cotton and Bear Hollow hurriedly reined in between some boulders in a thick cluster of cottonwoods, mesquite, and scrub brush with a trickling stream running through. They dismounted, and Bear tied his horse to a branch. Cotton's horse was trained to stand in place with a drop of the reins. Cotton told Bear to keep an eye on McMasters. He then made his way to the edge of the tree line, squatting behind the outcropping of granite boulders. Whoever had fired the shots he'd heard wasn't making any attempt to come closer. He looked over to make sure Bear stayed put, hunkered down behind the protection of rocks. McMasters was huddled uncomfortably beside him, avoiding any chance a stray bullet might find him. Bear kept a tight grip on the shackles. The usually abundant birdcalls were strangely absent, a dead giveaway that danger lurked nearby.

"You see anything, Bear?" Cotton moved back to where the other two kept cover.

"Nothing, Sheriff, but I got a strange feeling they didn't

throw some lead and then ride off. I don't figure they intend to leave us alone out here."

McMasters began to grin. "My boys ain't got you two tough rannies spooked, have they? Why they're just a bunch of softhearted fellas with a hankerin' to make friends. Haw haw."

Cotton gave him a cold stare that was a silent order to shut his mouth. McMasters didn't stop grinning until Cotton cocked his Colt and pointed it straight at his head.

"You bring them boys down here with your bellerin' and I'll finish you right here and now with a little frontier justice. I'm in no mood for your tough talk. You'll learn soon enough that I don't spook easily, and I don't take crap from murderin' jackasses like you." Cotton turned back to continue his scan of the hills for any sign of movement. Bear was also keenly surveying the landscape, his Sharps at the ready.

Several minutes later, Cotton thought he saw a glint in the sunlight from across a shallow dip in the terrain. Soon thereafter, two shots rang out. Bullets thudded into the dirt about twenty feet short of their position.

"They must be using sidearms, Bear. Guess they figured they could get close enough to be effective with a six-shooter. Why don't you haul out that Sharps buffalo rifle and plunk one of them cannonballs into their position over there behind those rocks and cactus that look like a bunch of hens with their chicks. Don't try to hit anyone until we know what we're facin'."

Bear raised the rifle and blasted off a .50-caliber shot right where Cotton had told him to. A man burst out of the brush and scrambled for more substantial cover in the boulder-strewn hills higher up.

Cotton grinned. "That ought to tell them something about our firepower. Maybe they'll think twice before tryin' again."

"That they should, Sheriff."

"You get a chance to see that fella well enough to know whether he's a miner or a townie, Bear?"

"He was movin' too fast to get a good look. It looked a little like Orville Digby, a clerk at the general store."

"If that's true, then we're looking down the barrels of folk who want our prisoner dead," said Cotton. "Probably not a real gunslinger among 'em."

"Easy to understand. The marshal was a fine fella. He was one of us, not a trained lawman, just a common, good-natured sort. Then this rattler had to murder him for no reason at all. Ain't that the way it was, McMasters?" said Bear, his face growing red with anger as he glared at the prisoner.

McMasters scooted back as far as he could to avoid Bear's rumored explosive temper. Cotton saw the same change in Bear's demeanor and knew he had to step in. He placed a hand on the big man's shoulder.

"Bear, don't forget what we're out here for. This man has to stand trial for what he did. I'm sworn to uphold the law, and I intend to do just that."

"Don't worry none, Sheriff, I ain't goin' to turn traitor on you. My word's good. I promised to help you get him to Apache Springs safely, and I will. It's just that I ain't keen on shootin' at my friends, that's all."

"Ain't any too fond of it, myself," said Cotton.

It was midday, with the blazing sun turning the desert into a furnace. As long as they could remain where they were, Cotton and Bear could hold out for some time. The townsfolk holed up in the rocks on the hill had no trees for shade and nearly a quarter of a mile of flat desert between them and their quarry. Cotton was consumed with what those men might be thinking. Would their resolve to get even with McMasters be diminished by the gathering heat, or would their hatred for the man drive them to hold out until they accomplished their task at all costs? And what could Cotton do to affect the outcome of their intentions?

Suddenly, Cotton's thoughts were interrupted by a number of riders coming into view on the road to Silver City. As soon as they got close enough to identify, McMasters jumped up and began yelling. They were his men. Bear had been right about the men on the hill, who were, Cotton saw now, undoubtedly citizens from Silver City.

Gunfire erupted from the hillside. The miners found themselves caught in a potential cross fire, and they dove for cover in the brush alongside the road. So far, it appeared no one had been hit, but Cotton knew it was only a matter of time. The two sides began trading sporadic fire. Some of the lead thunked into the trees and ricocheted off the rocks where Cotton and Bear were hunkered down. All of the shots seemed to have been aimed high.

Cotton stayed low, not firing back. He told Bear to do the same. "We're tied up tighter than a calf at brandin', pardner. We can hold out for a spell, but sooner or later, we'll have to make some hard choices."

As Cotton pondered his possible options, he noticed a slowing in the two sides trading gunshots. After several minutes, McMasters suddenly yanked free of Bear's grip and jumped up, making a dash for the group of miners that had dug in along the road to the south. Before Cotton could reach him to drag him back, McMasters had burst through the tree line and was running for all he was worth straight for his own crew.

"Damn! I'm sorry, Sheriff. I reckon I wasn't payin' enough attention to that scoundrel and his wily ways," Bear said with a look of guilt on his broad face.

"It ain't no more your fault than it is mine, Bear. But it sure looks like we've lost any chance at hustlin' McMasters off to trial."

All the two of them could do was watch the murderer escape into the hands of his own men and freedom.

But as McMasters neared his men, waving and shouting triumphantly, one of them popped out from his cover behind some low rocks and mesquite and raised a double-barreled shotgun. In one single smoky blast, he pumped a shotgun round into the oncoming McMasters. Struck squarely in the chest from the twelve-gauge's double-aught pellets, McMasters stumbled backwards. He fell to the ground with a groan and lay still, an expression of disbelief etched permanently on his grizzled face. He'd been blasted into eternity by one of his own men.

"What the hell did we just see, Sheriff?" said Bear, his eyes wide with surprise.

"An execution. Plain and simple."

As Cotton, Bear, and the townsfolk held their fire, several miners emerged from cover, took hold of McMasters's corpse, and dragged him to an awaiting horse. They threw him over the saddle, mounted up, and started back toward their mining camp. The townsfolk slowly eased down from the safety of the foothills and joined Cotton and Bear as they collectively stared incredulously after the departing miners.

"I'll be damned" was all Cotton could think to say.

Cotton and Bear watched as the miners began to ride off with the body of McMasters. One man reined his horse, then rode back, stopping in front of Cotton.

"Name's Hicks. I 'spect we owe an explanation for what we done."

"Wouldn't mind one, if you've a mind," said Cotton, still clearly bewildered by what had happened.

Hicks leaned forward on the pommel, hands stacked. "McMasters was one mean son of a bitch. When he wasn't kickin' the stuffin' outta one of us, he was taking his bad temper out on someone in town. He shot the marshal for no reason except sheer meanness. When we saw how the townsfolk was lookin' at us like we was no more than a bunch of rabid skunks, fit only to be shot, we took a vote, and the majority decided it was time to set things right. But we couldn't let someone else do what needed to be done, so we come out here to do it ourselves. No offense, Sheriff, but if he got to a judge, he coulda got off scot-free. Ain't that right?"

"It's possible, but not likely. There's no doubt he was guilty, sure as hell," said Cotton. "He was bound to hang."

"We couldn't take the chance. If he had escaped justice, like as not he'd have come back and commenced where he left off, and this time some of us mighta paid the price.

We need the town as much as they need us. We deal with
our own when they step outta line. There's only a handful
that feels different. We'll deal with them as need be," said
Hicks.

"Who'll run the mine?" said Cotton.

"I reckon the bank where McMasters borrowed the
money to buy the mine in the first place will find a new
owner. The mine'll survive. There's too much ore there for
it not to." Hicks tipped his hat, spun his horse around, and
trotted off to catch up with the others.

Cotton had never run across anything like this before in
his career as a lawman. These men had committed murder
themselves by shooting down an unarmed man. But, on the
other hand, McMasters *was* guilty by his own admission,
and would have hanged. Since Cotton had no authority in
the matter anyway, being outside his county, his thoughts
turned to more pressing matters in Apache Springs. He
stuck out his hand to Bear.

"It looks like your services are no longer required.
Thanks for your help, Bear. Maybe we'll meet again."

Bear shook his hand and began to mount up. "Anytime,
Sheriff. If you ever need someone to back you with a big
gun, gimme a holler," he called back as he joined the other
townsfolk. Cotton felt a wave of relief that he could now
return to Apache Springs and set about freeing Emily
Wagner.

Chapter 31

———◆———

Jack looked around carefully as he brought the buggy to a halt in front of the stone porch of the Brennan ranch house. He leapt out and rushed to the front door. Doc Winters followed uneasily. Wu Chang opened it before he had a chance to knock.

"Prease hurry inside, sirs, Missa Hank up stair in bed," Wu Chang said, leading the way with hurried steps.

When they entered the bedroom where Hank Brennan lay twisted and groaning, Doc Winters seemed to sober up almost in an instant. He went to Hank's side and began pulling medical devices and bandages out of his bag. He turned to Wu Chang and asked that he boil some water and bring it in a large bowl. The Chinaman left quickly, pulling the door shut behind him. Jack grabbed the door before it closed and let himself out of the room.

"Wu Chang, has anyone seen this Cruz fella or any of his men since we got back?" Jack asked barely above a whisper.

"No, no see. That velly good, too, yes?"

"Yes, it is. Have you seen Cappy?"

"I get him for you, Missa Jack." Wu Chang ran down the stairs hollering for Cappy, as Jack went back inside the bedroom to learn what he could about Hank's condition.

"How does it look, Doc? Is he goin' to be all right?"

"This old bird is too tough to succumb to a trifling fall down a cliff, all night in near freezing temperatures, and no food or water for a day and a half. He'll be healing up for quite a spell, but he'll make it. It's going to take a bite out of Cappy's and Wu Chang's days just fetching after his needs, though, if I know Hank Brennan." The doctor had fashioned splints for both of Hank's legs and his right arm, and was wrapping his ribs with cloth bandages.

Cappy eased into his father's room, stopped, and looked aghast at his father. "Damn! You look like one of them Egyptian mummies, Pa."

Hank attempted a weak smile. Jack pulled Cappy aside while the doctor finished up.

"What do you plan on sayin' if that Cruz fella you told me about comes back and sees the doc here? You gonna tell him your father is alive? He might be tempted to try to kill him again."

"I don't know. I, uh, ain't had time to think on it. You got any suggestions?"

"Does Cruz have any reason to be comin' into this house?"

"No, but he don't live by other folks' rules, either. So I can't say he *wouldn't* just bust in anytime he took a mind to."

Jack rubbed his chin for a moment. Deep in thought, he failed to hear horses approaching, as Cappy went to the window and drew back the curtains.

"It's too late. Cruz and Blade Coffman are comin' into the yard right now. What should I say?"

"We'll both step out on the porch. You're going to introduce me as a new hand you hired because you were short-handed. Then you'll say that the doc is here because Wu Chang took ill from some bad food he ate. Say he'll be fine in a day or two, but the men will have to look after themselves till he's up and around. Then you can ask if he's seen Hank, since he's been gone for a couple days and nobody's seen hide nor hair of him. Got that?"

"I-I think so. Would you really consider hiring on for a spell, at least till we get my father back on his feet so he can deal with Cruz?"

"I'll hang around for a while, if you'd like. I hate to admit it, but I need a job. Like I said before, I *was* on my way out to your place because the bartender said you maybe could use an extra hand."

"Well, then consider yourself hired." Cappy stuck out his hand, relief showing on his face. "I ain't good for too much around here, but I can sure as hell do this."

"Thanks. Oh, and don't forget to tell Wu Chang he'll have to lay low for a day or two."

When Virgil and Blade dismounted in front of the porch, Jack and Cappy stepped out the front door to meet them.

"Hey, Cappy, what's the doc's buggy doin' out here. Everybody's all right, ain't they?"

"Wu Chang came down with, uh–"

"A touch of rotten food," said Jack. "I came on him down the road apiece. He was trying to make it to town on foot. Poor soul was bent over in pain, groaning and holding his stomach. I rode to town and fetched the doc."

"And just who the hell might you be, mister?"

Jack stepped off the porch and extended a hand to Virgil. "I'm Memphis Jack Stump. New to these parts. I was passin' through when I saw your man Chang. I reckon it was lucky I came along. Doc said he coulda died."

Virgil and Blade looked at each other, then back to Jack.

"Well, I'd suggest you keep on movin', Mr. Stump," said Blade. Virgil nodded.

Cappy broke in. "Well, you see, since the Tulips is gone, and Hank rode off two days ago and ain't come back, I hired Mr. Stump to help out for a spell. Us needin' the help and all."

"I do the hirin' and the firin' around here, sonny. And no snot-nosed kid's gonna do it for me, understand?"

Jack could see Cappy was all out of options and completely unable to stand up to his foreman. He figured he had little choice but to do a little pushing back himself. Jack let his hand fall to his Remington. He stepped off to the side and motioned for Virgil to walk with him. Virgil frowned at Blade, then walked to where Jack had stopped behind the doctor's buggy.

"Fact is, Mr. Cruz, I'm wanted for a little trouble with a bank in Arizona. I could use the work until I can get back on my feet. I had a few unfortunate hands at the poker table and lost what pitiful amount I came away with from that pissant town's vault. So if you could see your way to lettin' me stay on for a couple weeks or so, I'd be damned grateful."

Cruz thought that over for a minute. "How do I know you're on the run?"

Jack reached into his pocket and pulled out a folded-up piece of well-worn parchment. He handed it to Cruz. It said, "Wanted. Memphis Jack Stump for robbery. $300 reward. Contact Sheriff Benson, Cochise County, Arizona Territory."

Cruz studied the dodger for a moment, his eyes narrowed in thought. He handed it back to Jack. He started to turn, but spun around, drawing his revolver as he did. What he found staring him in the belly was unnerving to the gunman. In a flash, Memphis Jack had his Remington already out, cocked, and aimed directly at Cruz's vitals. Cruz grinned nervously.

"You're a fast hand with that thing, mister."

"You're pretty fast yourself."

"Yeah, well a man's got to keep his skills honed. Times are tough in this rattler-snake infested hole. Can't take any chances," said Cruz.

"I agree," said Jack, still holding his Remington on Cruz, who let his Colt drop back into its holster.

"I don't reckon you'll be needin' that thing."

"Well, it's available if the need should arise," said Jack, letting the Remington roll on his trigger finger then slipping it smoothly into the holster with one quick motion.

"Uh, after givin' it more consideration, maybe we *could* use a man of your talents, Mr. Stump. In fact I got something lined up that might suit you just fine," Cruz said.

"Thanks. I appreciate the opportunity. You won't regret it."

Cruz and Blade mounted up and started for the bunkhouse. Cruz turned in the saddle and said, "Bring your bedroll and follow us. I'll show you where you can bed down."

Jack nodded and smiled. He'd tossed out the bait, and now it appeared he'd set the hook.

Chapter 32

———◆———

Emily rolled onto her side so she could better watch Dogman and any attempt he might make to do to her what his deranged brother had been intent on doing several times. But he continued to quietly sit at the table dealing cards for three hands, playing each hand as if he were different people. Watching his interest in the game gave Emily an idea. It was a long shot, yes, but one worth trying, considering the options that had presented themselves thus far.

"Excuse me, Mr. Dogman, but I can't help noticin' you playing cards with yourself. Wouldn't it work better if you had someone to take another hand?"

"I reckon it might be. But you don't see no one around just beggin' to sit in, do you?"

"There might be someone a lot closer than you think. If you were to loosen these ropes, I could take a hand. I love to play poker."

"If I was to let you loose and Virgil found out, I'd be a dead man. Sorry, lady, nothin' doin'."

"How far could I get? You're so much bigger and faster than I am. If I tried to make a break for it, you'd catch little old me without even getting out of breath. And where would I go? I don't even know where I am. C'mon, I need to go to the outhouse anyway."

Dogman stopped dealing and began stroking his chin, deep in thought. His eyes darted about the dark corners of the cabin as if the answer might be hidden there. He frowned as he looked over at Emily.

"I don't know about cuttin' you loose, missy. Virgil Cruz shows up at times when you'd think he was miles away. The man's like a spook, passin' through walls and all."

"He said you could untie my ankles, didn't he? So, he must have figured I could never escape your watchful eye. Anyway, you can always listen for him to come ridin' up the trail. I've noticed there's a loose board on the steps, too, that's a dead giveaway. All you have to do is listen carefully. I'll even help by jumping back onto the cot if we hear anyone coming. What do you say?"

"Well, I—"

"I've got enough money at my ranch to pay any pot I lose. I'll even give you a marker for it. You can't make any money playin' by yourself, and you might win big. You can always use extra cash, can't you?" Emily put on her most innocent face.

"Aww, well, all right, but you gotta promise not to make a break for it. Virgil wouldn't like it none if I was to have to shoot you." He untied Emily's ankles first and then her wrists. Her relief came out in a great sigh.

"Thanks, that feels real good. Now, if you'd allow a lady the use of the outhouse, we can get to that game," she said, finding she had to grab the doorpost to steady herself. Her balance was unsure, her legs weak from being unable to move about for so long. She knew she would have to play by Dogman's rules until she regained sufficient strength to even attempt to make a break for it.

Besides, how bad could a few hands of cards be anyway?

*   *   *

"Now, Keeno, tell me what's got you so upended? Cruz hasn't pulled anything yet, has he?" Cotton asked as he watched his nervous deputy wringing his hands.

"No, not yet. But he's a-fixin' to any day now. I can feel it in my bones. That scoundrel is mighty tight with that Blade Coffman feller, and Ben Patch, too. Neither of them is good for a thing except makin' trouble. Mark my words, there'll be hell to pay, and soon."

"What about this gunslinger you mentioned? What do you know about him?"

"Name's Red Carter. I ain't laid eyes on him face-to-face, but I know the law's a-lookin' for him. Billy tells me he's been palaverin' some with Cruz. Billy's the one who told me who he was." Keeno leaned over the desk and shuffled through some of the pile of papers that had collected since Cotton left town. "I looked around and found this dodger on him, Sheriff, that says he's wanted." Keeno pulled the paper from a stack on the desk. It had no picture, just a description.

"Hmm. You say this fella has been huddlin' with Cruz? Any notion of what might have transpired between them?"

"No, but the gunsmith said Carter thought one of Cruz's men was following him and he slipped out the back door to shake the man from his trail. Sounded like Blade Coffman from the description."

"Why would Cruz have him followed if they're in cahoots? That doesn't make much sense. I better look up this Carter fellow. Any idea where he might be?"

"Most likely at this time of day he'll be at the saloon. Want I should tag along, Sheriff? Just in case he gets itchy with his trigger finger?"

"You mind the store, Keeno. I won't be long, and I don't anticipate any trouble."

With that, Cotton strolled outside toward the saloon, the place Keeno figured he was most likely to find Red Carter. When he pushed through the swinging doors, One-Eyed

Billy Black, the bartender, met his gaze. Cotton could tell by Billy's expression that someone in the establishment was making Billy nervous. He walked to the polished oak bar, leaned on his elbows, and motioned Billy over.

"Hello, Billy, you look like a snake is about to strike. What's got you all lathered up?"

"It's that fella over in the corner, sitting all alone. I'm bettin' money that's Red Carter, and if it is, his bein' in here is enough to raise the hair on anyone's neck. If it ain't him, there's *somethin'* mighty peculiar about that owlhoot. I'd be careful if I was you, Sheriff."

Cotton ordered a beer, then carried it over to the table where Carter was sitting.

"Mind if I join you, mister?"

Carter looked Cotton over, then his eyes fell to the badge. He nodded for the sheriff to take a seat.

"Obliged," said Cotton. "You must be new to Apache Springs. I don't think we've ever met. I'm Sheriff Cotton Burke. Welcome to our peaceful little town."

"Why thank you, Sheriff. I've come to like the peace and quiet myself. Been thinkin' maybe I'll settle here. A man has to put down roots sometime, and it could be my time has come."

"You never know. Where are you from, Mister–uh . . . ?"

"Carson. Folks call me Burt. I'm from over near Abilene."

"What line of work were you in, Mr. Carson?"

"Oh, you know, a little of this and a little of that. Nothin' special."

"Why'd you leave Abilene?"

"Things was kinda dead there, so I decided to come a little farther west, maybe hire on with an outfit hereabouts. Know anyone lookin' for a good hand?"

"I imagine it all depends on what you're a good hand at. That Colt of yours looks pretty well used. That your line of work?"

"Naww. I just like to keep my hand in, that's all. Practice is good for the soul. But I expect you already know that, Sheriff. In case you're wonderin', I ain't aimin' to stir up any trouble. I'm a peaceable man with nothin' but good intentions. I hope that settles your mind some."

"I really wasn't concerned, Mr. Carson. I didn't figure you for anything other than an upstanding citizen. I hope the folks in town make you welcome."

"Well, that's mighty considerate of you, Sheriff. I thank you. You can be sure I'll repay your trust."

Cotton stood up, reached over and shook Carter's hand, then carried his beer to the bar. He set the glass down, winked at Billy, and went out, whistling as he went.

Carter's either very smart or very stupid, he thought. *I reckon he's worth keepin' an eye on; however, I don't see him gettin' too close to Cruz. Two rattlers in the same hole usually don't work out so well.*

Chapter 33

Jack's luck at getting in with Virgil Cruz and his gang had been better than he could have hoped for. Now all he had to do was gain their confidence enough for them to tell him where Emily Wagner was being held and what the object of their crooked intentions was.

He was brushing his gelding when Virgil came stomping past him, grumbling to himself. He slammed the door to the bunkhouse. Jack could hear him shouting for Blade. Getting no answer, he stormed back outside.

"Hey, Jack, or whatever the hell your name is, where'd Blade Coffman get to?"

"It's Jack Stump, Virgil, and I didn't see where he went. He was here only a few minutes ago."

"Well, I want him back here, pronto. I got a job for him. You find him, and be quick about it. Oh, and another thing, since it appears I'm stuck with you, for the time bein' at least, I'm *Mr. Cruz* to you. Don't you forget it, neither."

"Right, Mr. Cruz. Anything you want me to tell him?"

"Yeah. Tell him to ride into town and round up Ben

Patch and meet me here in two hours. Also, I hope you can cook, or that Chinaman is goin' to have to get his butt back in the kitchen, sick or not. Understand?"

Jack nodded and started off to find Blade. He had an idea where he'd gone, but he wasn't about to tell Virgil. In just the few words that had passed between them, Jack could see how contentious the man was, and how he'd have to be very careful with every word he said. The two times he'd had a verbal exchange with Cruz, he'd learned something about the man. He hadn't liked any of it.

Jack wandered down behind the corral, where the land slanted toward a winding creek. A stand of cottonwoods dotted the bank, and Jack thought he'd seen Coffman headed that direction. When he heard some shots, he was certain that's where he'd find him letting off some of the steam that had been building up. As he neared the creek, he stepped out from behind a boulder and started to speak. Blade spun around with his six-shooter cocked. He eased the hammer down when he saw who it was.

"You lookin' for a bullet between the eyes, Stump, sneakin' up on a man like that?"

"Cruz sent me to look for you. He wants you to go find Ben Patch and then meet him back at the bunkhouse in two hours. Sorry if I startled you."

Blade said nothing but started back to the corral. Jack fell in beside him.

"I saw you shooting. You're pretty good with that thing."

Blade frowned. "I'm better than pretty good."

"Look, I ain't aimin' to cause you no grief. I'm just a fella down on his luck temporarily and needin' a job. Once I get a little money in my pocket, I'll be movin' on. No need for us to get off on the wrong foot," said Jack.

For a moment, Jack thought he saw Blade soften a little, but his expression quickly returned to its former stone-cold facade when he saw Cruz coming toward them.

"Where the hell you been, Blade? This fella tell you I want you to round up Ben and get back here, pronto?"

"Yeah, Virgil, he told me. I'm headin' out right now. It

won't take me long to get to town, but I don't think we can get back in two hours."

"You better bust your ass tryin' or you'll know what for." Cruz seemed to be pushing Blade as far as he could and for no reason that Jack could understand. There was increasingly bad blood between these two, which didn't make any sense, since it appeared they had ridden together for a long time, and they seemed solidly in cahoots in some nefarious plan. But as long as they argued and sniped at each other in plain sight of others, Jack figured that made his job easier. Or more dangerous.

Blade mounted up and spurred his horse to a gallop through the gate. Cruz turned to Jack and said, "Go see how that damned Chinaman is doin'. I'm near starved, and I don't aim to wait much longer for some grub."

Jack headed for the house at a trot. When he got inside, he saw Cappy Brennan coming down the stairs from Hank's bedroom.

"How's you father doin'?"

"He's growling something ferocious. I imagine he's on the mend. So, you got any ideas on what we do, now? I'm afraid Cruz will find out Hank's alive and storm in here to kill him." Cappy's look of bewilderment was tinged with fear. It was clear to Jack that this boy was inexperienced in the art of subterfuge, and the risk of him spilling everything was an ever-present reality. He had no choice but to make Cappy believe everything would be all right as long as he held firm and didn't let anything slip about his father still being alive.

Just then, Wu Chang came into the large living room with a bowl of soup to take upstairs to Hank. Jack knew he was walking a thin line with his whole scheme. The only thing he could think to do was to take the Brennans into his confidence—a major risk. But one that had to be taken if he was to come out with his skin intact.

"Cappy, Wu Chang, come and sit down over here for a minute. I have something to tell you, and it's probably best you're both seated when you hear it. I'm about to place a lot of trust in you both." The little terrier came up, sniffed at Jack's pant leg, then returned to his bed near the fireplace.

Cappy and Wu Chang sat down as they had been asked, each wearing a puzzled expression. Jack leaned on the mantel as he began to tell them about why he had come to the Brennan ranch and what he needed to do. Cappy's eyes grew wide as Jack told about his being sent by the sheriff to gather information on Virgil Cruz. Wu Chang smiled and nodded, relief showing in his eyes.

"I know fum sta't you no like that man an' his bunch. He no good like snake, but you got eye and heart of eagle. You count on me, okay?"

"Okay, Wu. I'm counting on you from now on. First, you need to rustle up some grub for the men. Make it simple, like you were too weak to fix a full meal. I'll get them to understand. Tomorrow, you can say you are feeling fine and everything will be okay. Don't let anything slip about Hank being alive. That's critical to remember. Not a word to anyone, understand?"

"I unnastand, Missa Jack. I you man." Wu Chang got up and went upstairs with the soup bowl. Cappy seemed dazed at Jack's confession. He stared at the floor for several minutes before speaking.

"Mr. Stump, what'll happen if Virgil *does* find out my father is alive?"

"He tried to kill him once, don't think for one minute he won't finish the job if given half a chance. It's clear he wants Hank out of the way for some reason. Any idea why?"

"N-no. I've never liked the man, but I didn't figure him for a murderer. Reckon I underestimated him."

"You can't afford to make that mistake again. Remember, if he tried to kill Hank to get his hands on the ranch, then he won't stop before he's gotten you out of the way, too."

"You think he'd try to kill me?" Cappy's eyes were wide with surprise. Perspiration began to dot his forehead.

Chapter 34

Cotton sat with his elbows on his desk and his chin in his hands, worry etched on his face. As if he didn't have enough to worry about, at that moment Keeno came storming through the door with more bad news, the type of news the sheriff had never gotten used to hearing. Someone had found a body lying out back of the corral, and it wasn't one of the town's drunks sleeping off too much redeye. With a muffled curse, Cotton grabbed his hat and followed Keeno out. The two of them hurried down the street toward the livery. It became evident pretty quickly that something noteworthy had gotten the public's interest. There were a dozen people standing around, speculating in animated conversation as to what had happened and who might have committed such a dastardly deed.

The liveryman, a man named Horst, was telling people to stay back, as he led the two lawmen out behind the barn, where fouled straw and manure were piled high, out of sight of most passersby. Several curious townsfolk tagged along behind, each muttering their best guess as to who the killer might be, including every known outlaw from Billy Bonney to Dave Rudabaugh.

"You the one that found the body, Horst?" asked Cotton, staring down at the bloody corpse.

"Nope, ol' Kettle done it. Sniffed him right out first thing this mornin'."

"By Kettle, do you mean that skinny runt hound of yours, Horst?" said Keeno.

"Now, Keeno, you know damned well what I mean. Why'd you ask such a fool question?"

Keeno looked away, embarrassed.

Cotton bent down and turned the man over. It was the man Keeno had identified as Red Carter. The same man who'd introduced himself as Carson to the sheriff. He'd been knifed once in the gut, then had his throat cut. The man's gun was still in its holster, and his pockets didn't appear to have been searched. Cotton found several dollars still on the body. He stuffed them back into the dead man's pocket.

"It doesn't look like a case of robbery. So there had to have been another reason. You got any ideas, Horst?"

"No, Sheriff. I hardly knew the man. He brought his horse in about three days ago, had me feed and board him till he come for him. Said he'd be around to collect the horse and pay any past fees on the sixteenth. Never got a name."

Cotton rubbed his chin, muttering to himself, "the sixteenth," over and over. "Keeno, see if you can find someone who might have seen him with anyone in the last twenty-four hours, then get the undertaker over to haul the body away. I'll be heading to the saloon as soon as the undertaker gets here."

Keeno rushed off to get the answers the sheriff had asked for, even though he thought he knew who might have done it. *Ben Patch carries a large knife and some say he don't hesitate to use it when necessary,* thought Keeno.

Horst's admonishment of him for his earlier attempt at detective work was still ringing in his ears. Being shown up again might push him over the edge and force a lengthy visit to the saloon for himself. He went to the gunsmith to verify his suspicions.

When he entered the gunsmith's shop, he found the prune-faced man hunched over a small milling machine, staring intently through a pair of glasses that rode low on his nose, painstakingly engraving scrollwork on the frame of a Winchester. The gunsmith got up, wiping his hands on his apron.

"What can I do for you, Keeno?"

"Uh, well, that gunslinger that's been hangin' around town for a couple days, the one I figure to be Red Carter, the one you told me about the other day, have you seen him in the last ten, maybe twelve hours?"

"Nope. The last I seen of him was when Blade come in askin' about him. Blade seemed to be keepin' an eye on him for some reason I never did figure out. Why'd you want to know? He causin' some sorta trouble?"

"Not anymore. Thanks for the information." Keeno tipped his hat and left the shop. On his way to rejoin the sheriff, he stopped at the undertaker's store and asked him to bring his cart to haul back a customer.

"Undertaker's on his way, Sheriff. The gunsmith says he ain't seen anyone hangin' out with Carter. I did hear Blade's name mentioned as havin' an interest in the man's comin's and goin's, though." Keeno puffed himself up with pride at having accomplished all that the sheriff had asked for. It hadn't escaped Cotton's notice, either.

"Good job, Deputy. Thanks."

"Uh, Sheriff, what's all this business about the sixteenth? I noticed you perked up when the liveryman mentioned it."

"Why, uh, nothing important. Just that more'n one jasper has been mentioning that date lately, and I aim to find out why."

Keeno looked bewildered but remained silent.

The undertaker arrived minutes later with a two-wheeled cart. Cotton and Keeno watched as Carter was loaded onto the bed of the cart and covered with a blanket.

"I hope there's enough money in his pockets to bury him, John. Don't go over whatever amount you find there. The county don't have the cash to make up any difference."

The undertaker quickly emptied Carter's pockets and found forty dollars and a silver watch. He called out to the sheriff, who by then was halfway down the street. "Looks like he's got just the right amount, Sheriff. It'll do just fine." A satisfactory smile spread across his face. A top-of-the-line funeral could be had for fifteen dollars any day of the week in Apache Springs.

Henry Coyote was growing weary of sitting around waiting for the sheriff to contact him, and he felt as if the walls of the empty bunkhouse were closing in. He'd convinced himself that Cotton Burke wasn't going to lift a finger to rescue Emily Wagner. He hadn't seen any of the other cowboys at the ranch for several days, not since Emily disappeared, so it looked as if it was up to him to find her and bring her safely back to her ranch. There was no point in putting it off any longer. He was determined to start out the next day before dawn. Day six. The day Sheriff Cotton Burke told him he'd be released from his word not to interfere.

He would need to raid the cook shack for some beef jerky. And he knew he'd better take at least two canteens of water. He made sure his well-worn Spencer rifle was loaded and that the bandolier of cartridges that hung across his chest was full. He would set off on foot to cover every inch of Wagner land in search of where Emily might be hidden. His curiosity as to where the other Wagner hands had gotten to was of concern, as well, because he could use their help. What if they knew nothing about Emily's abduction and were simply working at the farther reaches of the ranch? If he found nothing of her on Wagner property, did he dare venture farther? And what if he found no signs of the other wranglers? His confusion over their disappearance was growing. He could fathom no reason for their absence.

He knew the next ranch to the north, the Brennans' spread, was full of caves, gulches, ravines, and rocky promontories that offered a great many perfect hiding places to stash a helpless woman, with scant hope of anyone stumbling across her. The Double-B would be worth searching. As long as he stayed out of sight of any of Cruz's bunch, that is.

Henry was keenly aware of the consequences of being caught and what it could mean to Emily Wagner's safety. She was a woman to whom he owed much. It was because of that debt that he felt compelled to strike out on his own, not waiting for word from the sheriff. He left no message to indicate where he was going or when he'd be back. It made no sense since he had no idea where the other men were. Of course, he seldom shared much with others anyway. Most of the men knew better than to press the Apache too hard about his activities. If Emily Wagner trusted him, that was good enough for them. Hard, though, for white men to trust any Apache when Geronimo was once again creating all sorts of trouble not far to the west, in Arizona Territory. But Henry Coyote didn't owe his allegiance to any Apache leader, especially since he was fairly certain it was another Indian that had tried to kill him those years ago, probably for serving the U.S. Army as a scout. Now he owed everything to Emily Wagner, and he vowed to honor that debt.

While he preferred living in the white man's world, Henry was fully Apache. He let it be known that no one should ever mistake that. He wore traditional Apache garb: the high-top moccasins with fringe up the side, a long, loose-fitting, patterned shirt, and a headband woven of

earth colors—with a single, wide red band wandering un-
evenly through it. He had explained that the blood-colored
band represented the reality of death that surrounds everyone. Never more than now was that reality a factor as he
squatted on the porch to await the safety of darkness.

Chapter 35

———◆———

Memphis Jack was all too aware that something was about to happen as Virgil Cruz and his men were suddenly running roughshod over the other hands. Cruz had taken to barking out orders left and right as if he were not only the foreman but also the new ranch owner. He made no attempt to hide the fact that he figured something had happened to Hank. He also made it clear he had no intention to look for him. "I didn't hire onto this half-assed outfit to waste time scouring the countryside to find an old man that shoulda stayed put."

Cappy could do little but stay out of Cruz's way. If Cruz was willing to kill Hank with no more thought than waiting for the right opportunity, Cappy stood almost no chance of survival. It was clear to everyone that Cruz assumed that Hank Brennan wouldn't be coming back, although he hadn't admitted to having had a hand in it. Jack was keeping a low profile as much as possible, but that didn't mean he could stand by and not ask questions whenever he saw tensions rise between Cruz and his henchmen. Blade was

Jack's choice for information as the gunman was clearly chafing under Cruz's relegating him to near obscurity. Something had gone down between them, and although Blade had remained tight-lipped about the circumstances surrounding his disenchantment with Virgil, he was still the best chance Jack had to break through the wall of silence to learn about either the impending robbery or the whereabouts of Emily Wagner. He didn't care which he stumbled onto first, as long as it was soon.

While he would have preferred to simply aim his Remington at Blade's head and threaten to pull the trigger, he had a strong feeling that it would take more than a threat to his life to loosen Blade's tongue. About two hours later, Jack was contemplating his options as he sat at a bunkhouse table cleaning his revolver, when Blade stormed in and threw himself on his bunk.

"Looks like you got a burr under your saddle, Blade. What's got you so riled?"

"It's none of your damned business. I can handle it myself."

"Of course. No one ever figured you for a man that needed help from anyone."

"You're damned right about that, gunslinger."

"But it don't hurt none to talk about a situation, in fact it sometimes helps to clear the air. Lets you see the problem in a different light. That's all I was sayin'."

"What does all that hogwash you're a-spewin' mean? You ain't makin' fun of me, are you? That'd be a big mistake." He let his hand ease toward his sidearm.

Quick to see he had to defuse the situation, Jack kept his voice calm and made no move to take a defensive posture.

"Look, Blade. No one's makin' fun of you, least of all me. I sure as hell don't want to be your enemy. But it don't hurt a man to talk about what's eatin' at him, that's all I'm sayin'."

Blade eased his hand back off his gun and seemed to relax a little. He chewed on his lower lip and frowned. He took his hat and slapped in on the bed beside him.

"I reckon a man just gets tired of bein' pushed around by a son of a bitch like Virgil Cruz. We was friends for a while, then he got too uppity when he got the idea for this big job he's planning. Now he thinks he's some sort of king or something."

"Yeah, I know what you mean. He's playin' his cards a little close to the vest for me, too. But I figure I'll hang around and see what comes of it all. After all, a man like me is always in need of quick cash," said Jack, hoping not to spook Blade by saying too much, yet still keep him talking.

"Yeah, well, he's goin' to push me a mite too far one of these days and he'll end up getting just what he's handing out. If it weren't for him havin' that Wagner woman stashed away, the sheriff would have already blowed him away."

"The sheriff?"

"Yeah. Cotton Burke. You may have heard of him. He's real slick with that Colt of his. He could take Virgil without thinkin' about it. Might even be faster than me. But I ain't aimin' to find out. Soon as we hit that train, I'm headin' for Montana with my share."

"Been to Montana myself a time or two. A fella needs to keep a sharp lookout for Indians, though. They're thicker than fat fleas on a small dog." Jack hoped that steering the conversation away from Blade's revelation of a train robbery would make it appear he knew more than he did. How long that would work, he wasn't sure. Blade seemed like a man who was driven by how he felt at the time—not very intelligent, but quick on the trigger.

"You got yourself a woman up there, Blade?"

"Naw. They's mostly just whores or army-camp followers. Not many available for marryin', if that's what a fella's got a mind to do."

"That what you're gonna do with your share of the take, get hitched?" Jack said.

"Don't reckon I'm much for gettin' no wife. But if I was, that Emily Wagner would be a real fine woman. Purty as

she can be. Ain't right Virgil got her holed up in that old
line shack like that. But he ain't one for makin' a woman
feel at home and all. Far as he's concerned, she's just a way
for him to stay clear of the sheriff. That's probably good
thinkin'."

"She's a good-lookin' lady, huh? Maybe we ought to
take a ride out there and take a look for ourselves. Maybe
take her some flowers or somethin' pretty," Jack said,
snickering at the idea. He thought for a moment he saw a
flicker in Blade's eye that maybe he favored the idea. But
just as quickly, his demeanor returned to the surly frown he
had when he came in.

"Naww. If Virgil found out, he'd gun us down like
he done them Tulip brothers. I don't figure to give him a
chance to put a bullet in *my* back."

"Well, I don't know a thing about any Tulip brothers,
but if what you say about that Emily lady is right, I got
a hankerin' to lay eyes on her myself. Only if she's a real
looker, of course. Don't cotton much to them whores in the
saloons, though," said Jack.

"I'll give it some thought. But don't go gettin' your head
set on it. Virgil ain't goin' to want any of us wanderin' off
afore he lays out the plan."

"When's that goin' to be?"

"First thing in the mornin' is what he said." Blade
stretched out on his bunk, fingers interlaced behind his
head.

If he could get away long enough to ride into town, Jack
could bring Cotton a great deal of the information he'd
been sent out to the Brennan ranch to collect. Things had
been going easier than he'd ever imagined. Maybe a little
too easy. As he stood up to wander outside, he ran smack
into Virgil, who, it appeared, had been hanging around
just outside the bunkhouse. *How much of that conversation with Blade did the cagey rattler overhear?* Now it was
Jack's turn to get nervous.

Chapter 36

The saloon grew ominously quiet as the sheriff pushed through the batwing doors. He stopped and looked around before taking a seat near the front window. He motioned for Billy to bring him a beer and one for himself. Billy never turned down an offer for a free drink. While he was actually the owner of the place, he was wise enough to know that drinking up one's own profits was never good business. So he drank only when someone offered to buy. Billy brought two beers and sat at Cotton's table. He was wiping his hands of some foam that had overflowed the glasses.

"Billy, why is the place so quiet?"

"I'm not sure. Could be several reasons."

"Name some of them."

"Why do you care if it's quiet? Seems you'd like it better than if those rannies were all whoopin' and hollerin' and shootin' up the place."

"I should, but I'm suspicious when things aren't normal. And they certainly aren't right now."

"Well, there has been some talk goin' around that you're afraid of facin' up to Virgil Cruz and his men. There's also some that's sayin' Cruz has kidnapped Emily Wagner and you ain't lifted a hand to get her free. Now, a' course I don't believe a word of it myself, but that's what's driftin' across the bar." Looking nervous, Billy took a swig of his beer.

Cotton leaned back in his chair. He held the beer glass with both hands then sipped it. He stared at the wet rings that had been left on the tabletop.

"Reckon folks has a right to their opinions, Billy. I don't pay much attention to ignorant cowpokes. But I'm curious who's been doin' all the speculatin.'"

"No one in particular. Mostly a bunch of fools just let-tin' off steam and keepin' themselves busy blabberin' a passel of nonsense. That's all it is." Billy took an even big-ger swig of beer. Two cowboys came in and walked to the bar. They stood for a second, looking for Billy, then one of them pounded on the bar.

"Hey, bartender, how about some service for a couple of thirsty coyotes?"

Billy got up hastily and went around the bar to serve the cowboys. "What'll it be, gents?"

One of the men said he'd have whiskey and he dropped two bits on the bar. The other one ordered the same, then leaned over and in a near whisper said, "Say, ain't that our chickenshit sheriff you was drinkin' with? Don't you have no pride, Billy?"

Billy didn't even blink when he answered, "Gents, if I was you, I'd let that notion of him bein' a coward blow away with the wind and not bring it up in public again. That is, unless you want to be facin' down one of the fast-est Colts this side of the Rio Grande. Just a piece of advice from a friend."

The cowboys looked at each other, downed their whis-keys, and left in a hurry. Billy had a smirk on his face as he returned to Cotton's table.

"What was that all about?"

"Just some more of the ignorance that's goin' around. Pay it no mind."

"Billy, have you any idea who was last seen with Red Carter?"

"Red was real chummy with Virgil at first, then all of a sudden they was chafing at each other somethin' awful. I expected gunplay before it was all over, but nothin' happened. It appeared as though they were cookin' up some sorta deal, then Red seemed to get himself a change of mind, and whatever the deal with Virgil was, it kinda went sour."

Melody was sick and tired of waiting around for Memphis Jack to return to Gonzales and her bed. She had made up her mind to do something about it. She went to the sheriff's office and asked if he knew anything about a man named Cotton Burke and where he might be found.

"Why, hell yes, Melody, he's the sheriff up in Catron County. Straight north 'bout a hundred miles. You plannin' on goin' up there for a wee visit?" he said with a smirk.

"Don't go gettin' all righteous, Sheriff. I ain't goin' nowhere to see that skunk Cotton Burke. I got other fish to fry. I thank you for the information." She turned and left the sheriff's office in a huff.

Reckon I will take a little trip up north, and when I see that Cotton Burke, maybe I'll just plug him, she thought.

She hurried back to the hotel to pack and arrange for one of the fallen angels who worked for her to be in charge while she was away. Melody made sure to pack some of her most alluring clothes—that would make Jack sorry he left—and her derringer—that was to plug Cotton if he tried to stop her from taking Jack back.

When she was packed, she dragged her suitcase over to the stage company office to buy a ticket. She dropped her luggage just inside the narrow room.

"I'd like a ticket to Catron County on the next stagecoach going that way," she said to the mousey man behind the counter. She pulled out some money from her handbag, unfolded it, and prepared to shell out whatever the man said the price of the ticket was. It didn't really matter the cost, she was too anxious to get Jack back to worry about such mundane matters. Besides, she could make it back in a few of days. And with her looks and the number of woman-starved cowpokes in Gonzales, she'd be even more in demand, and the money would flow like wine as it always had. Which was one of the reasons Jack had taken up with her in the first place. She had no illusions as to the scope of Jack's interest.

"Would that be Apache Springs you're goin' to for a visit?" the man said.

"Is that the only town in Catron County?"

"Only one where the stage stops. Couple of dirty little crossroads further north, but nothin' that amounts to more'n a pile of dung."

"Then I reckon it's going to have to be Apache Springs. When does it leave?"

"Tomorrow morning, 'bout eight-thirty. Be out front with your luggage. I'm shorthanded and I ain't got no one to fetch it from the hotel."

"I brought it along. I'll leave it right here inside the front door. You just keep an eye on it. And make sure you lock up tight when you leave. I'll be back first thing in the morning." With that, she turned and danced out with her shoulders thrown back, a spring in her step, and a wide smile on her lips.

Watch out, Cotton Burke, you're about to get the surprise of your life.

Chapter 37

———◆———

"Where the hell's Blade?" Virgil bellowed in Jack's face.

"Inside." Jack threw a thumb over his shoulder.

Virgil pushed Jack aside and stormed into the bunkhouse. "Blade, why the hell didn't you bring Ben back from town?"

Blade sat up on his bunk, ran a hand across his stubbly face, and scowled at Virgil's blustering manner.

"He wasn't there. And I ain't his nursemaid."

"You are now. Get your sorry ass outta that bunk and go find him. He's gotta be somewhere." Virgil turned and stormed outside. He was soon heard berating one of the other ranch hands for not unsaddling his horse fast enough.

Jack came back inside just in time to see Blade go for his revolver and start to aim it at Virgil's back. Jack grabbed Blade's wrist and pushed down. "Whoa, pardner, that's no way to handle this. You'll get yourself hanged for backshootin' the man, no matter how bad he deserves it. How 'bout we go do what he wants done? Give him enough rope, he'll end up hangin' himself. But you shouldn't have to pay for it," he said.

The fury in Blade's eyes told how tightly wound he was. Jack could see that Blade's loyalty to Virgil Cruz ended pretty much right where the almighty dollar began, and that was possibly the only thing keeping Cruz alive. *This robbery they're planning to pull off must really be big,* Jack thought. *It could work in my favor if I play my cards right.*

Blade squinted as he stared Jack straight in the eyes; then, reluctantly, he released the hammer and jammed the gun back in its holster. "Maybe you're right. I want the son of a bitch dead, sure enough, but I reckon another time will work just as well. C'mon, we'll ride out and see if we can find Ben."

Jack was pleased with Blade's turnaround in attitude. Maybe he'd gotten someplace with his efforts to talk reason to him. He knew Blade wasn't very intelligent, and a couple of times it had been questionable whether Jack had gone too far, risking his own neck in the process. It appeared Blade was beginning to trust him. But Virgil wasn't the trusting sort, as Jack quickly found out. When they began saddling their mounts, Virgil stormed up to Jack.

"Where the hell do you think you're goin', Stump? I didn't say nothin' about you leavin', did I?"

"Why, er, no, I reckon not. I just figured it would be easier if two of us went lookin' for your friend. That's all." Jack could see the blood in Virgil's eyes. This man was right on the edge of exploding, like nitro in the hot sun.

"Well, you figured wrong. I want you here where I can keep an eye on you. I ain't decided whether I trust you yet."

"How will you know if you don't let me do some work for you?"

"I'll know, all right. I got me a keen eye for rattlers. I know when they're about to strike long before I hear the sound. Same with men, I can tell when they're about to turn on me long before they make the mistake. Now, unsaddle that gelding and make yourself comfortable. When the others get here, we got some plannin' to do." Virgil stomped off toward the corral.

Blade scowled at Virgil's back as he left. Blade's anger was smoldering like a three-day-old barn fire. Jack knew that if he could keep Blade from jumping too soon, he might have an ally when the time came. But that time wasn't now, and he knew he had to be patient and keep his mouth shut. Blade rode off in the direction of the rough country where Jack had stumbled onto Cappy and Wu Chang, very near where they had found Hank Brennan's battered body.

As Jack began unsaddling his horse, Virgil yelled at him from across the barnyard. "Hey, Stump, run up to the house and see if that damned Chinaman's got us some vittles yet. I'm starving."

A perfect opportunity to look in on Hank. Also, he could tell Wu Chang to get back to cooking full-time. He could no longer get away with feigning weakness from stomach problems. Cappy could devote his time to helping his father. Virgil would assume Cappy was too afraid to show his face and would gladly let the younger Brennan stay inside out of his way. Cappy met Jack in the large entry hall.

"Mr. Stump, I sure am glad to see you. What's that bastard Cruz got up his sleeve?"

"I don't know yet, but it ain't got nothin' to do with ranchin', of that I'm certain. How's your dad getting along? Can I go up and see him?"

"Yessir, he'd be glad to talk a bit. He's cantankerous about havin' to stay put until he heals enough to face the bastard that tried to kill him."

"You must keep him out of sight, no matter what happens. Cruz won't hesitate to put a bullet in him if he finds out he's alive. If Hank talks, Cruz will hang, and he knows it."

As they walked into Hank's bedroom, Jack stuck out his hand. Hank took it with his good hand and a weak grin. "Thanks for helpin' save my worthless hide, son. Cappy here told me what all you done and your plan to keep that son of a bitch Virgil Cruz in the dark. I'm beholden to you."

"I know Cruz is plannin' something big, a robbery or something. I already told Cappy I was sent here by the sheriff, Cotton Burke, to find out what Cruz is up to. It's important Cruz doesn't find out you're alive. You have to lay low until we can either bust up Virgil's plans or put him behind bars for something he's already done. You gettin' pushed off that cliff could be that somethin' if I can get word to Cotton."

"Hey, I could ride into town and tell the sheriff whatever you want me to," said Cappy.

Jack thought about that for a minute. He couldn't allow Cappy to put himself in danger. Without Cappy to look after Hank, the whole plan could crumble. But then, how else was he going to get the word to Cotton? He knew Cruz wouldn't allow *him* to go riding off by himself. Besides, he needed to be around when Virgil disclosed the plans for the robbery. Just then, an idea formed.

"Cappy, what if you were to tell Cruz you have to take the buckboard into town for supplies? Tell him if he wants to eat, Wu Chang needs beans, flour, potatoes, bacon, coffee—you know, all the stuff he usually gets in town."

"That's a great idea. I'll get right to it." Cappy jumped at Jack's suggestion. Sitting around the big ranch house with the heavy drapes drawn must have been beginning to get on his nerves.

"One thing, Cappy. Don't let any of Cruz's men that might be in town see you talking to the sheriff when you get to Apache Springs. One or two could have ridden in earlier, and you might not come back alive," said Jack.

Cappy took his time digesting Jack's words for a moment before smiling weakly and nodding his understanding. Jack saw fear in the boy's eyes. He didn't like sending this innocent young man into a potentially dangerous situation, but it was the only thing he could think to do at the moment. He slapped Cappy on the back.

"You'll do fine."

Chapter 38

———◆———

Cotton looked up from cleaning his Colt when a buck-board pulled up across the street. He saw Cappy Brennan jump down from the conveyance and step onto the plank walk. Cappy hesitated for a moment, glancing across at the sheriff's office, then continued on inside the general store. Cotton was intrigued by the boy's curious behavior but went back to his cleaning.

The door flew open and Keeno blew in like a desert sandstorm. "Well, Sheriff, I reckon we can write Virgil Cruz off our list of suspects who might've killed Red Carter."

"Oh. Why is that?"

"Well, several folks saw him leave town early in the day. He couldn't have been around when it happened." Keeno looked quite proud of his detecting abilities. He slipped into a chair with a satisfied look pasted on his unshaven face.

"When did it happen?"

"You mean the killin'?"

"Yep."

"Uh, in the evenin', I reckon. Ain't no way he was lyin' there all afternoon without someone seein' his body, right?"

"You better go check with the liveryman. Find out if he was there all day, and if he was gone any of the time."

"Uh, okay."

Keeno left with considerably less gusto than he had entered with. The disdain that showed on his face would have led most anyone to believe he didn't like facing the possibility that all his hard detective work might have gone for naught. He sauntered outside and took his sweet time crossing the street to the livery. When he got there, he saw the liveryman pitching hay up into a wheelbarrow.

"Howdy, Deputy. What can I do for you?"

"Horst, the sheriff asked me to come over here and find out if you was gone anytime when that fella might have been cut up out back. Was you?"

Horst scratched his chin for a moment. "Yep, I remember now. Reckon I *was* away most of the afternoon. I had to take a horse out to the widow Barnes's place. Her old mule keeled over and died. A neighbor came in and asked me to take her a substitute."

"So you might not have been here when the cuttin' happened?" Keeno wanted to make double sure there wasn't any mistake about the time Horst was missing.

"Likely I was four miles out of town. Didn't get back till late and went straight home. I told you it was ol' Kettle that found him the next morning."

"Uh, yeah, reckon you did at that. Well, thanks, Horst." Keeno felt dejected. He took his time returning to the jail, stopping off for a quick beer at One-Eyed Billy's. He even took several minutes to chat with the general store owner's wife, who was out front sweeping a week's worth of dirt and dust off the boardwalk in front of their store. When he returned, Cotton was reading a three-week-old newspaper. He seemed to have found an article that caught his attention when Keeno came in.

"Well, uh, Sheriff, reckon Cruz and his boys coulda done the deed to ol' Red Carter. Horst was away messin' with a dead mule for most of the afternoon. Guess that pretty well tosses my theory into a cocked hat, don't it?"

"It does open more gates than it closes, at that. Listen, Keeno, I want you to stay here while I go talk to the newspaper editor. I'll be back soon." At that, Cotton got up, folded the paper he'd been reading, and hurried out the door. Keeno watched with a frown as he disappeared down the street.

"Mr. Birney, it's Sheriff Cotton Burke," he called out to a seemingly empty office. "I wonder if I might ask you about an article here in your newspaper." Cotton looked around as the door closed behind him and a bell tinkled.

"One moment while I pull off this sheet and re-ink the platen," came a raspy voice from the rear of the room that housed the *Apache Springs Weekly Times*. After a few minutes of clanking and shuffling around, a tall, skinny man, wearing an apron covered with ink and wiping his hands on a filthy rag, stepped out from behind a high-backed table on which were flat boxes filled with tiny, lead letters.

"Afternoon, Mr. Birney. I was wondering what you could tell me about this little article that appeared a few weeks back. I found it buried in a stack of papers on my desk and hadn't gotten around to reading it until today."

Birney, the editor and publisher of the *Times*, squinted as he scanned what was written. He pulled out a pair of spectacles from his vest pocket and smiled, obviously recognizing the article.

"Ahh, yes. This was sent in by a reporter over in Tucson. I remember because it came in response to my inquiry about a rumor concerning a large shipment of gold that might be coming through soon from the San Francisco mint, bound for Texas. This reporter confirmed that, sure enough, there had been rumors that the mint was sending gold by way of the Southern Pacific to Fort Worth."

"Isn't that kind of information usually kept secret? What makes you think it's true?"

"Well, actually I don't know myself, but I can vouch for the veracity of the man who forwarded the information to me."

"What made you print such a story? Did you not consider it might cause some of the less law-abiding citizens to consider something dishonest, like a robbery?"

Birney wrinkled his nose as if something offensively odiferous had just been plopped in front of him.

"As a responsible journalist I cannot imagine who in this town would even consider such an outlandish act. Certainly not I, nor the banker, nor, nor . . . ," he sputtered. "I'm shocked you have such little regard for our honest citizenry."

"Uh-huh. Also, I noticed you included the date: the sixteenth of this month. Isn't it unusual to include such facts when divulging information that some might figure shouldn't be exposed to the public anyway? Would you run a story about the date and time of money coming into the bank?"

"Are you questioning my perspicacity or my motives, Sheriff? I assure you, I am not a gadfly, nor would I disseminate information that I felt inappropriate for public consumption. Besides, the public has a right to know these things. Now, if you'll pardon me, I am a very busy man. I must get back to this week's edition, so I will bid you a good day, sir." In a huff, Birney disappeared behind his California job cases.

Cotton stormed out of the newspaper office. His confrontation with the editor had given him a pretty good idea of Cruz's potential robbery target and the source he may have relied upon for his information. If he was right, it was an ingenious way to get word to the outlaws without arousing suspicion. Cotton's suspicions coupled with Birney's pompous attitude served only to further lessen what little faith the sheriff had in the Fourth Estate.

Cotton decided to send a telegram to an old friend in

Tucson, the editor of the daily newspaper there. His question was simple: Would you ever print a story about a big gold shipment prior to its safe arrival at its destination? He had a reply in less than an hour. It read: "Not unless I wanted to attract half the gangs in the territory to some easy pickings."

Cotton now wondered if Birney's story hadn't been printed for that very reason. Could this editor be in cahoots with Cruz? And how could he ever prove it?

Chapter 39

———◆———

Jack was nervous about Cappy accidently running into one of Cruz's men in town. Since Ben Patch hadn't been heard from for several hours, Jack figured he might have doubled back and gone to the saloon. He sat on a bench out front of the bunkhouse watching the activities at the corral, where Virgil seemed busy with several ranch hands, giving them orders and yelling at them when they moved too slowly. Just then, Cruz came storming out of the corral and toward Jack with fire in his eyes.

"I can't trust any of those fools to follow my instructions. I'd shoot them if I didn't need them for a little something that's coming up. I may have to trust you, Stump."

"That's what I'm here for, Mr. Cruz."

"Uh-huh, I wonder. Blade should be back here with Ben soon. If he ain't, I'm goin' to be a couple of men short because of premature death by bullet. You stay close by. Don't go wanderin' off. I may need you soon." Cruz raised dust with every step as he headed off toward Wu Chang's kitchen, cursing and grumbling.

I'm beginning to think this man isn't smart enough to run a Chinese laundry, Jack thought with a scowl. *How the hell is he going to pull off some big job, whatever it is?*

Cappy stood eyeing every person he saw after he'd loaded the wagon with the things Wu Chang had sent him for. Perspiration poured down his forehead, and he swallowed hard trying to work up his nerve to go into the sheriff's office and spill everything Jack had told him to pass on. Just then, the sheriff came out of his office and headed for the saloon. Cappy followed after him, hoping to catch him alone where they could talk quietly. As Cappy entered the saloon, he saw Cotton at the far end of the bar chatting with One-Eyed Billy. Cappy looked around nervously to see if anyone from the ranch was inside. He saw no one, and, encouraged, he stepped toward the sheriff.

"Uh, Sheriff. I'm Cappy Brennan, maybe you know my father, Hank," he said barely above a whisper. "Could we go to a table and palaver a spell?"

"Sure, I know Hank. How is he?" The two sauntered over to a table in the corner where no one could overhear what was being said.

"He ain't doin' so well, I'm afraid. Virgil Cruz pushed him over a cliff. Tried to kill him. With the help of a fella who happened along, we was able to get him back to the ranch. Doc Winters come out and patched him up good as he could. Dad's goin' to live, but it'll take a while to heal up them broken bones. This fella, Memphis Jack Stump, said to come in and tell you some things he's learned."

"That's good news, Cappy. Go on."

Cotton brightened at the news that Jack had gotten into the Brennans' confidence so quickly. He bent forward, eager to hear what Cappy had to say.

Ben Patch and Blade Coffman rode hard through the gate at the Double-B. They came to a dusty halt in front of the corral, both dismounting quickly. Blade took the reins of both horses and led them into the corral to unsaddle later. Ben headed for the bunkhouse, where he was met by a furious Virgil Cruz.

"Where the hell you been, Ben? I told you to keep an eye out for anything suspicious that might be goin' around. I didn't tell you to plan on havin' a vacation at the saloon. What happened? Where were you when Blade came looking for you?"

Ben held up his hand. "Hold on, Virgil, I gotta good reason for not bein' there when he come a-lookin' for me. I met up with a problem."

"What kinda problem?"

"I ran across Red Carter. He started jawin' on me about the train and all, and sayin' he knew what we was up to. He said *he* was goin' to put together some men and take a shot at that train comin' through on the sixteenth himself. He was getting too loud. I figured if we was overheard, someone might go to the sheriff. I had to handle the situation the best way I knew how."

"Did you kill him?"

"Had to. Cut him up real good. He won't do no more figurin' on cuttin' in on our job."

"Do you think he talked to anyone else in town before you got to him?"

"I don't know. I reckon not, because he kept sayin' he was gonna send off a telegram to some owlhoots he knowed back in Santa Fe. After I done it, I hightailed it out of town."

"Anyone see you take him down?"

"Naww. I was real careful. Carved him up out behind the livery. I took the long way just in case someone saw me and put the sheriff on my tail. I waited in ambush for him outside town for a spell. He never came. I musta been outta sight when Blade come for me the first time. I was on my way back to the ranch when he come a-yellin' you wanted to see me in a hurry."

"He was right. And about what you had to do, it was for

the best and good riddance. I never liked the man, anyhow. C'mon, we got to round up the rest of the boys and have our little meeting." Virgil motioned for Blade to gather the others at the bunkhouse.

"How about that Stump fella?" said Blade.

"Yep, him, too."

"How do you know you can trust him?"

"Don't make no difference. After the job is over, you're gonna shoot him. That way, neither one of us has anything to worry about ever again." Virgil laughed hard at the thought as he led the way to the bunkhouse. Jack was already there, waiting out front. He stood up as the others arrived, and Blade grabbed his arm and shoved him inside. The other hands who'd been gathered for the meeting began to settle around the room, some at the table, others on bunks, a couple leaned against the wall.

"Well, boys, the time has come for me to tell you what my plans are for the sixteenth. I been puttin' off layin' out the whole thing 'cause I needed to ponder all the unpredictables. So here it is. We're gonna rob a train. It'll be the biggest haul in the history of the railroad, and we'll all ride away rich men. There's talk of near to a million dollars in gold and greenbacks on the Southern Pacific coming from San Francisco. It'll pass by ten miles north of Apache Springs. It's headed for Texas and the cattle markets in Fort Worth. But that ol' wood burner is goin' to take a little detour," Virgil again laughed at the thought of such a conquest.

"How'd you find out about such a shipment, Virgil?" asked Ben.

"Never you mind, Ben. I know things that you ain't privy to, that's all, mostly 'cause I can read. And you can take stock in it when I say it."

Chapter 40

———➤◆➤———

Jack sat in silence as Virgil outlined his plan to rob the Southern Pacific of a million dollars. Darkness had set in, and the only light in the bunkhouse came from three kerosene lanterns hanging from pegs in the walls. The shadows cast by the lanterns revealed the faces of hard men, men to whom life had dealt a cruel blow, men for whom the future held little or nothing. Only three of these men had any experience in what they were about to ride into. Most had never held up a store, or a bank, or a stagecoach, or even a single rider on horseback. And now they were being asked to risk their lives for the promise of great wealth and a future filled with ease. Of those in the room, only Virgil, Ben, and Blade were real criminals, and Jack sensed that the others had been included to convince the railroad of the gang's resolve to actually go through with something as daring as holding up a train. A couple of the younger ones were looking about with eager anticipation of what would come their way with very little effort. That was Virgil's promise. The way Virgil had put forth his strategy, any man could easily be brought under his spell, his guarantee of easy pickings.

Cruz's intent to rob the Southern Pacific was a carelessly constructed, poorly thought out jumble of "ifs" and "maybes." Virgil's information about the gold shipment came from the newspaper. His source was the editor of the newspaper, a man he'd beaten often at poker. He had promised to forgive the man's markers if he'd print whatever he came across concerning potential targets for his gang. Birney had been an easy and gullible foil for Virgil's evil intentions. Virgil had even promised him a small share in the loot for his contribution. Birney had jumped at the opportunity because he saw no way anyone would be able to prove complicity on his part.

Even if the robbery does come off, that fool Birney will come up empty-handed, thought Jack. *And these other rannies, if they live through it all, they'll likely be shot afterwards for their trouble.* Virgil had given no guarantee of sharing the loot. Jack wasn't sure that Ben and Blade would get away with anything but a bullet, either. Virgil Cruz didn't seem the kind to take great stock in friendship or sharing. His recent animosity toward Blade made that theory even more tenable in Jack's mind.

"Now, look at this piece of paper, boys. This here's the route we're gonna take to where we make the strike. I got special instructions for each one of you. Memorize them and you'll know what's expected of you. Any questions?" said Virgil.

One cowboy held up his hand nervously. "Mr. Cruz, I cain't read. Would it be okay if Billy read it to me?"

Virgil hung his head in despair as he grumbled, "I don't give a damn who reads it to you, you idiot, just know it by heart. Do you all understand me?"

Red-faced and ashamed, the cowboy nodded.

As Ben handed out the assignments to each man, Jack watched, uncertain as to whether Virgil was planning to include him and equally uncertain how much longer Cotton expected him to go along with these outlaws, putting his neck on the line. He now had enough information about the robbery itself, but getting the specifics into Cotton's hands was going to be difficult. Virgil seemed to be watching him like a hawk. Also, if Jack did manage to leave the Double-B ranch, how certain could he be that Virgil wouldn't find out about Hank's still being alive and living not more than a hundred feet away? Jack was sure Hank wouldn't last ten minutes if Virgil found him alive.

Things were becoming increasingly complex, and Jack hadn't gotten any closer to finding where Emily was being held. Cotton had made it clear that Emily's freedom was a priority, and Jack understood the deep feelings that went into such a decision. As he sat pondering Virgil's ill-defined venture, the crafty foreman pulled a surprise on all of them.

"Now, listen up, gents, because this is where it gets serious. This here is how we get that lumbering monster to come to a screeching halt, which will make our grabbing the loot as easy as milking a cow," said Cruz. "Blade, go outside and fetch in the crate by the door."

"How come I gotta do all the fetchin'?"

"'Cause I said so, that's why. Now, git to it."

Jack could sense that Virgil's hammering away at Blade was taking an ever increasing toll on a man already stretched too thin. When Blade returned a minute later with a medium-size crate cradled in his arms, things went from bad to worse. Blade dropped the crate at Virgil's feet.

"You clumsy idiot. You coulda killed us all. Now, go sit down over there with the others. Now!" screamed Virgil. Blade had reached his limit. His hand went to his gun. He started to draw it, but before he could clear leather, Virgil had grabbed his own six-shooter and, in one smooth motion, cocked it and stuck it no more than an inch from Blade's nose.

"Either do what I said or finish your draw. I've had all of your dumb decisions I can take. Make your move." Virgil was cool and deadly. Only a fool would not take him seriously. Blade backed off and slumped onto a bunk across the room, his gun still firmly in its holster.

Jack swallowed hard. Virgil was proving to be a more able adversary than he had first thought. He'd have to make sure that if the time came to go up against him, he'd make no mistakes and take no chances.

"All right, now, listen up, gents. This is what's goin' to make this little job a cinch." With those words, he pried open the top of the crate with his knife, reached in, and brought out several sticks of dynamite, fuses, and primers. He held them up for all to see. A collective gasp rose from the hands as they realized just how close they had all come to being blown to smithereens by Blade's oafish mistake.

"Son of a bitch. Do you know how close you came to sendin' us all to our maker, Blade?" said Ben, red-faced and also clearly fed up with Blade's tantrums.

Blade's eyes were wide open as his face turned white from fear, then pink from embarrassment. He hung his head as every eye in the room glared at him. Finally, he shot up from his bunk and stormed out of the bunkhouse. Jack considered following him. This would be a perfect time to turn Blade into giving up information about Emily. But he knew Virgil was too smart to allow his departure. So instead he decided this was as good a time as any to find out what his role in the robbery would be.

"Excuse me, Mr. Cruz, but I didn't get one of them pieces of paper. I'm wonderin' what you want me to do," said Jack.

"Why that's easy, Mr. Stump, you're goin' to kill someone for me."

Chapter 41

———➤◆◄———

Henry Coyote had obeyed Sheriff Burke's admonition to remain at the Wagner ranch and not leave in search of Emily Wagner. For six days now he'd done what he'd been asked to do: nothing. Cotton had insisted it was all in the name of assuring Emily's safety. Her well-being and ultimate release from the clutches of kidnappers was predicated on no one nosing around trying to find her. "She's gonna be safe and sound as long as . . . you stay away from the Brennan place until after the 16th," said the note tacked to the sheriff's door. It was the sheriff's reliance on the word of a kidnapper that worried the former Apache scout the most. Both Henry and the sheriff figured Virgil Cruz and his cutthroats were the ones behind this despicable act. It was as Henry sat pondering the situation that his patience finally stretched to the breaking point.

It is time to go, Henry thought as he rolled up a blanket, packed a leather satchel with a few provisions, picked up his rifle, and set out on his quest.

He left the Wagner ranch in the middle of the night. It

had gnawed away at him that no one had been around when the Cruz gang rode in and grabbed Emily. He felt personally responsible because he had insisted on checking some fence in the farthest corner of the property, so far away that he couldn't have even heard gunfire. Why weren't any of the other hands there when it happened? If there was a traitor among the hands, someone who sold out by getting all the cowboys away from the ranch so the kidnappers could ride in with no attempt to stop them, he wanted to know who it was. Whoever was involved in the kidnapping scheme, he knew he'd have to watch his back trail carefully.

Henry's keen understanding of tracking told him to stay off all known trails. Besides, he knew Cruz would be too smart to hide his prisoner where a posse might be expected to look. Posses tended to take the easiest paths when chasing outlaws. Virgil Cruz was far too clever to make it easy to find Emily. And hadn't he warned against any attempt to free her before the sixteenth? Cruz would have hidden her away where his men could keep a sharp lookout for anyone riding in to free her. That meant a hideout that was reasonably inaccessible, easy to defend, and almost impossible to approach without being seen. But Cruz wasn't counting on an Indian to attempt a rescue. That would play in Henry's favor, and he fully intended to use all his native skills to achieve just that.

If Cruz was keeping Emily anywhere within the Double-B ranch boundaries, he would have chosen the area north of Saucer Valley, an almost inaccessible place, unusable for any of the activities normally associated with ranching. Craggy mountains, narrow passes, and sheer cliffs made it no place for cattle or horses. In fact, Henry saw no reason for any man to seek out its dark, foreboding dangers, unless, of course, he had ill intentions, such as holding a defenseless woman captive.

When Henry reached the Wagner ranch boundary, he slung his bedroll over his shoulder and set off for the mountains far to the west. Those mountains, now shrouded in darkness, formed the northern border of the Double-B and were the best place to begin his quest. A full moon was his only companion. He smiled as he started off on what he considered the most important thing he'd ever undertaken in his life: saving a kind and generous woman from the evil that had stolen her freedom, an evil that clung to Virgil Cruz like smoke from a campfire. As the eastern sky began to lighten before dawn, Henry broke into a trot, his spirits rising in anticipation of a successful venture.

The stagecoach pulled into Apache Springs, leaving a dusty trail behind. As the coach came to a halt, the driver jumped down and opened the door.

"Watch your step, ma'am. It'd be mighty easy to turn that pretty ankle," he said with a leer.

Melody ignored the driver's obvious attempt to ingratiate himself as she stuck her head out. She had been the only passenger, and she was tired, dusty, and bored from having no one with whom to share even a convivial conversation. She was in no mood to be seduced by the disingenuous advances of a stagecoach driver. She was also angry from having to make the trip in the first place. Cotton Burke had no right to take her lover from her, and she was damned well going to let the world know what a snake the Apache Springs sheriff was. As she glanced around at the wooden and adobe buildings that constituted the center of town, she spied a hotel that appeared to be a likely place to put her things, get a bath, and eat before setting out on her mission to make Sheriff Cotton Burke's life a living hell. Ignoring the offer of help from the driver, she marched off like a soldier with a bag under each arm, straight for the Garfield Hotel and its peeling green paint.

"I'd like a room, please," she said to the balding man at the counter. The slight smile on his face was one she'd seen a thousand times, always from a man who expected favors for any kindness.

"Why, yes, ma'am. Happy to oblige. Will you be staying long, I hope?"

She sighed and signed the register. "Only long enough to corral a snake."

"Oh? And to whom might you be referring? Anyone I might know?"

"Never mind. I'll be cutting off his rattle soon enough. Then you'll know." With that, she hoisted up her two bags and began climbing the stairs to her room. At the landing, she turned and asked, "Where can I get some hot water for a bath?"

"Oh, why I'll just fetch you some and bring it up to the last room on your left. There's one of them big copper tubs sent all the way from St. Louis last spring. It'll take about a half hour. I'll knock on your door on my way up with the water. Will you be needin' soap, too?"

Melody couldn't believe that anyone would desire a bath without soap, but since that seemed a possibility in this godforsaken town, she nodded, "Yes. Thank you."

Two hours later, clean and dressed in a blue silk dress with puffy sleeves, lots of lace around the low-cut neck and three petticoats, Melody set out across the street to confront Cotton Burke. She stormed into the jail with her derringer tucked nicely into the pocket of her dress. When she pushed open the door, she came face-to-face with Deputy Keeno Belcher. Keeno was pleasantly surprised at having the usually drab sheriff's office suddenly brightened by a beautiful woman. He grabbed his rumpled hat from his head and tried to smile.

"Uh, howdy, ma'am. Can I be of service? I'm Deputy Belcher."

"Why, you surely can, Deputy," she said, dripping with sweetness. "I'm looking for my fiancé, a man named Memphis Jack Stump. I believe he's here."

Keeno scratched his head, then mumbled, "I-I'm right sorry, ma'am, but I ain't never heard of no Memphis Jack Stump. That's a name I'd surely remember. Nope, not in Apache Springs. I could ask around for you, if you'd like."

"I know your sheriff rode this way several days ago. They rode together." Her tone was losing its syrupiness.

"Cotton rode in about three days ago all right, but he come alone. I seen him with my own eyes."

"Damn! Well just where *is* your sheriff?"

"I 'spect I could round him up. How about you sit for a spell, and I'll go fetch him. If that's all right with you." Keeno had replaced his hat and was starting out the door when he stopped and scratched his chin. "Anything I should tell the sheriff when I find him?"

"Tell that miserable coyote I aim to shoot his pecker off if he don't come right away. I'm in no mood to cool my heels for a no-good scoundrel like Cotton Burke. Tell him if he don't come, he'll find me down at the nearest saloon just singin' my sad tale like a wounded canary." The syrup had been completely replaced with vinegar.

"Sad tale?"

"Yes. About how that miserable coyote yanked Memphis Jack right outta my bedroom and outta my life. And I aim to get him back. I'll tell the world if I have to."

Chapter 42

Cotton was tossing down the last drops of a shot of whis-key when Keeno burst through the saloon doors. The deputy looked like he had a wildcat on his tail and couldn't shake him. He rushed up, sputtering.

"Sheriff, there's a gal over to the jailhouse and she's lookin' for you. She's a real looker, I'll tell you, and she ain't the least bit happy. Say's she's lookin' for some feller named Memphis Jack Stump. Said you come and took him from her bedroom. I told her it didn't sound right to me, but she insisted it was true. Said you two had been friends at one time."

Cotton's eyes grew wide at the prospect of Melody be-ing in town and in a position to blow Jack's undercover assignment all to hell.

"Don't ever mention that name again," Cotton said, shushing the mouthy deputy. "Now, turn right around and walk back to the jail with me, and not another word of this to anyone. Understand?" Keeno nodded and fell in behind the sheriff.

"Uh-huh. Yessir. My mouth is shut tight." He followed Cotton out of the saloon.

Back in a dark corner of the room, a man had been sitting with a half-empty glass in front of him. When he'd overheard the name "Stump," he'd strained to pick up more of the conversation while gulping down the last of his drink. He now walked over to the door to watch as the sheriff and his deputy disappeared into the jail office. Blade Coffman's eyes narrowed at the prospect that he'd overheard information that Virgil would certainly want to know. It appeared that Memphis Jack and the sheriff knew each other. That could explain why Jack showed up at the Brennans' place when he did. Blade mulled over whether to tell Virgil about what he'd seen in order to get back into his good graces, or sit back and wait, see what developed. He was still stinging from Virgil's rebuke and his condemnation over the dropped box of dynamite. And at the moment, at least, he wasn't all that certain he cared whether or not Virgil got warned that he might have a spy on the payroll. While Blade considered his options, he called for another whiskey.

When Cotton pushed open the door to his office, a violent, angry woman abruptly set upon him. Melody spewed venom like a cornered rattler, her eyes ablaze. She stormed up to him and began pounding on his chest.

"What in the hell have you done with Jack, you bastard? Tell me, or I'll blow a hole in that hard head of yours!"

Cotton grabbed her by the wrists and sat her down on a straight-backed, wooden chair. Hard. There was fire in *his* eyes, too. Her showing up in Apache Springs couldn't have come at a worse time.

"Sit there and shut up, Melody. If you screw things up, I'll lock you away for interfering with the law. I could get you sent to prison for what you've already done. Now, what the hell are you doing here?"

"I told you. I came to get Jack back. You stole him, and I

aim to take him home with me. If I don't see that he's fit as a fiddle in the next few minutes, every decent, law-abiding citizen in this mud-hole will know of your treachery, 'cause I'll holler it at the top of my lungs."

"You'll do nothing of the sort, you loudmouthed bitch. I'll not have you interfering with things. Now, you can get right back on that stage, or you can spend the night in jail. It's up to you. What'll it be?"

"You don't have the balls to stick a lady in your filthy jail."

"You, a *lady*? Ha! I'll do it all right, if that's your decision. And let it be known right now, I certainly ain't never considered you a lady. I hope you got nothin' against rats, though. I hear they like to gnaw on silk." Cotton looked over at Keeno, who appeared surprised at hearing about rats in the jail.

Melody sat stunned at what he'd called her. After all, the two of them *had* been lovers at one time, although it seemed like a hundred years ago. She couldn't believe he'd forgotten that. How could he call her a bitch? Her knuckles were white from clenching her fists tightly in her lap. Her face was flushed with the anger boiling up inside her. Cotton knew her well enough to see she was about to explode.

"Melody, you've put me in a dangerous position, which I'm willing to forget if you get right back on that stagecoach and hightail it out of here. And no talking to anyone. Not one word. Otherwise, I have no choice but to lock you up until this is all over."

"Until what is over? I need an explanation before agreeing to anything from you. I also need a drink." Melody said.

"I can't explain it right now. But your big mouth could get Jack killed if the wrong person overheard you. You go ahead and call my bluff if you've a mind, but—"

"Pardon me for buttin' in, ma'am, but I know he don't bluff. And that's a fact." Keeno grinned from ear to ear, obviously proud of himself for putting in a good word for the sheriff.

Melody stared Cotton straight in the eye. Her whole body shook with hatred for him at that moment.

"You wouldn't dare put me in one of those filthy jail cells, Cotton. Not after what we've been through together."

"What's your decision goin' to be? I need an answer right now before the stage pulls out for Gonzales."

Cotton looked out the grimy, dust-covered window. He squinted as he watched the stage driver put the last of the luggage on the boot and tie it down. "They're about to leave. I need an answer, Melody."

Suddenly she stood up defiantly. She clutched her handbag tightly and pursed her lips. She glared at Cotton as she spit out her next words. "You do whatever you must, but I'm not leaving here without Jack. And that's final." She stomped her foot for added emphasis. She had thrown the challenge back in the sheriff's face. It was now up to him as to whether he had the guts to put a woman behind bars for chasing after her missing lover and speaking her mind.

She remained glued to her spot as Cotton mulled over the position she had put him in. Her arms were crossed defiantly. Considering her well-known unpredictable and stubborn nature, he could see her doing just what she'd threatened to do: blabbing to everyone within earshot that Memphis Jack Stump, an old friend, was being held against his will somewhere in this town. She'd tell anyone who would listen that she would swear to what she claimed.

Cotton took one quick step toward her, snatched her handbag from her hand, tossed it on the desk with a thud, then removed the jail keys from the desk drawer.

"Put her in the first cell, Keeno. She ain't leavin' until I say so." He turned and stepped outside, closing the door behind him, as he watched the stagecoach make its way down the rutted street and out of town.

The sudden panic on Melody's face said she'd met her match, and her expression said she didn't like it one damned bit.

Chapter 43

—————◆◆◆—————

Virgil was in a foul mood. He had no idea where Blade had made off to, and he didn't like it when his men left the ranch without his knowledge. Blade had been with him for some time, but lately Virgil had gotten a sense that the man was capable of stupidity beyond that which he'd ever known. A scheme as big as a train robbery required careful planning and a crew that followed orders without question. Blade seemed to have been questioning Virgil's every move from the start. Maybe it was time to get rid of him and not take a chance on his blundering during the robbery. Too much was at stake. That's when Virgil decided it was time to put Jack's skills to the test, in the one way that could assure the loyalty of all the others, while at the same time getting rid of a thorn in his side.

Virgil went to the bunkhouse to look for Jack. When he got there, one of the hands said Jack had gone to the cook shack for some coffee because someone had stomped the living daylights out of the coffeepot they had.

"Now, who'd go and do a fool thing like that?"

"I, uh, believe it was Blade, Mr. Cruz," said the hand.

"That figures." Cruz stormed out to find Jack in conversation with Wu Chang outside the cook shack.

Wu Chang saw him coming and whispered a warning to Jack just as Virgil came up to them.

"Get back inside and start rustlin' up some grub, Chinaman. I got hungry men out there." Virgil made a shooing motion with his hand to dismiss the cook. Wu Chang grumbled something in Mandarin but went inside as instructed.

"Now, Memphis Jack, or whatever the hell they call you, I'm ready for you to do that little piece of work I mentioned. The time has come for you to prove your worth."

"I'm ready, Mr. Cruz. What is it you want me to do?"

"Go into town and find Blade."

"All right. Do you want him back here?"

"Hell no. I want the buzzard shot. Can you handle that? He's fast."

Jack stood frozen at the prospect of having to kill a man just because Virgil Cruz said so. But did he dare question a madman like Cruz? Jack was no murderer, but it appeared he'd just been handed an opportunity to go to Apache Springs, look up Cotton, and tell him what he'd learned. It was the first time since arriving at the Brennan ranch that Cruz seemed willing to let him out of his sight. Jack just shrugged.

"I think I can take him, Mr. Cruz. Anything else?"

"Yeah. Go to the newspaper office and tell that editor, Birney, that it's time to get out of town. He'll know what you mean." Virgil grinned his gold-toothed grin and sauntered off as if he'd simply stopped to ask for a light. "Oh, and don't forget to hightail it back here as soon as you get the job done. I'll need every gun I can get. Tomorrow is the sixteenth," he called back over his shoulder.

Jack didn't like the prospect of leaving the ranch without warning Hank that he needed to be on the lookout for Cruz coming into the main house unexpectedly. But Cappy wasn't around and Wu Chang was inside preparing a meal for the hands. Time was short and he knew he had to do something quickly. He had gone to the corral to saddle his horse when he saw Cappy riding in. Jack stalled around as much as he could while Cappy got close enough to get word to him of Jack's leaving for a while. Cappy reined in beside Jack's horse and dismounted.

"That rattler Cruz sent me out to check some fence. Hell, there wasn't a thing wrong with it. He just wanted me out from underfoot so he could talk freely about whatever it is he's got planned. If I ever get the chance, I'm gonna blow that skunk to kingdom—"

"Forget that right now," Jack whispered. "I have to go into town. Cruz's crazy, and I wouldn't bet on his stayin' out in the bunkhouse. He's been actin' like he already owns this spread."

"How long you gonna be gone? I couldn't take him alone. He's too fast, and besides, I ain't real good with a gun," said Cappy.

"I'll be back as soon as possible. Load up that shotgun I saw next to the fireplace. That'll even the odds a bit. Don't be afraid to use it, either, if it comes to that. Give Hank a Colt, too. He's got one good hand, and I'll bet he's eager to get even with Virgil." Jack wanted to get mounted up and ride off before Virgil saw him talking to Cappy.

But Virgil had seen them together, and as Jack rode off, he stopped Cappy.

"What was you two jawin' about?"

"Wh-why, he asked me how long a ride it is to town, since he ain't never been there before. That's all," said Cappy. His nervousness gave away that he was lying. Cruz just grunted as the boy hurried off in the direction of the house.

Virgil rubbed his chin as he pondered what to do with Cappy now that Hank was dead. Should he stick around after the robbery and make the Double-B his? He could shoot the kid and no one would be the wiser for a long time. He'd sell off all the livestock, and after he rid himself of those that might bear witness against him at some time in the future, he could sit up there in that big house and live the life of a rich man. Sounded good to him right at that moment. In fact, why wait until after the robbery? Why not shoot the kid right now and be done with it?

Virgil drew his six-shooter, half-cocked it, and rolled the cylinder through. Fully loaded. He'd about made up his mind to go to the big house and make himself at home when Blade came riding through the gate hell-bent for leather. He'd taken the shortcut from town.

"Virgil! Hold up. I got somethin' you're gonna want to hear." Blade's frothy horse came to a dusty stop as he yanked back on the reins. He dismounted like he'd been shot from the saddle.

"What the hell's got you actin' like your ass is on fire?"

"Where's Jack Stump?"

"Why, I, er, sent him to town to, uh, look you up. Why? Didn't you pass him on the way in?"

"Naww. I took the back trail anyway. And he ain't who you think he is, neither. He and that sheriff are tighter than wet leather in the sun."

Virgil's face turned red. He spit on the ground. He'd been made a fool of and that didn't set well. Not well at all. "Ride up to the line shack and bring back Scat. Then, the two of you ride into town and gun down Mr. Stump. Maybe you'll get to him before he can let on to the sheriff what he knows."

"Who'll watch over the woman?"

"Leave Dogman there. He ain't all that good with a six-shooter, anyway. Liable to shoot himself in the foot. Just you get to doin' what I said. And do it now!"

Chapter 44

———✦———

Henry Coyote had been scouring the streambed that led up into the steep crags of Blue Mountain. He'd seen some fresh tracks of a horse that appeared to have been paralleling the creek bed within the past couple days. Those tracks matched the ones he'd seen at the ranch house. The tracks split off and headed into a narrow canyon. The way was confining, in places barely wide enough for one mounted horseman to squeeze between the jagged boulders. If he were seen, he would have little chance to escape. Rather than follow the tracks, he decided to embark on a treacherous climb to the rim.

The steep walls made the going difficult even for an Indian. It was said an Apache could climb a sheer wall of granite and not be out of breath at the top. The thought of the many myths surrounding his ancestors brought a brief smile to Henry's lips, just before he lost his grip and nearly tumbled into a crevice that could have killed him. But he grabbed onto a jutting slice of sandstone, worn smooth by the rains and blowing winds, and by spreading his power-

ful legs to either side of the split, he stopped his descent.
His elbow had slammed into the stone and the pain of it
shot up his arm. He ceased his climb long enough to catch
his breath and to rub his bruised elbow.

As he gripped the rock with one hand, glancing about
for possible handholds farther up, he spotted a shadowy
split in the rocks above him that he hoped would be a cave.
He headed for that darkened hole.

With a bandolier of .50-caliber cartridges carried across
his chest, and his Spencer rifle with a handmade strap over
his shoulder, Henry began the arduous task, climbing the
tricky face of rock that would lead him to the top of the
plateau. If the dark impression turned out to be a cave, he
would rest in its cover while still remaining out of sight,
watching for any riders to come through the gorge. When
his hands finally got sufficient grip to give him leverage to
pull himself onto the ledge, he hoisted his weary body up.
He could just make out what he hoped would be a cave of
sufficient size for him to rest and watch from. His hope was
fulfilled as he glanced over the ledge into a large depres-
sion that likely had been, at one time, a hideout for others with the same desire as he: a safe lookout for any who
would try traversing the gorge below.

As he climbed inside and eased his burden by removing
his rifle and the cartridge belt, he set about checking the
cave for any signs of recent activity. He had no illusions
that Cruz and his bunch might have used this place to hide
Emily, as access would have been too difficult. But if it was
still in use by others, for whatever reason, he didn't want
to wake up looking down the barrel of a rifle or, worse, not
wake up at all.

Near the rear wall he found evidence of a fire, one that
had warmed the occupants of this cave many years in the
past. And they had certainly been Indians, most likely
Mescalero Apaches, like himself, or possibly Chiracahua.
Markings and designs indicated an attempt to relay a message to whoever might use the cave after them. Unfortunately, Henry Coyote had been associated for too much of

his life with the white man's world to have knowledge of the ancient signs. To him, the symbols were no more than decorations, meaningless to furthering his quest to save a woman's life. He lay back on the soft, sandy floor to rest. Anyone coming through the gorge would be traversing nearly solid stone, stone that would echo each step of a shod horse. He could hear and react in time. Sleep would not interfere with his vigil.

But sleep would not come easily. He felt a pang of guilt for not telling Sheriff Burke that he intended to leave the ranch and look for his mistress. Cotton Burke had told him the consequences of any rash action, that, if discovered, it could result in harm to Emily Wagner, something neither of them dared chance. But he couldn't wait around doing nothing. A woman's life was in danger, and he owed it to her to make every attempt to save her, no matter what the cost. It never occurred to him that he might be putting his own life in jeopardy in the process. But that really didn't matter. In Henry's mind, he already owed Emily his life, so it would be a fair exchange. In deference to the sheriff's request, he vowed to be particularly careful as he searched for wherever the Cruz gang had her stowed.

He drifted off into a light sleep but awakened often to noises that seemed foreign. They always turned out to be merely the wind, which, as it whipped around the rock face and across the cave entrance, created a forlorn moaning. He'd been out all night and half the next day, and as the afternoon sun was creating deepening shadows across the canyon face, another sound reached his ears. Neither wind nor wild animal nor the flapping of birds' wings could simulate this sound. It was the sound he had waited for: the unmistakable clacking of a shod horse echoing off the walls. He crawled to the ledge and peered over to see a lone man making his way up the canyon. He had seen this man before. He was one of Cruz's men. The mean one—Blade Coffman.

Henry watched for several minutes as Blade disappeared on the winding trail. *There can only be one reason that man is going up into that canyon*, Henry thought. *He's going to where Emily is being held.* The smart thing to do would be to wait until he came back. That would give a good idea how far away their hiding place was. He had waited and watched for nearly a half hour when he heard the same distinctive hoofbeats coming back down through the narrows. Only this time, Blade wasn't alone. A rough-looking man with a sallow face, whom Henry had never seen before, followed closely behind Coffman. As they passed, Henry began to make a plan for the best way down to the canyon floor. Looking over the ledge, he saw that it would be even more treacherous descending than it had been making his way up. Then a thought struck him. If his ancestors had used this cave on a regular basis, there had to be another way out, something less adventuresome than a tricky descent down the face of the canyon walls. He went deeper into the cave, feeling his way along the smooth, cool cave surfaces until he found what he'd hoped would be there. Just ahead, a shaft of light indicated a small open-ing leading to the top of the plateau. Small, yes, but large enough for a man of his slight stature. Up he went into the afternoon light.

Chapter 45

When Jack got to town, he headed straight for the saloon and the only man he thought might be able to get a message to Cotton: One-Eyed Billy Black. He draped his heaving gelding's reins over the rail and went inside, looking around briefly to see if he could spot Blade. He wasn't there. He hadn't seen Blade's horse outside, either. He knew Blade enough to know he'd come straight into town, most likely to drink off the guilt of being a clumsy fool with a box of dynamite. Blade had had no inkling of the box's contents, so he couldn't really be blamed for dropping it. But in Virgil's eyes, a blunder was a blunder. And Virgil's idea of making people pay for blunders was usually a bullet for the guilty party.

Jack ordered a beer and asked if Billy had seen Blade Coffman.

"Yeah. He was in here earlier, but he left in a hurry right after Keeno came rushing in and told Cotton about some screechy woman I saw get off the stage."

"What! What did she look like?" Jack started sweating

bullets at the possibility that Melody had followed him to Apache Springs.

"She was a looker, a little whorish, though. She had long blond hair. Had on a blue dress that was right pretty. It showed her bosom off nicely. Oh, and she carried one of them frilly parasols. Cotton came back later and said he'd had a run-in with her."

Jack knew instantly that his worst fears had come true. Melody was in town and had probably already screwed everything up so bad he'd be lucky to get out with his life.

"Billy, could you go to the sheriff's office and ask Cotton to meet me here right now?"

"Sure. If anyone wants a drink, collect for it on the spot. No credit," said Billy, removing his apron. He then handed Jack his damp towel and strolled through the swinging doors like he'd been given a day off. The two men at the one occupied table looked at Jack like they'd like to order another round, but after seeing the look of dismay on his face and the twitchy way he kept stroking his gun butt, they decided to wait for Billy to return.

Ten minutes passed before Cotton burst through the doors to the saloon. He motioned for Jack to join him in the back room. They hastily closed the door behind them. Cotton started to speak but was interrupted by Jack.

"Is Melody here?"

"Yes, I'm afraid so, and she may have blown our plans all to hell with her big mouth."

Jack hung his head. "Son of a bitch. Did Blade overhear anything that could do me in?"

"Maybe. I don't know for sure, but I think it's likely. Your whore started bitching as soon as she stepped foot in this town, loud enough for the whole town to hear."

"Billy said Blade rushed out as soon as you and Keeno left. Where'd you go?"

"To the jail. I ordered her to get back on the stage or I'd stuff her ass in a cell. She refused, so that's where she sits, fuming, mad as a wet cat. And that's where she'll damned well stay until this thing is over. Did you learn anything about Cruz's plans?"

"Plenty. Tomorrow is the sixteenth and they plan to hit the train on the north side of Gambler's Pass, where it starts up the incline into the narrows. He's got himself a box of dynamite, and he aims to use it."

"Damn! You find out anything on where they're holding Emily?"

"No. Not one word was ever said about where she is except I heard the words 'line shack' and an admission that they *had* snatched her."

Cotton began pacing, stroking his chin and muttering. Jack broke the silence with an idea that sounded as feeble as his faith that he could turn Blade from an enemy to a friend.

"Hank Brennan is lying up there in that big ranch house all busted up from Virgil's attempt to kill him. What if you go up there and arrest Virgil? Hank'll back you up in front of a judge. That oughta keep the bastard in jail for a long time, at least. What d'ya say? I'll back your move," said Jack

Cotton shook his head. "I'll let them rob a hundred trains before I'll take a chance on Emily's life."

"Say, it sounds like you're really sweet on that gal. I never knew you to be this serious about some who—"

Cotton grabbed Jack by the collar with his left hand, yanking him forward, while he drew his Colt and jammed it in Jack's belly.

"Don't finish that sentence if you don't want to be stuffin' a cork in your gut to keep your food from spillin' out. Emily is the finest woman I've ever known. And that's all you need to know. Understand?"

Jack quickly held up both hands in surrender. "Whoa, Cotton, I didn't mean nothin' by it. Never met the woman, so how would I know anything about her? I apologize. That good enough?"

Cotton released Jack's shirt and slipped the Colt back into its holster. He just shook his head. "Yeah, apology accepted. I'm sorry I let my concerns for her welfare color my judgment. We gotta stop these bastards and now. Before they can get their filthy hands on anyone else's money or take another life."

"We?"

"Since Melody has busted up our plan, you can't go back to Brennan's place. You'd be so full of lead you'd sink in the bathtub. I'm goin' to deputize you. That way, anything that happens from here on, you'll be covered by the law."

"You figure that'll make a difference to ol' Virgil when he comes gunnin' for me?"

"No, but at least you can shoot first without the court demandin' I plunk you inside those bars alongside Melody."

"I thought you said my lawman days was over. Wasn't that what you said?"

"A man has a right to change his mind. And I'm changin' mine. You're my new deputy, as of now, whether you like it or not. We'll walk over to the jail and fetch you a shiny tin star," said Cotton, eyes narrowed to show he meant business.

"What if I don't want to be your damn deputy?" said Jack.

"Then I'll arrest you for conspiring with known criminals and toss you in the clink. You'd probably be safer there anyway."

Cotton and Jack had no sooner stepped inside the jail than Blade Coffman and Scat Crenshaw rode into town, stopped in front of the saloon, and dismounted. They pulled their guns, rolled the cylinders through to assure six shots apiece, and stomped onto the boardwalk. They looked around before going inside.

"Hey, bartender, you seen Memphis Jack Stump lately?" Blade said.

"Not for a while. But if I do see him, I'll tell him you're lookin' for him," said Billy, as he continued wiping a glass without looking up.

"Think he's lyin'?" asked Scat. The look on Blade's face told him all he needed to know. They both drew their guns just as Keeno came in through the back entrance. The smoky explosions were only a blink apart, sounding like a single cannon blast. With a look of shock, Billy flew backwards into the stack of glasses on the back bar, glasses he'd never again have to polish. His limp body crashed to the floor, blood spreading across the shattered shards beneath him, mixing with spilled, watered-down whiskey. Keeno dropped to the floor in the rear doorway, clutching his chest, his revolver still holstered.

"That oughta bring 'em both to us," said Blade. Scat grinned as he built a smoke. He grabbed a bottle off the bar and headed for a table where he could watch the front doors.

Chapter 46

———◆———

Emily Wagner was seated at the table with Dogman Crenshaw, five cards splayed out in her hand. An hour earlier, his brother, Scat, had ridden out with Blade Coffman. When Dogman had heard Blade's horse approaching, he'd quickly wrapped rope around her hands and feet as if she were still tied up. Scat had stayed outside ever since Dogman had almost had to pull him off Emily. He still had every intention of taking her, even over Virgil's explicit orders not to.

Now that Scat and Blade were gone, Dogman was free to continue his card game with Emily, something he'd been talked into by her gentle, convincing argument that she was no threat to him. Besides, where would she go? She didn't even know where she was being held. Being an eager card-player and armed with the prospect of taking some of her money, Dogman seemed content to shuffle the pasteboards in anticipation of some big pots, which he fully expected to walk away with.

But Emily Wagner was nobody's fool. She didn't care

a whit whether she won or lost, and in fact, she hadn't the slightest notion of paying off if she did lose. Kidnappers should not be rewarded for their treachery. She had feigned an interest in poker simply as a ruse to convince Dogman to untie her, thus affording her a better chance to escape, if such an opportunity presented itself. Her obvious femininity aside, she was no stranger to the grit it took to survive in the harsh New Mexico frontier.

Dogman dealt the first hand. He grinned at the cards with an eagerness that told Emily she was sitting across from an amateur, a man for whom it was clear "poker face" meant nothing. After ten hands, Dogman was astounded at the woman's good fortune. She had displayed no emotion at all, hand after hand, yet managed to win seven of the games. He was in debt to her to the tune of sixteen dollars, and he wasn't happy about it. Emily could see his displeasure mounting. If he was as quixotic as his brother, Dogman might turn from an amiable cowboy to a desperate rattlesnake with the turn of a card. She had to keep him playing but not make it too obvious that she was letting him win more often. Even a gunslinger had pride. She purposely lost the next hand.

"You're a pretty good player, Mr. Crenshaw. But I need to make a trip outside, if you'd be so kind."

"Yeah, sure. I'll have to walk outside with you, though. You wouldn't try to make a run for it, would you, Miss Emily?" Dogman snickered.

"Not while I'm winnin'," she answered.

Henry Coyote made his way along the rim of the cliffs that wound around in a confusing series of switchbacks and dips, large crevices that had to be jumped, and patches of shale broken off in storms or ancient earthquakes. The going was rough, even for an Indian. But he figured that as long as he could keep the trail below in sight, sooner or later he had to come upon the place where the two men he'd seen riding back through the gorge had met. That meeting

place was likely the kidnapper's hiding place. Night would
come in a few hours. He knew he must make better time
or risk missing the place Emily was being held. He pushed
on with the fortitude of a young buck, and although he was
over forty years of age, nothing could turn him back.

When he came to a break in the crags, he looked down
to see a small, crude cabin tucked neatly back in some
pine trees. The trail he'd seen led right to the door. He saw
only one horse in a rough corral of sorts, made mostly of
ocotillo spires wired together. He crept to the edge of the
rim, keeping low so as not to be seen before he could fully
assess the situation and make his plans. If this cabin was
where Emily Wagner was being held, he must make sure
that when he made his move, he didn't miss. He couldn't
allow her to be put in greater danger. He made certain his
Spencer was loaded, then lay still, waiting until someone
came out of the cabin.

After a half hour's wait, the door opened and a man
stepped out, leading Emily. Her hands weren't tied, and
she was free to walk, or run, if need be. Henry was filled
with joy that she appeared to be unharmed. The man carried a sidearm, but it remained holstered. The man's confidence was unmistakable; his prisoner would not dare try
to escape. They walked toward an outhouse ten feet to the
rear of the cabin. When Emily went inside and closed the
door, the man was alone, fiddling with the makings of a
smoke. He made a perfect target. But could Henry hit him
with one shot? He didn't dare chance a miss. A second try
would surely give the man plenty of time to scoot behind
the outhouse and use it for cover. Then Henry couldn't
shoot for fear of hitting Emily. What if she were to come
out just as he fired? She might actually step right into the
path of his bullet. Should he try to get closer? His choices
were limited, and he knew it. He would never get another
chance with the same degree of certainty. The decision
came as the moments ticked away. He wiped perspiration
from his brow, lifted the rifle to his cheek, and braced the
barrel against a rock. He aimed slightly high to allow for a

bullet's tendency to drop at that distance. The man turned toward him casually, as if he had all the time in the world. He showed nothing but confidence that he was alone with his captive. Just then the door began to open and Dogman glanced around. No more time.

The Spencer bucked as Henry squeezed off his shot. Dogman Crenshaw was slammed to the ground, a gaping wound in his forehead. He hadn't let out a sound. The smoke was still drifting from Henry's rifle when he stood and shouted to Emily to stay put; he was on his way down.

The shock of seeing Dogman's head explode right before her eyes overcame Emily's emotions in an instant. She screamed as she dropped to her knees and burst into tears. Her sobs showed just how grateful she was to be free of the animals that had been holding her captive for what seemed an eternity. The nightmare was over. She was free from the humiliation of being under the power of degenerates, men without conscience or principles. Men for whom self-gratification was paramount.

Free!

Chapter 47

———————◆————————

"Okay if I go back and see Melody? I should let her know I'm alive," said Jack, as he polished the badge Cotton had handed him. He pinned it on his shirt with a wry smile.

"I s'pose. But you can damn well tell her for me that she isn't getting out unless she agrees to get her butt on the next stage and keep her big mouth shut. I can't have her underfoot screwin' up anything else. Make her understand that, Jack."

Jack nodded and went back to where three cells stood in a row. Melody was sitting in the first cell, on an adobe slab with a thinly stuffed mattress. She was bedraggled, her hair falling down, and her eyes puffy and dark. All the toughness she was famous for had evaporated. She was defeated; tears had drawn dark streaks down her cheeks. She looked up at the sound of the door opening, expecting to see Cotton ready to try once more to bend her to his will. When she saw Jack, she cried out, rushing to the steel slats that kept her prisoner. She reached through to grab on to him.

"Oh, Jack, sweetie, thank God you're alive. I knew you'd come. Get me out of this awful place. That bastard Cotton Burke had the nerve to put a lady in jail. I hope you've taught him a lesson," she sobbed. "Whatever you had to do to him, he deserved it."

He reached through the bars to touch her face and wipe away her tears. But she could tell there'd been a change in the man she thought she knew so well. He hadn't shown the eagerness to hold her and kiss her that she had been expecting.

"Hi, Melody. I, uh, I'm afraid Cotton was right to put you in here. Why'd you have to come to Apache Springs anyway? As much as I sure do love layin' eyes on you, I'm afraid you've put a lot of lives in jeopardy."

"Wh-what? I don't understand. All I did was come looking for you, to bring you back with me. I've been so lonely without you. I just wanted you back. What's so awful about that?"

"Well, it seems you spouted off that Cotton and I knew each other. Some very dangerous men found out about it. You see I had gotten in with a gang that plans to rob a train. I was gathering information so Cotton could stop it. Now that they know who I am, well, they'll be gunning for me."

"And I did all that?"

"I, uh, I'm afraid you did."

Melody hung her head and returned to her pallet. She put her head in her hands and began sobbing again.

"Cotton says if you don't agree to get on that stage in the morning, you'll stay put until this is all over. There's not much I can do, I'm afraid."

Melody didn't look up as Jack walked out of the cell area and went back to where Cotton was checking a shotgun.

"She going?"

"Didn't say. I didn't push it. You figure Cruz will send someone in after me or wait until I ride back to the Brennans'?"

"If I was to guess, he couldn't take the chance you'll return on your own. We should be prepared for visitors."

"Cotton, I'm not so sure I can leave old man Brennan at the mercy of those cutthroats. He won't stand a chance if they find out he's alive," said Jack.

Cotton walked to the window. He hadn't figured on Hank Brennan turning out to be an innocent bystander in Cruz's plot to rob the railroad. Somehow, he'd figured that Brennan at least suspected what Cruz was up to. He had to be aware that the whole Cruz gang was as crooked as a juniper limb. But if Brennan's life *was* in danger, Cotton couldn't ignore Jack's admonition.

The roar of gunfire brought them both to high alert. Cotton tossed Jack a rifle, pulled a shotgun from the rack, and they both started for the door. Cotton stopped before stepping outside.

"That could be some of Cruz's men. From the shots, I'd guess there are two of 'em. They may be trying to draw us out the front door so they can gun us down. We'll go around back and down behind the livery," Cotton said, grabbing Jack by the arm.

"Sounds right. Blade is sure as hell goin' to be one of them and the other, well, I don't know. I doubt that Cruz will risk a showdown here in town with all that money just a day away," said Jack. "But I'm certain they want at *me* real bad."

Cotton opened the back door slowly. He was in no hurry to present a target to someone who might have guessed he'd come out the back and be ready for him. Seeing no one, they eased into the shadows behind the jail and moved quickly down the alley toward the livery. The way was clear, and they sprinted for the safety of the next building. That's when bullets rang out, tearing chunks of pine from the livery's walls.

Jack dove for the safety of some barrels. Cotton barely made it to the other side before several bullets dug into the dirt behind him. He peered around the corner. A bullet embedded itself in the siding two inches from his head.

"It looks like they're in the saloon. Not easy to get to. The distance across the street is too damned far to make a run for it. We'd never make it from here to the saloon alive. Billy's got a shotgun behind the bar. Maybe he'll get a chance to use it on one of them buzzards," said Cotton, hunkered down about fifteen feet away from Jack's position.

"What if one of us was to get on top of one of these two shacks? The sun would be to our backs and in their eyes. Maybe we could squeeze off a few rounds. That'd at least make 'em keep their heads down until one of us could rush the place," said Jack.

"You're the one with the rifle. Easier to keep them pinned down with a few forty-four slugs pouring down on them than buckshot, which might not even get that far."

"Okay. Try to cover me with your Colt while I shinny up the tree behind the livery. If I don't fall out of the damned thing and bust my fool neck, I'll keep 'em busy for a while," said Jack, not waiting for a reply.

As Jack struggled to get a grip on one of the lower limbs and pull himself up, Cotton began firing at the front of the saloon. "I wonder what's keeping Billy from joining the fray," Cotton mumbled as he emptied his Colt and began reloading. Just as he took aim on a shadowy figure inside, Cotton heard three quick reports from atop the building adjacent to where he was holed up. He figured Jack's aim must have been pretty good because there quickly came a yelp from inside the saloon. Cotton decided in a flash that now was the time for him to move. He burst out from behind the building, firing as he ran toward the saloon.

He quickly regretted it.

Chapter 48

Henry Coyote half-slid, half-jumped as he came crashing down the split in the incline above the cabin where Emily had been held captive. His hurried descent rained down dirt and rocks from the steep sides of the canyon walls. He lost his balance more than once, tumbling into boulders that spared neither bruises nor cuts. But the pain of his awkward slide was nothing compared to the joy of seeing Emily Wagner safe. Until he reached the flat ground where she sat sobbing, he had not given any consideration to the possibility of there being more than one of Cruz's men at the shack.

He stood up, dusted himself off, then, with a round chambered and his rifle cocked and ready for whatever might come, he cautiously approached Emily. When she saw him, her face lit up, her pleasure in seeing a friendly face overcame her, and she struggled to her feet to greet him.

"Henry, thank heavens you've found me. Are you alone?"

"Yes, ma'am. The sheriff tries to show he follows writing in note so you safe."

"What note?"

"One saying you captive. Not harm if he do as paper say."

"Did he send you?"

"Hmmm. He say act as nothing happen. His words carry doubt I would obey," said Henry.

"I am indeed gratified that you disobeyed, Henry. I don't know how much longer I could have held out. These men are a vicious lot."

She walked over to Dogman's body and stared down at the gaping hole in his forehead.

"He might have been the least devilish of them that seized me, but I fear he was still a rascal. He fully deserved the fate you have dealt him," she said.

Henry looked about as if the devil himself was on his trail. He was anxious as he spoke. "If we stay longer, we be found out. Should go now. Make way out by rim of canyon."

"Yes, Henry. You are right. But I am not certain I can make it up the steep wall you came down. And if we try to make our escape through the gulch, we would have no place to hide if someone were to come from the other direction. We would quickly be discovered and likely shot for our trouble. What shall we do?"

"I make way to top. I send down rope. You tie around waist. I pull you up."

"Do you think it will work?"

"It work. We hurry."

Emily nodded her acceptance of Henry's plan. Immediately he began his ascent of the tricky terrain he'd just come down. With some trepidation, he began scaling the crumbling sandstone. He faced only an occasional setback, one of which—a possible bruised rib—slowed his progress. But, after several minutes of struggle, he successfully reached the top, at which time he tossed down his rope and braced his foot against a solid boulder. Almost immediately he felt Emily's weight tug and stretch the hemp. His heart pounded and sweat broke out on his forehead as he prayed his strength would hold out until she reached the relative safety of the top. Once, he thought he heard the echo of horses' hooves on the rocky surface below, but no rider came into view and he assumed it had been a mule deer somewhere nearby, scurrying for the same safety that Emily aspired to reach.

As her hand reached up, he caught it and pulled her up with his last ounce of strength. He fell to the ground, his chest heaving, the muscles in his arms screaming for rest. But he knew there would be time for that only after they were well away from this place. And so he began to lead the way back in the direction of the Wagner ranch. As they walked, he thought to clear his mind of the questions he'd asked himself over and over since Emily had gone missing.

"Miss Emily, forgive words, but must know why other hands not at ranch when you taken. Can you tell me?"

Emily's scowl told him that she, too, had pondered the same question. She didn't answer for a minute, seeming to search for anything that might seem an acceptable excuse for them. By the time she spoke, she had found none.

"I've rolled that thought over and over in my mind, Henry. But I cannot understand any plausible reason for them all to be away at the same time, the very time that Cruz and his men rode in. I found I was quite alone. It was as if all the men I had hired had vanished into thin air. Have you asked any of them where they were?"

"No. I see no one since you gone."

"We shall look deeply into this when we return home."

"If safe, we stop at ranch to get horses. Ride to town and safety the sheriff provide."

Emily thought this over for a minute. "We shall do as you suggest, Henry. But I fear we must hurry because to-morrow is the sixteenth, the date those awful men kept referring to. Whatever is going to happen will happen then. Sheriff Burke must know that I am safe and that he is free to go after those scoundrels."

It took several hours to reach the Wagner ranch. The terrain was rough and rocky. Emily's shoes had been taken from her to prevent her from escaping. Her feet were bruised and cut, but she would not let that slow her more than necessary. Henry had volunteered to carry her on his back, but she refused. She could ask no more of him.

Both were tired, hungry, and eager to see Cruz and his men brought to justice. As they approached the gate, Henry grabbed Emily by the arm and pulled her back behind some shrubs. Something wasn't right. He made a sign that she was to remain silent and hidden while he scouted the area. He bent to make himself as small as possible, slipping down the dusty slope to get a better look at the ranch house. As he peered out from behind a clump of mesquite, his throat tightened at what he saw.

They were definitely not alone.

Chapter 49

———◆◆◆———

As Cotton sprang from behind the relative safety of the building across from the saloon, Blade saw him, took careful aim, and fired off a round. The force of the bullet knocked Cotton to the ground, his Colt flung aside as he fell. He lay still, assessing his situation. He'd been hit, that was clear from the searing pain in his side. How bad was it? It was a strange sensation, almost as if he'd taken a punch to the kidney from someone twice his size. He decided to lie there and catch his breath a little longer. A couple of minutes should do it.

Sprays of dirt were being hurled into the air in front of him. How strange it looked from his vantage point, flat on his stomach, staring at ants busily carrying on their work unmindful of the giant only inches away. He wanted to laugh. It was all so strange and at the same time embarrassing that the sheriff of Catron County should be lying in the street. And those dusty geysers, what in the devil was causing that? He felt a wave of nausea come over him and a spasm in his gut. Perhaps it was something he'd eaten. Damn that One-Eyed Billy if he'd slipped him some tainted beef. Or perhaps it was bad branch water Billy used to water down the whiskey. Either way, he'd get even with the wily bartender for his carelessness, just as soon as he took a little nap to let his energy build back up. It was getting dark out, anyway.

Cotton had barely closed his eyes when he heard a voice yelling his name.

"Cotton! Cotton, dammit, get up! They're shooting at you."

The voice was familiar, but he couldn't quite place it. Perhaps an old acquaintance, someone from his days in Texas. Yes that was it. But what was he saying about being shot at? Why would anyone want to shoot at a man taking a nap? He closed his eyes, again, and was overtaken by a foggy darkness.

Scat saw his opportunity. "Blade, I'll finish him. Cover me." He slammed through the saloon doors on a dead run across the street.

Jack could tell from his vantage point that Cotton wasn't moving and was obviously wounded. If he could tell that Cotton was down, so could the shooters in the saloon. He had no sooner shouted at Cotton to get up than he spotted a man bolting from the saloon, fanning his revolver at Cotton's position, kicking up clumps of dirt all around him. It appeared his shots weren't coming close, but then a *real* gunman wouldn't fan a six-shooter while running.

Jack took careful aim with the Winchester, leading the running man. He squeezed off a shot that caught the man mid-chest and dropped him. He fell in a cloud of dust and never twitched a muscle after that. Jack turned his attention to the remaining shooter, putting two quick rounds into the front window. But his shots remained unanswered. Within seconds he heard the sound of a horse pounding down the alley behind the saloon. The rider turned north, whipping his mount for all he was worth. Jack could tell by the man's clothing that it was Blade Coffman making his getaway.

Jack climbed down from the livery roof. As soon as his feet touched the ground, he ran to where Cotton lay. There was blood seeping from his side. A great deal of it. Several others began congregating around the two.

"Someone get Doc Winters and do it damned quick," shouted Jack. "And he damned well better be sober this time." Jack was also wondering where the hell Cotton's deputy, Keeno, was hiding out. Why wasn't he here when he was needed?

In minutes, the town's only doctor arrived on the scene, ordering some of the men to gently pick up the sheriff and take him inside the saloon. The crowd was growing as Jack and two others placed Cotton's limp body on a billiards table. Jack looked around for the bartender, but saw no one. As the doctor began fussing over the sheriff, Jack went behind the bar, intent on freeing up a bottle of brandy to calm his nerves. That's when he saw Billy Black on the floor with a bullet in his chest

"There's one behind the bar and another one outside, gents, but you'll need an undertaker for both," Jack said, pulling the cork out of a bottle of brandy, and taking a long pull on it.

As he went to a table at the rear of the room, he saw another sight that sent chills up his spine. A pair of boots was sticking out of the room where Billy kept his supplies, near the back door. Jack walked over to investigate. That's when his question was answered as to the whereabouts of Deputy Keeno Belcher. He'd also been shot, once in the chest. He, too, was stone cold dead. That accounted for the two shots that he and Cotton had heard earlier, the shots that had brought them into the fracas in the first place.

"This place reminds me of Shiloh," said the doctor, after steadily working on Cotton for about twenty minutes, his hands covered in blood. "What the hell's going on?"

"Virgil Cruz's gang has decided to take over. That's my assessment," said Jack, his feet up on a table, the brandy in one hand and a glass in the other. The quantity of brandy had gone down appreciably, and Jack's attitude seemed to be mellowing. "How's ol' Cotton doin'?"

"He'll live. Bullet busted a rib but didn't go far enough to do any other damage. I got it out. Lost a lot of blood, though. He'll be down for a spell, I reckon, unless he wants to bust open these stitches I'm puttin' in and come down with a fatal case of *excessive* bleeding." He stretched out the word "excessive" as if it were a whole paragraph.

"That's not much comfort, Doc. He'll need to be up and around by tomorrow if we're to stop this gang from blowin' up a train and stealin' a million dollars," said Jack.

The doctor turned to Jack, saw the badge pinned to his chest, and said, "Well, Deputy, this man shouldn't be going anywhere tomorrow. Unless, of course, you want him leaving a trail of blood wherever he goes. However, I'll wrap him as good as I can."

Jack's eyebrows knitted together like storm clouds gathering for a downburst. Just what was his stake in all this now? He didn't owe the town of Apache Springs a damned thing. He'd come at Cotton's insistence and a healthy dose of conviction that he'd be shot if he refused. But now that the sheriff was down with a bullet wound, who would expect him to stick around and risk getting shot to pieces himself? Why not just take Melody and ride out of town like he'd been nothing more than a casual visitor? Hell, that wasn't far from the truth, and there was certainly nothing in it for him anymore, if there ever had been in the first place.

Jack downed the remainder of the bottle of brandy, thanked the doctor, and headed back to the jail to mull over his next move. If the doctor was right and Cotton was likely to be out of action a while, and with Keeno dead, it looked like he was the man in charge. He could set Melody free without consequence. They could get a room at the hotel and take up right where they'd left off. That sounded so good, he quickened his steps. He hadn't realized how bad he'd missed having her lying by his side on chilly nights. Or warm nights, either.

Chapter 50

———◆———

Henry Coyote held his breath. Several men were gathered on the front porch of Emily Wagner's ranch house. Cruz's men. He recognized them. They were the ones who'd tormented him, called him offensive names, spat on him for being a filthy Indian. They'd tried to run him out of town on several occasions, but his quickness had allowed him to escape untouched. He always came back with the supplies he'd been sent for.

The townsfolk were generally accepting of the former Apache scout. Only Cruz and his men caused trouble. But what were these deadly men doing at the Wagner ranch? Just then, Ben Patch appeared leading several men, Emily's men, around the side of the house. They were tied together like a string of horses. Ben kept nudging the last of them with his rifle.

Henry slipped silently back to where Emily sat huddled beneath a boulder, kept hidden by a proliferation of brush that grew down the hillside.

"Who are they?" she asked.

"Cruz's men. They hold your cowboys prisoner. That why nobody here when you need help. Cruz round up before he take you. Keep hidden away from ranch."

"What are we going to do? These men are murderers. If they discover their man shot to death, and me gone, they will hunt us both down and kill us."

Henry scratched his chin as he thought about the predicament they were in. His mission to save Emily from the Cruz gang was not over, not by a long shot. Several horses were in the corral behind the house, but it would be impossible to get to them without being spotted. It was up to Henry to figure out a plan to get them both away safely. It wouldn't be easy, but his determination was strong, and his allegiance to Emily Wagner even stronger. If he crept closer, he might be able to make out what Cruz and his men were planning.

He told Emily he'd be right back and to remain silent. He then crawled through the narrow opening between the rocks and some mesquite, creeping ever closer to the group of men, who were milling around as if they were waiting for something or someone. Just then Henry heard a horseman approaching. The men came together as Virgil Cruz rode up with Blade Coffman at his side and dismounted.

"Well, men, I have some real good news. The sheriff is no longer a problem. Blade here shot and killed him. That's one gnat I won't have to swat after we blow up that train."

He said it so loudly that Emily overheard him. She buried her face in her hands and began to sob. She tried to keep her emotions under control, so that she wouldn't be heard, but it was difficult. She pulled her long dress up around her face to help muffle her crying.

"What'll we do with the Wagner riders?" asked one of them men, throwing a thumb over his shoulder.

"We won't need them after tonight. Ben, assign two men to keep 'em company and then shoot 'em once we don't have no more use for 'em."

Ben nodded and pointed to two of his comrades. "You

boys heard the boss. Put them in the barn and keep an eye on them."

"Blade, I want you to round up all the goose grease you can find. We're goin' to lather up the tracks starting at the base of the incline. That'll slow that smoke-puffin' son of a bitch down to a crawl. Then we blow the tracks in front of it with one stick of dynamite, and the express car with two sticks," said Cruz. "We'll surround her so no one can escape and get off a warning to someone foolish enough to try and stop us."

"Where'll we meet up?" asked Blade.

"Back at the Brennan place. I want to keep an eye out and make sure that fool son of Hank's don't get it into his mind to do something heroic, like gettin' the townsfolk together to chase us off the spread. He hasn't been a problem so far, but I don't want to take any chances. So mount up."

"D-did you hear what they said about Cotton? They said that gunslinger, Blade, killed him," sobbed Emily after the riders had left the ranch and Henry had rejoined her.

"I hear, but I don't believe. I must see with my own eyes," said Henry. "That sheriff one good pistolero. He not die easy."

Emily wiped at her reddened eyes with the hem of her skirt. She tried to smile at Henry's positive attitude, but it was easy to see she was crushed by the news. She, too, would have to see for herself, but the possibility that the man she had secretly loved for so long might be gone nearly overcame her.

"Henry, we must do something," Emily sniffled.

"Miss Emily, we free men held captive in barn. They help us," said Henry.

"How do we do that? Those men are gunmen."

"We wait for dark, then I go and free them."

"You might get one, but the other will hear the gunshot and take cover. Then he will be free to await your next move, and he'll shoot you."

"I no use gun, missy. I have this," Henry said as he held up his Bowie knife. The blade glinted in the waning sun as he turned it. It was razor sharp. He grinned.

As darkness overtook the valley, Henry prepared to free Emily's wranglers. He glanced her way, gave her a nod of confidence, and then slipped off into the dark. The barn was about two hundred yards from where he and Emily had spent the afternoon, hunkered down in the thick brush that skirted some boulders spilling down the hill. He took the long way around, keeping low so as not to spook the horses in the corral. When he reached the barn, he put his face close to the rough-sawn walls, listening for sounds that might indicate where Cruz's men were. A flickering light escaped the uneven boards and Henry could see a lantern hanging from a peg. It illuminated much of the inside. He could make out the men tied together and pushed back into a stall. Then he spotted Cruz's two gunmen, sitting on the floor, one blowing smoke rings from his hand-rolled quirly.

"Why don't you go up to the house and see if you can rustle up some grub from the lady's pantry. I bet you can find some coffee, maybe some salt pork or some beans up there," said one of the gunmen. "My belly feels like it's been abandoned."

"Yeah. Good idea. I'll be right back," said the other. He got up and stomped out of the barn and into darkness. Almost instantly, he was grabbed from behind and his throat slashed so deeply his head almost came off. He hadn't been able to make a sound.

Henry let the man's body slump to the ground, wiped off his blade on the dead man's shirt, and crept silently toward the barn. He waited outside for the other man to come looking for his partner. As hungry as the man claimed to have been, Henry figured he'd only wait a few minutes for the return of the other.

He didn't even wait that long. The knife's work was once again done in one clean swipe.

Chapter 51

———⟫•⟪———

Jack lay beside Melody in a squeaky iron bed at the hotel. He looked over at her, a satisfied grin on his unshaven face. "I gotta admit, I sure have missed that," he said.

"Hmmm. Me, too. So how long are we going to stay in this godforsaken town? I wanna go home."

Jack interlaced his fingers behind his head, leaned back on the pillows, and stared at the ceiling. Her question carried with it a puzzling number of other questions. What *was* he going to do about Cotton? After all, wasn't this Cotton's war? And what would become of Emily Wagner, stashed away somewhere, not knowing what fate awaited her? And Hank Brennan, what about him after Cruz pulled off his train robbery? And why was Jack feeling guilty about walking away, leaving Virgil Cruz and his thugs to do whatever dirty dealings they wished? He didn't owe this town anything, did he? Of course not. He was his own man, not obliged to follow anyone, so why were so many doubts gnawing at him?

"Aww, hell, Melody, I can't just up and leave these folks to the likes of that rattler, Cruz. Damn!"

"Wha-whatever do you mean, honey? What's this place ever done for you? And what about Cotton Burke? You can't be forgettin' that the jackass yanked you outta my soft and comfortin' bed and dragged you through who knows what kinda hell. You can't have second thoughts. And don't forget, he threw a lady in jail. Not just any lady, neither—me. I shoulda plugged him when I had the chance." Melody had worked herself up into one fine frenzy, and Jack liked it. When she took a bite of something she couldn't spit out, she got prettier by the minute, and sexier, too.

He rolled over and began smothering her with kisses. She dug her fingernails into him and pulled him so close he could hardly get his breath. They made love like they were half-starved for affection. After a half hour, Jack rolled back onto his side of the bed, wet with perspiration and thoroughly spent. Melody smiled as if she'd just been victorious over some phantom enemy. She felt certain she'd won him over to her way of thinking. He'd pack up and take her home now. She was sure of it.

But Jack had been immersed in a world, though not of his making, that had presented him with a look at some of the frontier's worst examples of humanity. And he couldn't bring himself to look away. Melody's lovemaking hadn't changed his mind any. He *had* to stay and help the town. Had to stop Virgil Cruz. Had to save Hank Brennan from a second attempt on his life. Had to find Emily Wagner, if only to look upon the face of the woman who could corral Cotton Burke. He jumped out of the creaky iron bed and pulled on his britches and boots. He stuffed in his shirttails and strapped on his Remington. Melody was aghast at what she was seeing. Her expression said he couldn't be doing what it looked like he was doing. But he was. She pulled the blankets up to cover her naked body and pouted.

"Wh-where are you goin', Jack?" she said with a whine.

"I got to finish what I started. You stay right there and keep the bed warm for me, you hear. I'll be back." He opened the door, then looked back at her. "Oh, and don't be prancin' around town so Cotton finds out you're not in jail. He'll kill me when he heals up."

When Henry had freed all of Emily's ranch hands, they gathered around with questions as to what they could do to even the score with Cruz and his bunch. Emily was much more herself now that the immediate danger of being recaptured had passed. Henry Coyote had saved her, but she still wanted to see Virgil Cruz and Scat Crenshaw pay for the torment and humiliation she'd endured at their hands. The shoe was on the other foot and she was ready to take charge.

"We've put up with the likes of Virgil Cruz and his cutthroats for too damned long. It's time we take our county back. I know it's bound to be dangerous, but what I'm about to ask, I'll only ask once. I intend to hold each and every one of you to your word if you sign on. Henry and me, we overheard one of Cruz's men say Sheriff Burke is dead, shot down by one of their kind. I aim to even the score. Before we're through, Cruz's gang will either be dead or hightailin' it out of Catron County."

"We're with you, Miss Emily," shouted one of the hands. Several others yelled their agreement. One cowboy stood silent, his hands to his sides. Emily noticed his lack of response.

"You know, gents, something has been puzzling me. Cruz and his bunch was able to saunter in here pretty as you please, and there was no one around to put up an objection to me bein' hauled off like a prisoner of war. Where were all of you?"

"Toby, here, said we was all to ride out to the north pasture and put up that fence you been talkin' about, ma'am," said one of the men, pointing to the one fellow who had remained silent. "We was all together, except for Henry, there."

"Tell me, Toby, why you'd give such an order? I gave no such instructions," said Emily.

"I, uh, sorta took it upon myself, er, knowin' it had to be done someday, and that day was as good as any, I reckon. Course, as it turned out, we rode right into a trap." Toby looked at his feet. "Those men held us under armed guard for all these days down in the cut beyond the north range. Couldn't so much as get up for a smoke without someone pointin' a rifle at our heads."

"I don't suppose one of you came into a little extra money about that time, did you?" Emily's face was turning red, her temper rising. The other men began staring at Toby like he was some sort of pariah.

"I-I didn't know it was gonna turn out like it did, ma'am. That fella said I was to get the men outta here long enough to bring you a surprise birthday present. And he said he'd give me ten dollars."

"It ain't my birthday, you damned fool. Who was this fella, anyway?" said Emily.

"It was that one they called Ben. Course he never did give me my ten dollars." The others groaned at Toby's stupidity. "I'm sorry I let you down, Miss Emily."

"Pack your things and scat, Toby. I won't have anyone that stupid working this ranch. And the rest of you, get yourselves armed and meet me in front of the house in a half hour. We're goin' hunting."

Chapter 52

———◆———

Cotton groaned as he tried to sit up. "Where the hell am I?" he mumbled. He raised his voice and tried again. There was no answer. The room was pitch-black and smelled of alcohol, or was it death? He stopped his struggle to sit up and just tried to let his head clear. *Am I dead? Is this what it's like to have your life snuffed out in an instant?*

Then a door creaked open and a weak shaft of light drove into the room. His eyes were slow to adjust, and he could barely make out a shadowy form standing in the glow.

"Are you awake, Sheriff?" asked a familiar voice in a whisper.

"Uh, yeah, I think so. That you, Doc?" said Cotton. "Where am I?"

Doc Winters came fully into the room and stood at Cotton's bedside. "I had you brought to my office. How are you feeling?" he asked.

"Sore, confused. Have I been drunk or sick or what?"

"You were shot, son. The man who did it is likely the one the deputy killed. An owlhoot named Scat Crenshaw. Ever heard of him?"

"I think so. Everything's sorta hazy right now. Where'd I get hit?"

"In the side. Plowed a furrow, but the bullet didn't get inside. Cracked a rib, and you lost a lot of blood. You'll be up and around in a few days. Just lie still and try to get some sleep. I had to give you some laudanum to keep you still so's I could get you sewn up."

"Could you send Keeno over so I can give him some instructions, Doc?"

"I'm sorry, Cotton, but Keeno is dead. So is One-Eyed Billy Black, both shot down by that Crenshaw feller and Ben Patch."

"But you said my deputy shot Crenshaw."

"I meant your other deputy, that Memphis Jack fella. Probably saved your life by pluggin' Crenshaw before he could get to where you were lyin' and finish the job."

Cotton mulled that over in his head for a moment or two.

"You say Memphis Jack is my deputy?"

"That's what that tin badge on his shirt says. You don't remember swearing him in?"

"No, uh, but that don't mean I didn't do it. Things are a little sketchy to me right now. Maybe if I could sit up and have some water things would clear a mite," said Cotton. He groaned as he tried to scoot into a more comfortable position. His ribs were bound tightly and his legs felt like they were full of angry hornets.

The doctor placed a lantern on a table beside Cotton's bed. The room was quickly filled with a pleasant orange glow, and Cotton could finally make out where he was: a couch in the doctor's operating room. Glass-fronted cabinets and trays of instruments surrounded him. There were several bloody towels lying in a heap near the rear door. He assumed it was his blood. The doctor handed him a cup full of cool water from the well. To Cotton, that was the sweetest taste he'd had for ages. But sitting up wasn't all he'd hoped for. He was still dizzy, and the thought of lying back down appealed to him greatly.

"What day is this, Doc?"

"Why, it's the sixteenth now. About one in the morning. Why do you ask?"

The day of reckoning had come. The day Emily was supposed to be freed. The day Cruz and his gang would probably try robbing the railroad. And he was lying there, doing nothing. *This isn't the way it is supposed to be*, he thought.

Memphis Jack had loaded every gun in the sheriff's office—shotguns, rifles, revolvers—everything that could spit out death. It looked as though he was fixing to take on an army all by himself. But, of course, he wasn't about to try to go after Cruz's little army alone. He needed help, and the only way he was likely to get it was to sound the alarm to the townsfolk, explain the situation, and hope they'd jump to his call for assistance.

He went to the biggest house in town, which he figured to be where the mayor lived, and pounded on the door. The house was dark, and it was several minutes before a skinny man with a beard, dressed in a knee-length nightshirt, came to the door, rubbing his eyes.

"What the hell do you mean waking a man in the middle of the night? Who are you anyway?" said the mayor.

"My name is Memphis Jack Stump, and I need your help."

"Help? Help for what? Are you some sort of lawman? That badge looks suspiciously like a deputy's tin. Where the hell is the sheriff?"

"Cotton's been shot. He's at the doc's. The other deputy is dead. Virgil Cruz and his gang are planning to rob the railroad today. I can't stop him alone. I'm asking you to rouse some of the townsfolk and enlist their aid."

"I'm sorry, son, but we're just a bunch of storekeepers

and merchants. They aren't any gunslingers hereabouts. We'd be about as useless as fleas on a rock. I'll bid you a good night and wish you all the luck in the world and remind you that this is what you were hired for." With that, the mayor promptly shut the door in Jack's face.

Jack stomped off in the direction of the jail, mulling over a proper response to the mayor's denial of help. His thoughts shifted to what he knew about Cruz's plans. He knew when and where they were going to hit the train. He knew how, and he knew about how many men would be there backing up the operation. He knew he was vastly outnumbered and that any thought of his successfully taking on the whole gang alone was tantamount to insanity. Only a drunk or a fool would even attempt it. He began to wonder which he was.

Jack stopped in front of the doctor's office. He saw a light in the back room. *What if Cotton has taken a turn for the worse, or even died?* he thought. He went up to the front door and knocked.

"Come in, Deputy. What can I do for you?" The doctor opened the door to let Jack enter.

"I saw your light, and I was hopin' you'd have good news about the sheriff. Sorry to intrude."

"Not at all, not at all. Come in. The patient is doing fine, drinking a sip, I venture."

"I could use a drink myself about now, Doc," said Jack.

"Well, I'm afraid you'll be disappointed in *his* libation. The sheriff is drinking water."

Jack's face turned red. "Can I see him?"

The doctor led him back to Cotton's bedside. Cotton opened his eyes just enough to see Jack through little slits. "That you, Jack?" he muttered.

"It's me, Cotton. And we got a problem. Today is the day Cruz is plannin' on robbin' that railcar, and I ain't certain I want to take on that bunch of jackals alone. Any suggestions?"

"Take the next stage out of town. It don't appear I'll be much help."

"Uh, I don't think you understand. I came here to participate in your little war. And even though I was dragged outta my comfortable bed against my will, well, here I am, and here I damned well intend to stay until this war, *your* war, is over. Hmmm. Cotton's War. I like that. Has a nice ring to it, don't you think?"

Cotton gave him a weak but insincere smile.

Chapter 53

At dawn, Virgil Cruz called his men together in front of the bunkhouse. He signaled them to hurry up and gather around him. There were eight of them. He was missing one man, Scat Crenshaw, and he was angry that killing the sheriff had cost him a good gunhand.

"All right, you hombres, listen up. Ben's carrying the dynamite for the express car. Blade is handling the explosives for the track, and the man with the goose grease has a whole bucket of the smelly stuff. The rest of you know where you're supposed to be, surroundin' that damned train, ready to plug the first man that tries to stop us. In about six hours, we're all goin' to be so damned rich, folks'll be bowin' and scrapin' as we walk by. Any questions?"

No one voiced any concerns. Every one of the men had a look of anticipation on his face, especially after Virgil told them how much money they'd have at the end of the day.

"Now, don't forget, after we hit the train, we light out eight different ways. Ain't no posse goin' to split up and come after us all. They'll know that if they tried that, we'd pick them off like a turkey shoot. No two of us go the same direction. I'll be carryin' the loot. We meet three days from now at the line shack up in the hills where we got the Wagner woman stashed."

"How come we don't split the money right off? That way we don't have to risk comin' back and gettin' spotted?" asked Blade.

"You suggestin' I can't be trusted with the money?" Cruz gave Blade a hard, squinty-eyed look. While others had the same thought, no one raised an objection. Even Blade let the subject drop after Virgil eased his hand to the butt of his revolver.

"We'll be headin' out just as soon as that good-for-nothin' Chinaman cooks us up some vittles. So head on over to the cook shack and start bangin' your cups on the table to let him know we're in a hurry."

The group started off, but Virgil went the other direction. Blade decided it was his business to keep an eye on the leader of the gang, a man that he had no trust in whatsoever.

"And we're s'posed to meet at the line shack?" he said.

"That's what I said, Blade. Now, get on over there with the others and start chowin' down. I'll be there directly."

Blade watched as Virgil went up to the main house and banged on the door. When Cappy opened it, Virgil stomped inside, coming nose-to-nose with Hank's son. Cappy tried backing away, but he was encumbered by having been shoved against a large leather sofa, with no place to go. The little terrier stayed beneath the table, growling lowly.

"Uh, what can I do for you, Mr. Cruz?" Cappy said.

"Well, for starters, since it's become apparent that your skinflint father has done took off, probably with the payroll, I figure you owe us about three thousand dollars in wages."

"Why, Mr. Cruz, you know I don't have that kind of money lying around. I'll have to go into town to the bank and make a withdrawal."

"Nope. You ain't leavin' here until I'm satisfied we're goin' to get what's due us. So, since your pappy's gone, that makes you the new owner, don't it? In lieu of the cash, you can sit right down at that desk and sign this IOU I had made up in case you came up with an excuse for not forkin' over the money. I put in there that if the full amount ain't paid by day after tomorrow, the ranch becomes the sole property of one Virgil J. Cruz, ranch foreman. Sign it!"

"I-I won't do anything of the sort. You can't bully me into turning over this ranch to you or anyone else. I'll go to the sheriff." Cappy attempted to push away, but the tough little man didn't budge an inch. Nervously, Cappy wiped perspiration from his forehead with his handkerchief.

"Well, that ain't goin' to help you none. One of my men saw to that by gunnin' Sheriff Cotton Burke down. So if you want to see the next sunrise standin' up, I'd say you'd better find it in your heart to do as I say, sonny." With that, Virgil slapped Cappy across the mouth. Cappy wiped at his mouth and came away with a smear of blood. He bent down and took a pen from the desk, scrawling his name at the bottom of the paper Virgil had placed before him.

As soon as Virgil left, Cappy rushed up the stairs and into his father's room. When he burst in, he found Hank snoozing.

"Poppa, wake up, we have a big problem." The old man stirred, then slowly opened his eyes. The flustered Cappy wasted no time in explaining what Virgil Cruz had demanded. Hank was fuming by the time his son told about turning the ranch over to Cruz.

"Slip out the back way and ride into town. Bring back the sheriff and his deputy. They'll not be so easily cowed by this madman," said Hank through gritted teeth.

Cappy looked down, shaking his head. "Virgil said that the sheriff is dead, killed by one of Cruz's men."

Hank chewed on his lower lip with a scowl. The tough old rancher knew he was in a difficult spot. There appeared to be little he could do to prevent Virgil Cruz from stealing his ranch. He couldn't even get out of bed to face him with a gun. And while he loved his son, it was common knowledge that Cappy Brennan didn't have the courage it took to stand up to *any* man with a gun, especially a killer like Cruz.

"Then it looks like we're whipped, son. If only I'd seen this comin' long before now. While I was healthy, I coulda done somethin'." Hank seemed to sink into himself. His will to fight had left him, and Cappy's expression showed there was nothing more he could do, either.

Cappy went downstairs slowly, shuffling his feet like an old man. *I just wish I had half the sand my father has*, he thought. Then he screamed, "Damn!"

For several minutes he stood at the window, staring blankly as Cruz and his men saddled up and rode off single file to the north, armed to the teeth, and looking every inch the ruthless, murderous outlaw band that they were. *The son of a bitch must be in a powerful hurry for something*, Cappy thought.

Chapter 54

Emily Wagner was mad, damned mad, madder than she'd been since the death of her husband. She was mad at Cruz for kidnapping her and humiliating her by allowing that scum Scat Crenshaw to paw at her. She was mad at the man who killed Sheriff Burke, and she was furious at herself for not plugging that pompous pig Cruz when she had first seen him riding up at the head of his little band of outlaws like he was Napoleon. And she fully intended to get even.

"Men, we have to stop these owlhoots. My intention is to ride into town and gather up whatever men there might be with spines stiff enough to drive Cruz and his bunch out of the county. Or hang the bastards. Whatever seems most fittin' at the time. Any of you that don't want to go, say so now or get to saddlin' up." Emily stood with her hands on her hips and a determined look on her face.

Every one of the men saddled his horse, strapped on guns, and shoved rifles into saddle scabbards. They left the Wagner ranch in a cloud of dust, with Emily and Henry

Coyote at the head of the column. They rode into Apache
Springs about an hour later. It was still early, and few stores
had opened for business. They arrived to nearly empty
streets.

Emily got off her horse and went straight to the sheriff's
office, hoping to at least find a deputy. She shoved open the
door and came face-to-face with Memphis Jack loading his
Remington. He looked up in surprise.

"Oh, I expected to find Keeno. Who are you?" she said.

"Keeno was killed yesterday, sorry to inform. I'm
Memphis Jack Stump. I'm fillin' in while the sheriff is on
the mend from a wound he received from an hombre I had
to shoot."

"Wha— You mean Cotton isn't dead? I heard he'd been
killed."

"He ain't up to dancin' to no fiddle, but I reckon you
could say he's pretty much alive. Everything considered."

"Wh-where is he? I have to see him."

"Just who might you be, ma'am?"

"My name is Emily Wagner, and Cotton, er, the sheriff
and I are, uh, friends."

"Emily Wagner! We thought you were being held prisoner by Virgil Cruz."

"I *was* his prisoner, but one of my men shot and killed
the man guarding me and led me to safety. I've come to
town with my men hopin' to gather some others willin'
to face down Cruz and even the score. Now, can I see the
sheriff?"

"C'mon with me, ma'am, I'll walk you over to the doc's
place. And about that recruitin' you're intent on, you can
forget it. I've already tried. Town's about to wet its britches
at the thought of goin' up against Cruz. I was fixin' to go
after him myself."

"Alone! You must be crazy to think you can go up
against that bunch by yourself."

"Crazy. Yup. That pretty well sums up the life and times
of Memphis Jack Stump. More'n one would agree with
you."

The doctor saw Emily and Jack approaching and opened the door. Emily pushed past Jack and rushed inside.

"Miss Emily. Damn it's good to see you're safe and sound. We was mighty worried about you, what with the sheriff's hands tied on freeing you and all," said the doctor.

"Thank you, Doc. Can I see Cotton, please? I'd heard he'd been killed."

"Sure. Sure. He'll be brightened up by seeing you safe and sound. About him bein' killed, well, it *was* close, and if it hadn't been for that fellow that came in with you, we'd be burying him by now. But he'll live to see many more summers."

Emily turned to Jack and said, "I'm grateful you saved the life of a good man, Mr. Stump. I personally offer my thanks." She slipped into Cotton's room and was shocked to see him struggling into his bloody shirt.

Sensing a presence, Cotton looked up. The sight of Emily brought a huge smile of relief to his face. His voice was weak and raspy, and a spasm of pain struck him as he reached out to touch her, causing him to wince. He took a breath and said, "Emily, thank God you're safe. How'd you get free?"

"Henry Coyote. He found me and shot Dogman Crenshaw for his trouble."

"Good ol' Henry. We talked a spell about the situation and how I couldn't head up a search myself. That was Cruz's warning. I asked Henry to wait for six days until I could put a plan in place before he set out on his own."

"Well, he did what you asked, and it worked out for the best. But enough about me, what happened?"

"I was shot, but ol' Jack here plugged Scat Crenshaw before he could finish me off. Blade Coffman got away, though. He's probably already told Cruz that I'm down. They'll figure they ain't got nothin' to worry about. Do they know you ain't their prisoner anymore?"

"Not unless someone came to the cabin. They probably figure I'm still there, all trussed up like a Christmas goose, just pining away for that handsome Scat to try fondlin' me some more. I'm glad to hear he's laid out cold."

"Did that devil Scat lay a hand on you?"

"He thought real hard on it, but fate seemed to step in each time he took a mind to."

"So you aren't hurt?"

"No, thank God."

She squeezed his hand. He pulled her closer, wincing in the process.

"What can we do now?" she asked.

"With Scat and Dogman both dead, Cruz has only Blade and Ben to handle the gun work, and a handful of other men, none of whom has any real shootin' skills," said Cotton. "You two help me out to my horse, and I think we can wrestle that critter to the ground."

"You're not up to any ridin', pardner," said Jack. "Miss Emily brought her crew in, and together I think we can mess up Cruz's plans easy. If the lady will agree to such an arrangement."

"The lady does agree, Mr. Stump. Go to it." Emily blurted out.

"I've got a stake in this, Jack, you don't. It's my job. So how about a hand here, ol' buddy?" said Cotton.

Jack turned and started for the door. "Not today, Cotton. Me and the Wagner bunch got our work cut out for us, and we got no use for a crippled sheriff taggin' along. Adios." He hurried outside to gather Emily's men and work out a plan to stop the robbery.

Cotton finished tucking his shirt in his pants. He took his gun belt off the chair and strapped it on.

"You should listen to your friend, Cotton. I have a feeling that Jack, Henry, and the rest of my bunch will prove a formidable force against Cruz's cutthroats," said Emily.

She saw an approving smile come across his lips as she took his hand, then kissed his cheek. The look on his face suggested he was feeling better, but deadly serious about his next move.

"I have a score to settle with Cruz for what he did to you, and I'll not let anything stand in my way. Tell me the location of the cabin where he held you."

"Why?"

"You're the hole card in this game, Emily. And Cruz intends on playing it. Believe me when I say if Henry hadn't come when he did, Cruz would never have let you live. If he escapes Jack's attempt to stop the robbery, he'll need a hostage to help him get out of the county. If I'm right, he'll come back for you. I aim to see this game play out to the end."

Chapter 55

—◆——

"Dad, they've just ridden out," yelled Cappy as he burst into Hank's bedroom.

"Good. We ain't got much time, so you gotta pay attention. First, tell Wu Chang to get up here with two loaded shotguns. Then, you ride into town and see if you can find that Memphis Jack fella. Tell 'im we got ourselves a passel of trouble out here and we need him, pronto. Got that?" said Hank.

"Yessir. I'll leave right away. You think you and Chang can hold Cruz off till I get back?"

"If he comes chargin' through that door, he'll get a face full of buckshot for sure. Now, git."

Cappy took the stairs two at a time. After giving Wu Chang instructions, he saddled up and tore through the gate like his britches were aflame. When he rode into town, he went straight to the sheriff's office.

"Deputy, it's me, Cappy Brennan. Where are you?" he looked back by the jail cells, then outside where the outhouse was. Unable to find anyone, he went to the saloon, to find it closed up, a board nailed across the doors. A paper was tacked to the door frame saying that the owner, One-Eyed Billy Black, had been murdered by Blade Coffman and that the burial would be today.

"Damn," said Cappy to no one in particular. He looked around, finding the town uncommonly quiet. He went to the middle of the rutted street and began shouting for someone, anyone, to come out. After several minutes, the doctor opened his door and peeked out.

"What's all the commotion, boy?"

Cappy ran up to the doctor's porch, out of breath, and told him of the happenings out at the Double-B ranch. The doctor told him to come inside and tell it to the sheriff.

"I heard the sheriff was killed."

"Not by a long shot, son," said the doctor.

When Cappy saw the sheriff bandaged up and a red bloom leaking through, his spirits dropped.

"What is it, Cappy?" said Cotton. Emily was seated beside him.

Gasping for breath, Cappy tore off his hat and began stammering out his story about Cruz's threat to take over the Brennan spread, and that Wu Chang was waiting by his father's bed with a shotgun in case Cruz came back and found Hank still alive, and Jack wasn't around to help, and—

"Whoa. Hold on there, son. I can't keep up with all this. Where is Cruz right now?"

"He rode off with all his men early this morning, soon after dawn. I think they're up to something, because I've heard talk of them all gettin' rich."

"Uh-huh. They're plannin' to rob the railroad up near the water stop."

"What are we goin' to do?"

"I reckon we're goin' to have to hope that ol' Memphis Jack comes through on his promise to bring Cruz down."

Cappy frowned and said, "Yeah. I reckon that's all we *can* do."

"Not quite. You ride on back to your father and be ready

to add your gun to his and Wu Chang's. The three of you should make Cruz think twice before bustin' in. But if Jack does what he says he's intendin' on doin', by sundown there won't be enough of the Cruz gang left to worry about. Now, go on, son, you can do it. I got somethin' needs doin', then I'll ride out your way."

When Cappy left, Emily leaned over to Cotton. "Isn't there anything I can do, Cotton?"

"Yep, there is one thing. You can take this over to the telegraph office and get it sent off real quick." He touched the end of a pencil stub to his tongue, tore off a piece of paper from one of the doctor's ledgers, and scribbled some instructions on it. He folded the paper and handed it to Emily.

"What's this?"

"It's something I should have done earlier. I been so damned worried about you, well, my head's been kinda foggy. It's a warning about Cruz's intentions. Send it to the railway stop at Gopher Crossing. That's the last water stop before the train reaches the pass. This'll explain the situation to the marshal. Maybe he can hold the train up until they can get a posse together. Jack would probably welcome the help."

"I expect he would at that," said Emily, as she hurried out the door.

Cruz had his men in position, awaiting sounds of an approaching train. If it was on time, it should be rounding the bend in less than thirty minutes, just before starting up the incline that would lead it into the trap that would relieve its express car of about a million dollars. One of Cruz's men had used a stick with a rag wrapped around the top to lather a healthy coating of grease on both tracks for almost a quarter mile where the tracks began their climb to the top. Blade was ready with his dynamite, and Ben had already placed his stick under the rail and was ready to strike a Lucifer to the fuse. They were all tense as they awaited Cruz's signal to start the operation. Cruz sat atop a boulder gazing through a single-lens telescope, hoping to spot the train long before it got to their position. He would wave a white handkerchief to tell those below that the train was on its way. But time was slipping away and there was no sign of a train.

"Virgil, what could be holding it up?" said Ben.

"Just be patient. It'll get here. The newspaper said so, and newspapers don't lie and neither do editors," Cruz added with a snicker.

Just then, Blade came rushing up. "Virgil, put your glass on that cloud of dust yonder. What the hell could be comin'? It ain't some cattle stampede, is it?"

Virgil whirled around, peering through his telescope. "Son of a bitch. It looks like we're about to have a war on our hands."

"Who is it?" said Blade.

"I'd swear it looks like that Memphis Jack fella, and he's got the Wagner bunch with him. How the hell'd they get loose? Limber up your gun hands, boys, and prepare for a shoot-out."

"What about the train, Virgil?" said Ben. "We can't handle them both at the same time."

"Wait a spell, then blow the track, Ben. Half of you men get ready to board 'er when she comes to a stop. The rest of you come with me. We'll put a stop to that bunch of cowpunchers and that meddlesome Memphis Jack in short order."

Chapter 56

———◆———

The desert leading to where Jack had figured to find Virgil and his men was rocky and rutted from the runoff of storms that blew through during the monsoons. As the ground slowly rose to finally reach a plateau, the railway came into view, and Jack saw why Cruz had chosen this particular location to hit the train. The tracks turned to avoid an area of building-size boulders in their path then continued up a long, steep grade to the top.

"Well, boys, it looks like ol' Cruz found himself a pretty good spot for an ambush," Jack said, turning in the saddle. He pulled out his rifle, levered a cartridge into the chamber, and grinned broadly. "But we aren't goin' to put up with that nonsense, are we?"

"You bet your ass we ain't," one of the cowboys shouted to the agreement of the others.

"Then, let's hit 'em hard. Maybe even surprise 'em some. If we can pick off a few before the train gets here, the whole plan might crumble before that devil's eyes."

The first shots were fired from horseback as Jack and the

Wagner boys came straight at Cruz and some of his men who'd tried to seek protection behind a copse of trees and rocky outcroppings. One of the Wagner bunch was knocked off his horse by a well-aimed rifle shot, but most of the firing from six-shooters went wild. Jack could see that Cruz's men weren't prepared for a cavalry-style charge against their position, and a couple of them broke and ran back toward where Blade and Ben were hunkered down near the tracks. When Cruz saw this, he started screaming at them, calling them cowards. He fired a warning shot and accidentally hit the one closest to him in the back. The man tumbled to the ground, blood burbling from his mouth as he died.

Jack signaled to his men to hold up and dismount.

"We'll go in on foot from here. No sense getting our horses shot to pieces," he shouted. "Follow their trail uphill. But watch yourselves, they'll be itchin' to fill us full of lead."

The men quickly dismounted and took up the chase. Cruz's men began firing haphazardly over their shoulders, killing nothing more significant than a few silver dollar cacti and chipping the occasional boulder. Henry Coyote drew up short, put his rifle to his shoulder, and squeezed off a shot at one of Cruz's men. The man was knocked off his feet by the impact of the bullet. He died facedown in the dirt, his body pierced by a thousand tiny barbs from the cholla cactus he had fallen into.

"Nice shootin' there, Henry," said Jack, as the two trotted side by side in pursuit of the outlaws.

"He shoot at horse. Unforgivable among my people. He had to pay," said Henry, with a wry grin.

When Jack and the Wagner men got to the top of a rise, they found that the Cruz gang was holed up in surroundings that would make it difficult to dislodge them without a prolonged gun battle. As he studied the natural fortifications behind which Cruz and his men had taken up positions, Jack's hopes for a quick victory needed a more realistic reevaluation. Jack motioned for his men to take cover and conserve ammunition.

"Make your shots count, men," he shouted, "and don't waste any bullets on gophers."

Henry crawled closer to Jack. "What we do now?"

"We bide our time, keep 'em pinned down, and be happy that train ain't on time."

"When iron horse come?" said Henry.

"By my watch, about twenty minutes ago." Jack snapped his watch closed and returned it to his vest pocket. He saw no sign of a train approaching. "I wonder if something's wrong."

Since Jack's men had slowed their firing, Cruz told his men to stay put also. The sun burned down with a vengeance. Jack watched a buildup of dark clouds rising rapidly over the mountains to the west. Dirt devils spun up from the thousands of acres of desert, heralding an increase of wind in front of the coming storm. It appeared that Cruz and his men could hold out in their present positions for a long time, and Jack could do little to change that. Throwing bullets in their direction would just be a waste of lead. He had to come up with a way to move them away from the tracks. He was shaken from his thoughts as an explosion threw dirt fifty feet into the air. A lingering cloud of smoke and dust came from the pass near the top of the rail incline.

"Damn! They've blown the track up ahead. Now, even if we could have kept them from jumping the train, the engine will either have to stop or be derailed," Jack growled. "And they're dug in all along the pass."

"Iron horse late," said Henry.

"Very late, Henry, very late. If this was a special express carrying a fortune, wouldn't you figure it would be on time?" Jack said, not really expecting an answer, because he suddenly thought he might already know. He called one of the Wagner bunch to come to his position.

"Yessir," said a tousled-hair young man.

"I want you to get your horse and beat it back to town. The sheriff might still be at Doc Winters's. I need to know if he had a telegram sent to stop the train somewhere west of here. Understand? Then get back here as soon as possible."

"Yessir" was all the man said as he took off at a dead run down the hill toward his horse. A few bullets were sent his way by Cruz's men, but the distance was too great for any accuracy, and he made a clean getaway.

"You know reason iron horse not come?" said Henry.

"Maybe. If Cotton somehow got the train stopped, that would keep the money out of Cruz's hands. But we still have to get rid of that scum."

"How we get behind them?"

"I don't know, but trying to hold us off while they wait for a train that may or may not be coming, with a storm brewin', can't be making them real comfortable. If I can get around that pile of rocks yonder, with you fellas throwin' lead at 'em, maybe we'll convince 'em to cut and run."

"I go with you," said Henry. Without waiting for Jack to answer, he passed the word on to the others of what was planned, then fell in behind Jack as he scurried off to find cover along a dry streambed that looked like it might lead around the hill the Cruz boys were camped out on.

A couple of Cruz's men saw Jack and Henry make a break for it and began firing their way. One bullet came close enough that Jack ducked at the impact in the dirt, lost his footing, and went tumbling down a gravelly slope and into a pile of dead cacti. After sitting for several minutes pulling dozens of cactus needles from his butt and leg, he cursed a few choice words then continued his quest for a way around the outlaws' position.

Henry shook his head at Jack as if he wasn't certain he should be following someone so clumsy.

The two of them reached a point where the ground sloped away steeply, with no way up to offer adequate cover from Cruz's guns. Only if they attempted an assault on a treacherous rocky incline on the east side of the pass could they hope to get to the top in a position to shoot down on their prey. Henry studied Jack's expression as he seemed to ponder the situation for what the Apache obviously thought was too long. Henry grabbed the roots of a long dead tree sticking out of the dirt and began pulling himself up to where he could get purchase on a slab of granite jutting from the side of the incline. Jack watched in wonder at the agility the Indian showed. Halfway up, Henry looked back at Jack as if to say, "What you waiting for?"

Jack got the message, sighed deeply, then began what he was certain would be a quick and painful trip to the bottom of the hill.

Chapter 57

—◆◆◆—

"That damned train ain't comin', Cruz," sputtered Blade. "I'm beginnin' to doubt there ever was a train full of gold."

"Are you doubting my word, you ignorant pig? I ought to blow your damned head off," shouted Cruz, his face red with anger. He spun around and stuck his gun in Blade's face, cocking the hammer as he did. Sensing Virgil's likely reaction to his comment, Blade did the same to Cruz. As they sat there, six-guns at each other's forehead, each within a microsecond of blowing the other to kingdom come, Ben shouted.

"There! Look out there! The train is coming."

The anger between the two of them quickly subsided as all eyes turned to the smoky trail being left by the approach of a powerful steam locomotive pulling two cars and a caboose as it snaked through the desert.

"I figured there'd be some passenger cars behind that engine, didn't you, Virgil?" said Ben. "I don't see but three."

"It don't make a damn bit of difference, does it? One of them cars must be the express car and that's all we care about. That and what's in it: a million dollars."

"How we gonna take the train while them cowboys is takin' potshots at us?" asked Blade.

"The train can't make it through the pass because Ben has already blown the rail. We stick to the plan. Soon as the engine comes to a stop, or derails and turns over, Blade blows the doors off the express car. The rest of you keep pluggin' away at those damned cowboys, that'll keep 'em hunkered down. That bunch ain't goin' to keep me from my money," growled Virgil.

"Don't you mean 'our' money, Virgil?" said Ben, with a suspicious look.

"Uh, yeah, that's what I meant." Virgil quickly turned away to avoid any further discussion on the subject.

Jack scrambled up and over some boulders where he could get a better view of the Cruz gang keeping under cover about thirty yards away across a shallow ravine. Henry moved to his side. As he reached a point where he could pick out each of the outlaw gang's positions, Jack looked up and saw the train approaching.

"Damn! Looks like Cotton didn't get it stopped, after all. I reckon it's up to us now. You got any ideas, Henry?"

"I follow you. You lead way."

I'm beginning to wish I'd never met Cotton Burke, Jack mused to himself.

"Okay, Henry, I count six of them. We'll try to take out those closest to us first, then work our way toward where the train will likely have to stop." He pointed to where he estimated the engine had to stop to avoid derailing.

Henry nodded, and without waiting for any further thoughts Jack might think of adding, he leapt from his perch and, keeping as low as possible to avoid early detection, began to snake around through the brush toward an outlaw who had settled behind a small pile of timbers left behind from when the rail was first laid.

Henry moved so quickly and quietly, he was on the man in seconds. The last sound the man heard was Henry slipping his Bowie knife from its scabbard. He died as his life's blood spurted from a deep slash across his throat, the shock in his eyes a testament to his killer's stealth. Henry was about to advance on another position when the locomotive reached the bottom of the incline. As soon as the wheels hit the thick globs of grease that had been applied to the tracks, the train slowed, as the big engine's drive wheels began to spin, unable to sustain sufficient traction to make the grade. Just when it looked as though Cruz and his minions were about to take the day, the wide sliding doors to two rail cars were flung open and four men in long, black trail dusters came out, blazing away with rifles and shotguns. Two of Cruz's men went down to the fusillade before they could even return fire. That left only Ben, Blade, and Virgil. Any thought of a successful robbery was immediately forgotten.

Virgil Cruz was mean through and through, but nobody said he was stupid. He did the only smart thing a man could do in this situation: he ran. Ran like the wind for his horse. Escaping those deadly guns was his only concern. The money could wait for another day. Ben and Blade were right behind him. They reached their horses almost simultaneously, leapt into their saddles, and spurred them to a dead run.

Jack watched as the three sped off across the desert. He and Henry and the others stepped out from their positions behind rocks or mesquite and joined the four at the open doors of the express car.

"You men sure do come prepared. Glad to see you," said Jack, holding out his hand to one of the men. "We were running short of ways to get them critters corralled."

"Your sheriff telegraphed the station at Gopher Crossing. Just so happened we had arrived by stage about an hour before. We're railroad detectives. We were headed to Fort Apache. Lucky we was close by when the help was needed."

"Glad to make your acquaintance. This bunch is down to just three; I reckon they'll scatter to the winds," said Jack. "Maybe I can pick off one or two before it's all over."

"We're going to have to get some help out here to repair the track up ahead. Got any ideas?"

"We can help if Mr. Stump don't need us," said one of the Wagner men.

Jack just shrugged. "Sounds all right. You fellas give 'em a hand, then head on back to the Wagner place. Probably got your work cut out for you there, too. Thanks for your help."

Henry insisted on staying with Jack to track down Cruz and his two cutthroats. Jack acknowledged he was grateful for the help. They rode off in the direction the outlaws had taken.

After they had made their way across the dry, hot desert for almost a half hour, Henry stopped, got off, and bent over some tracks. "They go different ways." He pointed to where the three had split off in what appeared to be two different directions.

Jack studied the tracks, scratched his head, and squinted at the way each man seemed to be headed. Then an idea struck him.

"If I got that low-down rattlesnake, Virgil Cruz, figured right, the opportunity to put a stop to his gunslingin' days is at hand," said Jack. "It looks like these tracks goin' off to the left are his, and I'll bet that's what some shot-up sheriff figured all along."

"You not follow Cruz?"

"Nope. Don't think I need to. Even all bandaged up and in pain, Cotton can take care of himself. He is one tough buzzard. Cruz don't know who he's up against."

"What you want me to do?" asked Henry.

"My guess is the other two are goin' back to gather their belongings and probably hit up Cappy Brennan for whatever cash the ranch has on hand. I'd like to head 'em off before the Brennans have to face them alone. Think the two of us can get to the Double-B spread before they get there?"

"They not Apache."

"I'll take that as a yes."

Chapter 58

———✦◆✦———

Henry and Jack urged their mounts over ground Blade and Ben wouldn't have dared tackle. The sure-footed pony carried the Apache with the precision of a bullet, allowing nothing—no obstacle, no incline, no rock-strewn hillock—to deter him. Jack's horse followed closely.

When they came to the top of the rise overlooking the Brennan ranch house, Henry stopped to look for signs that Ben and Blade might have arrived before him. There were no horses to be seen, none tied to the rail in front of the big house. Their horses began a cautious walk toward the ranch house. They'd no sooner gotten there than a man came running out waving a meat cleaver and yelling.

"No come here! Go way!"

Henry reined in, his eyes wide at the sight of the angry Chinaman. Jack held up his hand.

"It's me, Wu Chang, Jack Stump. The outlaws are on their way here. They'll arrive very soon. And they'll likely be lookin' for all the cash they can steal."

Wu Chang stopped, blinked. Then shook his head in dismay.

"So solly, Missa Jack. Old eyes not what they used to be. I no recognize from distance."

Wu Chang had been with the Brennans through many good times and bad, although trouble seemed to have engulfed the Double-B ever since the Cruz bunch signed on. Now, according to Jack, more of it was on the way. Chang's shoulders slumped. He shook his head as he motioned for them to get down and come into the house.

"I hide horses first," Henry said to Jack. He led their mounts around to the back of the house and tied them to the porch railing. Jack followed Wu Chang inside. As the heavy front door closed, Cappy ran down the stairs with a gun in his hand.

"Jack? Damn, I'm glad to see you. Did you kill all them scoundrels?" he said, waving the .44 in Henry's face.

Wu Chang spoke up. "He say bad men coming to rob us."

Cappy lowered his revolver. "Damn!"

"Ben and Blade are on their way. I figure on stopping them, with your help of course."

Cappy looked as if he'd been overwhelmed by sudden darkness. He glanced around for a way back into the light. "Uh, wh-what do I have to do? I-I ain't no gunslinger. Dad is upstairs, still all busted up, barely able to lift his head let alone hold off gunmen. Wu Chang is just a cook. He ain't never killed anything but chickens."

As Henry entered, Jack turned and said, "You two set up to defend the house. I'll go around back and come at them from the corral."

Henry nodded. He turned to Cappy and said, "You have shotgun?"

"Sure. There, by the fireplace." Cappy went over and grabbed it up. He broke the breech and checked to make certain it was loaded. It was. "Okay. Now what?"

"When men come, we be ready."

Even though fear gripped the young man and he was

shaking like a leaf, Cappy got the picture real quick when
Henry went out on the stone porch and squatted down, out
of sight of anyone approaching. Cappy did the same on the
other side of the steps to await Ben and Blade's arrival.

"What if I miss? They'll shoot me quick enough. I ain't
never been in a gunfight." Cappy's nervousness was getting
the best of him. Those who had called him a bookworm
were right. His only heroic adventures had come while
reading James Fenimore Cooper.

"You stay down. I shoot first. If miss, use shotgun, defend self and father."

Cappy had started to say something else when the
sound of horses approaching at a fast pace reached their
ears. Henry checked his Spencer. His rifle would be much
more accurate at a greater distance than the six-guns of
Blade and Ben. He could get off two or three shots before
they were close enough to hit anything from the back of a
racing horse.

When the distance was right, Henry leapt to his feet and
cranked off a quick shot before Ben and Blade could get
their guns out and return fire. His bullet missed its mark,
but got the outlaw's attention. Both men yanked back on
their reins, urging their mounts to get out of the line of fire,
so they could dismount and find cover. Their expressions
showed surprise at anyone's having the spine to attempt to
thwart their intentions to rob the ranch.

Henry chambered another round, quickly squeezed
off another shot, and Blade went down that time, blown
from his saddle and dumped on his back in the dirt, dead.
Urging his mount to a run, Ben got two quick shots off
as Henry chambered another round. But Cappy suddenly
stood up from behind the stone railing and pulled both
triggers on the scattergun. The spread of buckshot, while
somewhat off target, crashed into Ben's right shoulder,
knocking him off his horse. He lost his six-gun in the
dirt. He scrambled to find his revolver and get to his feet
before either Henry or Cappy could get another chance
at him.

Ben was about fifteen feet from the porch now, and on foot, stumbling about, fumbling to get a firm grip on his gun. He kept on the move, making himself an unreliable target. As he struggled with his revolver using his left hand, stumbling left and right with his uneasy horse as cover, he was shocked to suddenly come face-to-face with Jack, the Remington aimed right at his head. Ben tried to cock and fire, but Jack beat him to it.

Ben's expression as the bullet struck him in the forehead was a mixture of shock and dismay. Drenched in his own blood, Ben tried to mutter something before crumpling to the dirt. The Cruz gang was now all but decimated. Cappy sat on the steps and began to shake; the shotgun clattered to the ground. Tears of relief flowed down his cheeks. "I told you I wasn't a gunslinger," muttered Cappy.

"You no coward," said Henry, putting his hand on Cappy's shoulder. "You ready when needed. Good man."

Wu Chang shook his head and clucked his tongue at the sight of the two bloody corpses.

Jack motioned for Henry to get their horses. "We'd better get to town and see what's befallen my ol' buddy, Cotton."

"Wait, no go yet," said Wu Chang, "Missa Hank want to thank you. Come into house, prease."

They stopped, thought about that for a second, then followed the Chinaman. Upstairs, Hank was all smiles when Wu Chang told him of the exchange that had just occurred in his own front yard. And how Jack, Henry, *and* Cappy had risked their lives to protect the ranch, killing at least two of the men who had been involved with the attempt on Hank's life.

"I swear I wish I had twenty men just like you two. You fellas ever want a job, with good pay, you come to me. I owe you that and more." Hank winced as his movements became too exuberant, and he dropped back onto his pillow.

"You have a brave son, Hank," Jack said. "You need *him* now."

Hank looked at Cappy and nodded. "I reckon I do, at that."

"I owe much to Emily Wagner. Must return to her." Henry turned on his heel and strode from the room and down the staircase as a man with high purpose. He had been saved from certain death by the Wagners; he had returned the favor by risking his life to save Emily Wagner. His debt was paid. He now would return to the ranch and stand tall among the white cowboys. From now on, if it had ever not been so, he would be regarded as an equal in all respects. His pleasure at how the events of the day had played out showed in his smile as he rode through the gates of the Brennan ranch.

"That Indian risked a lot to help us out. You suppose he'd accept some money?" Hank said.

"I doubt he wants any reward. He only wants to get back to the Wagner ranch and take up where he left off before Cruz and his bunch tried to pull off the biggest haul in the territory. At least that's what they thought."

"What do you mean?" said Cappy.

"One of the railroad detectives on the Southern Pacific told me there *wasn't* any money on that train. When the railroad got wind of that article in the newspaper about the million-dollar shipment, they changed their plans and sent it out a week ago. It arrived safe and sound. It may turn out that the whole thing started when a newspaperman with not enough facts and a big mouth got too big for his britches. Or *maybe* he had something else in mind, like a way to come into some quick money," Jack said, raising one eyebrow.

Cappy said, "What will you do now? Would you consider staying on and becoming our foreman? It was Hank's idea."

"Thanks, Cappy, but I'm afraid hard work just isn't my style. I'm goin' home and take up where I left off with a gal that thinks I'm near perfect. I only hope she never learns the truth."

Chapter 59

———◆———

Cruz figured he wasn't whipped yet. He still had one card he hadn't played: the woman in the cabin. Emily Wagner. While Cotton Burke was alive, he wouldn't have let anything happen to her. Now that the sheriff was dead, she would still serve as Cruz's hostage, his shield for a clean getaway. The townsfolk would let him pass because they wouldn't want a dead woman on their conscience. Then he figured he'd kill her just for good measure.

Cruz kicked the mare into a dead run through the canyon and up the narrow draw to the shack where Emily Wagner was his prisoner. As he pulled up, Cruz jumped from the saddle and raced up the steps to the cabin. He knew he couldn't be more than a few minutes ahead of whoever would be following him. *Probably that damnable Jack Stump.* He gritted his teeth at the thought. Dead silence surrounded the cabin. Only the incessant buzzing of flies filled the air. And the stench of something dead. He burst through the door to the darkened room. A shaft of light spilled in. He instantly saw what was missing: his captive.

Furious, he screamed, "Where the hell is that bitch? With my bare hands, I'll kill the man who let her go! Dogman, you bastard, where are you?"

From behind him, back deep in the shadows, a voice said, "He had another engagement."

Cruz spun around, pulling his .44 from its holster, his eyes fighting to adjust to the dark as he searched for the source of the voice that had challenged him.

A single shot rang out.

The bullet hit Cruz in the right shoulder, spinning him to the floor. His tumbling body knocked over the table, spilling plates and cups with a clatter, and sending the lantern crashing in a puddle of kerosene. Cruz lay groaning as he clutched at his wound, struggling to free his right hand, which still held the six-shooter.

Sheriff Cotton Burke stepped out of the dark and into the light from the open door. He stopped a few feet from where Cruz lay. The outlaw's mouth twisted in hatred as he glared up in shock at the man who had shot him.

"You! You're supposed to be dead! You bastard! You killed my brother and now you want me, too. Ain't no surprise to see you in cahoots with a ringer like Jack Stump. I shoulda blown you both to hell myself." Cruz spit out the words as if they had been caught in his throat.

"Yep. I reckon you *should* have played your hand the way you saw it, Cruz. But it's a mite late now. The way I see it, the only chance you got now is to let that gun drop to the floor and let me take you in to see the doctor. He'll get that shoulder patched up good enough for you to spend the rest of your days in a lonely, cold prison bustin' rocks." Cotton let a twisted smile cross his face, a smile that couldn't hide his hatred for Cruz.

"Uh-huh. You ain't aimin' to turn me over to no prison guards; you figure to patch me up so you can drag me out to get my neck stretched. Ain't that right? Since you're a lawman, you cain't collect no reward, can you?"

"'Fraid that's about the size of it, pardner. Maybe you're right. A necktie party would be more fittin' than prison. Besides, any reward on you wouldn't be worth dry spit. Anyway, I owe you for what you did to Emily Wagner."

"Where is the bitch?"

"Safe. And she'll stay that way."

"But what about that Stump fella? He's wanted. He had a poster on himself. I saw it with my own eyes. What about that three hundred dollars on *his* head? How the hell could he be workin' both sides of the fence and not get caught?"

"Twenty-five cents and a friend in the printing business can get a man all the wanted posters he needs. Money wisely spent, I'd say. Now, for the last time, how about lettin' that hogleg drop to the floor."

"I knew I shoulda gone ahead and killed that Wagner woman. I planned to anyway."

Before Cotton could say anything else, Cruz twisted his body around and brought the six-shooter up in Cotton's direction. The second smoky blast left no doubt that Virgil Cruz was not going to be taken into Apache Springs to stretch hemp *or* go to prison. A dark red splotch spread over his filthy shirt where Cotton's bullet had struck him in his chest—dead center. His dying spasm squeezed off one shot that nearly took his own foot off. One final, burbling gasp and Cruz slumped back, his body jammed between the stove and the wall, staining the rotting wood with his life's blood.

Cotton slipped the Colt back into its holster and walked outside into the sunlight. He pulled a cigarito from his vest pocket, struck a lucifer, lit it, and drew deeply of the smoke.

As he rode, Jack figured that by now Cotton would be up and around, probably being well tended to by Emily Wagner, a thought that brought a picture to mind that amused him: Cotton Burke tied to a woman's apron strings. It was all turning out to be a pretty satisfactory outcome. The Wagner boys and the railroad guards probably had the train back on its way. And he was off the hook for whatever it was Cotton figured he owed him. He'd done what he'd agreed to, and he could now get back to doing those things he liked most: gambling, drinking whiskey, and snuggling up to that sweet Melody every night she wasn't engaged in making money. He smiled at the thought as his horse continued retracing the way back to Apache Springs.

Chapter 60

———◆———

Cotton was still moving gingerly as with each labored movement Doc Winters's stitches tugged at his flesh. Loading Cruz's dead body onto his horse had taken every last bit of strength he had. The ride back had further taken a toll, and he looked forward to just sitting still for a few days. He rode into Apache Springs leading Virgil Cruz's horse with his corpse draped across the saddle. Emily and the doctor rushed out to greet him.

After Cotton told her about what had happened at the line shack, Emily's mood seemed to brighten appreciably. She was whistling as the two of them went to gather up his belongings from the one-room house the town had supplied its sheriff. She began stuffing clothing—shirts, pants, socks—into two bags she'd hastily purchased from the general store. Cotton tried sitting, standing, and leaning on the door frame—none of which afforded much relief from the discomfort he would be saddled with for at least a couple of weeks; that's what the doctor had told him. That is, if he didn't do something foolish, tear open the stitches, and end up bleeding to death.

"Emily, I still don't see why I need to—"

"Hush, Sheriff. You need someone to look after you while you're on the mend. The Wagner ranch has plenty of room, and I can take care of you until you're all healed."

"And then?"

"Well, I suppose we'll have to discuss that, won't we?"

Cotton broke into a sheepish grin that made Emily laugh out loud. The two of them had grown close after her husband's death, both as a result of Cotton's having been the instrument of fatal punishment for Otis Wagner's killer, and from a mutual attraction that had perhaps been there longer than either had wanted to admit.

Cotton was lost in his memories of their burgeoning relationship when a knock came at the door. The door creaked open as Emily called out for whoever it was to enter. It was Jack and Melody. Cotton's surprise at seeing Melody was a mixture of embarrassment at having a lady of the evening come into close proximity with the love of his life, combined with a still simmering belligerence at Melody's impulsive actions that played a part in his being shot by Cruz's gunman.

"Hey, Cotton, ol' pal, how're you doing?" Jack said.

"I'm getting' along, Jack. I see you sprung our prisoner."

Melody's face turned sour and her eyes narrowed at Cotton's obvious slight.

"Uh, yeah, I found myself in need of friendlier company than a broken-down sheriff. But now that the job I came here for is done, reckon Melody and I will be headed back to Gonzales. Just wanted to say so long. Oh, and don't you owe me some pay for being a deputy?"

"I spect I do, at that. I seem to recall your agreeing to pin on that badge as a deputy. I don't know if you bothered to look at the fine print or not, but I'll enlighten you with the contractual language anyway. You have signed onto an obligation to the town of Apache Springs for a period of six months, to be extended if either party desires . . . and so on. Well, you get the idea. You have exactly five months, two weeks, three and one half days left to serve, pardner. So you might as well get settled into this here room, which is owned by the town for the use of the sheriff or, in your case, his deputy. Since I'll be recuperating out at the Wagner ranch for a spell, and you'll be the only law in town, you can move in here. Any questions?"

Jack's eyes were wide at Cotton's declaration of an obligation he had no knowledge of ever agreeing to. Melody's jaw tightened, indicating a storm was brewing. She looked first to Jack, then to Cotton. Finally, her pent-up anger burst forth like a stampede.

"Cotton Burke, you rotten, no good son of a bitch, you can't get away with this. Jack's going home with me, and that's final. Now, move outta our way. We've got a stage to catch."

She stormed out of the room, then looked back to see Jack staring at the floor, her fury suddenly tempered with fear.

"Jack, honey, I'm leaving. Jack—"

"Melody, you know I want to go back with you, but if I signed a contract, even if I don't remember it, well, I don't see how I can go back on my word." He shook his head.

Emily was watching the whole charade with great amusement, which she kept carefully hidden behind a lacy white handkerchief. Her lower lip was quivering as she turned away at Jack's response to Melody's demands. Cotton remained straight-faced, although he, too, was trying mightily to contain a smirk.

Melody stormed off, slamming the front door. She started across the street, stopped, as if in deep thought, then timidly turned around and came back and eased open the door. She hung her head, sighed, and slumped into the one and only chair. Her silk dress rustled as she folded her hands in her lap. She looked up meekly at Cotton.

"Do you suppose the town could afford two in the same room?"

Cotton could no longer contain himself. He burst out laughing, followed by Emily and Jack.

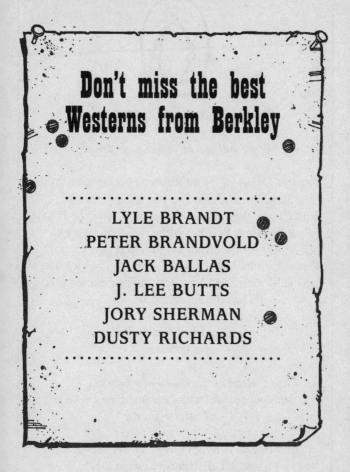

Don't miss the best
Westerns from Berkley

· ·

LYLE BRANDT
PETER BRANDVOLD
JACK BALLAS
J. LEE BUTTS
JORY SHERMAN
DUSTY RICHARDS

· ·

penguin.com

Penguin Group (USA) Online

What will you be reading tomorrow?

Patricia Cornwell, Nora Roberts, Catherine Coulter,
Ken Follett, John Sandford, Clive Cussler,
Tom Clancy, Laurell K. Hamilton, Charlaine Harris,
J. R. Ward, W.E.B. Griffin, William Gibson,
Robin Cook, Brian Jacques, Stephen King,
Dean Koontz, Eric Jerome Dickey, Terry McMillan,
Sue Monk Kidd, Amy Tan, Jayne Ann Krentz,
Daniel Silva, Kate Jacobs...

You'll find them all at
penguin.com

*Read excerpts and newsletters,
find tour schedules and reading group guides,
and enter contests.*

Subscribe to Penguin Group (USA) newsletters
and get an exclusive inside look
at exciting new titles and the authors you love
long before everyone else does.

PENGUIN GROUP (USA)
penguin.com